I0687666

HEARTS OF FIRE

EMPIRE ASUNDER BOOK II

MICHAEL JASON BRANDT

EMPIRE ASUNDER BOOK 2: HEARTS OF FIRE

Library of Congress Control Number: 2017916731

ISBN 978-0-9964984-5-6

Cover & Map Design: Autumn Birt and nuvue creative

Editing: LeeAnna Groves

For Terri

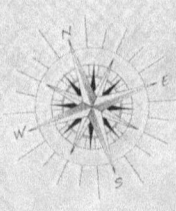

THE EMPIRE *of* Twelve Kingdoms

- ♛ = KINGDOM
- ☆ = Capital
- ● = City
- ✳ = Village

✳ Neverdann

Shadow Glen

FALKENREACH

☆ Varborg

DAPHINA

Darleaux ☆

LINIZA

Tarento ☆

Koshi Mahini ☆

YOSHINI
(The Western Isles)

☆ Valo

0   50   100   150   200 Miles

map design by nuova creative

Black Ice Wastes

Feuersten Mountains

LORESTER

☆ Chisenhall

☆ Kleinricht
※ Parca

NUROSTERLEND

Soul's Pass ✗

• Allstatte

Stormere Mountains

AKENBERG   ☆ Neublusten

VILNIA

Northgate ☆   Halfsummer   Sky's Pass ✗

Valma River

Qiver River   Triumph Mountains

Cormona ☆   GOTHENBERG

ASTURIA

Threefork

☆ Oren   •

Sea's Pass ✗- - - -

BULDOVA

☆ Livu Brada

CARTHA

Naru

A larger, full-color map is available to readers for free. Please see the Kings Club offer at the back of this book for details.

GLOSSARY

(Space restrictions require this to be a partial list. A free complete guide to the people and places of the empire is available to readers. Please see the Kings Club offer at the end of this book for details.)

Nobility
Emperor - the highest authority in the Empire, dominion over all twelve kings
King - ruler of a kingdom/province, swears fealty to the Emperor
Duke - ruler of a duchy within a kingdom, swears fealty to a king
Baron (Hern in some provinces) - ruler of a barony within a kingdom, swears fealty to a duke or king
Count (Landgrave in some provinces) - ruler over two or more lords, swears fealty to a baron, duke, or king
Lord - landed gentry with Imperial holdings

Military
Soldiers are divided between recruit ranks, drawn from the commoners, and officers, generally drawn from nobility or esteemed veterans of the recruit ranks.

A standard squad (squadron for cavalry) is 10 privates plus a corporal.

A standard company is 4 squads (3 for cavalry) led by a captain.

Officer Ranks
General - commands an army, reports to the king
Commander - commands a regiment or detachment, reports to a general
Captain - commands a company, reports to a commander

Recruit Ranks
Corporal - recruit in command of a squad, reports to a captain
Private - recruit, reports to a corporal

Provincial and Town Officials
Chancellor - a position of authority over administrative or financial matters within a province, appointed by king
Retainer - personal follower of a specific member of the nobility, sometimes themselves of lesser nobility
Magistrate - chief judicial and executive official in a city, town, or significant village, usually appointed by lord, count, or baron
Clerk - chief administrative official in a city, town, or significant village, usually appointed by magistrate
Historian - librarian overseeing Archives, usually appointed by magistrate

Other
Swordthane - member of the Order of Swordthanes
First of Swords - singular head of the order
Second of Swords - one of two thanes obedient to the First of Swords
Third of Swords - one of six thanes obedient to a Second of Swords

Housethrall - servant for life in the employ of nobility, town official, or prominent family
Fieldthrall - worker for life employed on one of the many farms dotting the Empire

Cards of a Harpa Deck
Suits
Battle Standard - Combat
Crown - Nobility
Dagger - Betrayal
Heart - Love
Lyre - Happiness
Map - Curiosity; Exploration
Plague - Sickness
Scroll - Knowledge
Shroud - Death

Colors
Black - Unwanted
Blue - Personal
Green - Transcendent
Red - Adjacent

DRAMATIS PERSONAE

(Space restrictions require this to be a partial list. A free complete guide to the people and places of the empire is available to readers. Please see the Kings Club offer at the end of this book for details.)

Akenberg
King Hermann
Prince Nicolas (Nico), Hermann's second son, a Swordthane and commander of The Threeshields
Prince Markolas (Marko), Hermann's eldest son, killed in battle at Allstatte
Renard, retainer to Prince Nicolas, killed in battle at Cormona
General Koblenzar, in command of all Akenberg forces
General Freilenn, in command of the Second Army
Captain Reikmann, in command of Hermann's Royal Guard

The Threeshields, Akenberg cavalry company
Corporals Ezra, **Manus**, and **Mickens**
Private Lima, Nico's aide
Private Mip, twin of Pim, killed in battle at Cormona
Private Pim, twin of Mip

Asturia
King Anton
Princess Letitia (Leti), Anton's daughter
Prince Tobias (Toby), Anton's son
Captain Gornada, in command of Anton's Royal Guard
Corporal Leonid, an officer in Anton's Royal Guard
Private Zenza, a Swordthane and member of Anton's Royal Guard

Neverdawn
Jak, a housethrall
Calla, the historian's daughter
Kleo, Kevik's sister, the clerk's daughter
Kluber, the magistrate's son
Riff, a housethrall
Kevik, the Corrupt, Kleo's brother, the clerk's son
Disciple Lukas, caretaker of the Shrine of Tempus, killed at Winter Festival
Acolyte Bashir, former caretaker of the Shrine of Tempus

Vilnia
Private Yohan, a soldier and half-Oster
Commander Jenaleve (Jena), King Volocar's eldest daughter
Corporal Mercer, in command of Vilnian escort
Private Brody, a soldier
Private Redjack, a soldier and scout

Harpa
Summersong Maple (Summer), caravan leader
Patrik, Summer's betrothed
Fairmeadow Sonnet (Meadow)
Silverson Goldthrush (Silvo)

THE STORY SO FAR...

Book I: Three of Swords

Nicolas and the Civil War

King Hermann of Akenberg and his eldest son, Prince Markolas, discuss the sudden abdication of Emperor Eberhart and a plan to dominate imperial politics and install the prince as Eberhart's successor. The key element of the plan sends Hermann's younger son Nicolas to the rival kingdom of Asturia under the pretense of arranging a marriage between Markolas and Asturian princess Letitia, with the expectation that the Asturians will execute Nicolas when they discover that the marriage was a ruse to distract them while Akenberg and her northern neighbor, Lorester, prepare for war.

But even the best laid plans go awry. Fresh off earning his membership in the prestigious Order of Swordthanes, Nicolas takes command of a cavalry company called the Threeshields. His diplomatic mission leads to helping Asturian King Anton defeat a rebellious duke and earning Nico a hero's celebration within the halls of Anton's castle. In return, he warms to the people of Cormona, begins mentoring awkward Prince Tobias in the art of swordplay, and forms a rivalry with Zenza, a disrespectful local Swordthane. He also develops a complicated connection to the princess betrothed to his brother.

A messenger from Akenberg arrives to recall Nico to Neublusten, informing him that Markolas was caught in between a surprising combined attack by Lorester and western kingdom Daphina, and subsequently killed in battle. Suddenly, Nico is in line to succeed his father as king. Letitia overhears the news of his brother's death and comforts Nico, and the two of them fall in love even as King Anton learns that King Hermann instigated the recently quashed rebellion.

Unaware of his own father's and fallen brother's intrigues, and warned by Leti of her father's growing hostility, Nico hurriedly escapes Cormona at the head of the Threeshields. His final promise to her is that they will never be enemies, whatever happens between their kingdoms.

Yohan and the Invasion

In response to rising tensions within the empire, a Vilnian infantry company led by Captain Marek and Princess Jenaleve is tasked with reoccupying long-abandoned forts in the Stormere Mountains. The company is ambushed by eastern barbarian tribesmen, who infrequently raid Imperial lands, in Sky's Pass. The only survivors appear to be Private Yohan and the princess, who receives a serious wound in the fighting.

Jena survives her wound but soon falls ill from infection, forcing Yohan to nurse her and protect them both from winter snows and aggressive beasts. He drives off an attack from hungry wolves, but not before the animals make off with the last of the survivor's food. One night, a solitary mountain tiger ventures into the camp and departs again as peacefully as a hunger-induced dream.

A distrustful relationship between Yohan and Jena eases somewhat as they face the prospect of starving to death in the frozen valley. Jena shares her anxiety about finding acceptance in the army, and the normally reserved Yohan opens up to her about his childhood. As she falls asleep for what he believes might be their last night alive, the tiger returns bearing the a miraculous gift of a dead goat for them to eat.

Restored by the mysterious act of kindness and made hopeful by a break in the weather, Yohan and Jena resume their journey out of the mountains. Finally arriving safely back at Halfsummit, they learn of one other survivor from Marek's company, a popular soldier named Redjack. Yohan reports to the general in command that the barbarians are not merely raiding, but coming in sufficient numbers to constitute an invasion, and are being led by the Chekiks, an evil semi-human race straight out of ancient legends.

Believing Jena to have already forgotten him, Yohan signs on with his new friend Brody to escort a trading caravan southward into Gothenberg. Meanwhile, Jena becomes frustrated by the bickering and inactivity of the officers in response to Yohan's warnings. She secretly cherishes his last gift to her, a small wooden horse figurine carved while she lay unconscious in the mountains. But when she decides to visit him in the soldier's barracks, she discovers that he and the caravan are already gone.

Jak and the Demons

In the far north of the empire, the tiny village of Everdawn celebrates the return of clerk's son Kevik from a prestigious academy in Varborg. Kevik's housethrall Jak, sister Kleo, and sweetheart Calla notice changes in the young man, whose drinking and boasting is out of character for the hero once known as Kevik the Kind.

At the autumn harvest festival, the villagers meet Third Rufus of the Swordthanes, who tells them of his quest to recover the

Sword of Yagos, God of Immortality, from the nearby mountains. His recitation of the legend is briefly contradicted by Disciple Lukas, the village's meek follower of Tempus, the local shrine's patron deity whose only duty involves burning all dead for reasons long forgotten.

Jak and Kevik spar just like old times, and the older boy breaks down and tells his thrall of the condescension and hazing he faces from the other students at the academy, all scions of more important families. Jak begins to understand the changes he sees in his friend, but when the two boys get into a simple fight with two outsiders and Kevik murders one, the thrall unhappily helps to hide the body and the crime.

When a delirious Rufus stumbles back into town carrying the ancient artifact he was seeking and raving about devils, Jak sees that his home is being swept up by important events beyond his understanding. Himself illiterate, he enlists the aid of Calla and her father to help him research the Sword of Yagos and the cult of Tempus. He learns of the jealous rivalry between the two gods and Tempus' fight to protect mortals from Yagos' corruption. He also learns of Calla's sudden engagement to Kevik, whom only Jak knows to be a murderer.

The wedding occurs during the festival of winter solstice, when the night is so long that its darkness lasts all day. The ceremony is interrupted by an attack of demonic bats that systematically slaughter the villagers. Jak, Calla, Kleo, and two others manage to escape by fleeing inside the Shrine of Tempus, where Lukas is able to briefly hold back the demons only by burning his own hand down to the stump. The disciple warns Jak that the unpurified souls of the dead outside will go unprotected by Tempus, though the thrall does not understand the precise significance. Leaving Lukas behind, Jak leads the five survivors through a trapdoor from the shrine into an unknown world below.

Meanwhile Kevik, separated from his friends and following

the magical compulsion of the Sword of Yagos, kills a mutated Rufus and takes the sword for himself. Despising himself for the weakness he showed at the academy, Kevik meets and swears obedience to the devil Nagnuaqua and begins planning revenge on the Empire.

"At last The Heart, that symbol of love both romantic and familial. The Heart reigns over the deck just as love reigns in life, for there is nothing more valued...and nothing more elusive, nothing more misunderstood. Therein lies a warning, for The Heart must be shielded from others who covet her. Loyalties, friendships, even crowns are heedlessly tossed aside in her pursuit..."

— IMPERIAL DECK STANDARD RULES

PROLOGUE

PURSUIT

The people of Cormona gathered early in the crisp dawn breeze in heady anticipation of an execution. They well knew their beloved King Anton's longstanding rivalries with two men—Duke Iago of Feana and King Hermann of Akenberg. At last, the son of one was to receive his final judgment for the sin of treachery on the hard stone block of the royal headsman.

The immense curved sword now in Uza's strong hands was called a falchion—both word and weapon remnants of Naru culture from a time when that southern country invaded the Empire of Twelve Kingdoms. Although twice the weight of a normal broadsword, the muscled figure held it comfortably poised before his chest, glinting brightly in the morn sunlight for all to marvel.

The youngster now entering the plaza chose not to look its way, however. His head was unbowed, defiant, but Captain Gornada noticed that the eyes deliberately avoided both falchion and the man wielding it. Instead the gaze swept over King Anton's assemblage, of which Gornada was a part. For a moment those eyes passed over his own, and in that instant the fear was palpable. Gornada fought the feeling of sympathy welling up within his bosom.

Then Duke Iago's son reached the block and knelt beside it, facing the generous crowd filling the city's central plaza. Saying nothing, he held himself as still as his trembling body allowed—a brave display by a lad whose solitary crime was to obey his treasonous father.

The crowd became silent in anticipation, some with nervous excitement, others with respect. Uza lifted the falchion high, King Anton nodded, and the blade swept down in a precise arc. The crowd broke their silence with a collective gasp.

For a few seconds, as blood jetted from the stump of the young traitor's neck, the front row of spectators pushed forward, a lucky few bathing their hands in the royal liquid. The macabre display caught Gornada by surprise, so contradictory to the respectful quiet of a moment earlier, but he casually dismissed the behavior as another bizarre manifestation of the idolization commoners held toward nobility.

He turned away, glad the ceremony was over, less bothered by the act of killing renegades as eager to get on with essential duties. His rapid soldier's stride propelled him from the ghoulish scene toward the castle. The captain's presence was required in the Royal Guard headquarters, where his corporals were already waiting.

By the time he passed beneath the languid banners of vermilion and gold overhanging the castle's main gate, Gornada had forgotten all about the execution. His mind was turning over the problem of the visiting diplomat turned renegade prince, but not with any particular anxiety. There was little enough chance of the Akenbergers escaping the kingdom. The greater question was whether force would be required to bring them back, or if Prince Nicolas could be reasoned with to recognize the hopelessness of his situation.

As expected, the five corporals remaining under Gornada's

command stood in the briefing chamber, awaiting their leader. Leonid had prepared for the captain's arrival by pinning an expansive map of Asturia to the large wooden table that dominated the room. Although the youngest of the corporals to survive the Battle of Cormona less than a tenday earlier, Leonid had quickly become Gornada's most reliable colleague and confidant. The lad's rapid progress brought joy to an old soldier's heart, for the young man always had been a favorite.

To begin the meeting, Gornada spoke for all to hear. "Our instructions are simple, but essential to Asturia. The king wishes the Akenbergers—or at least Prince Nicolas—brought back for judgment. We must locate them, intercept them, and subdue them, if necessary. The first two steps are trivial, the third a bit trickier." He stepped toward the table and gestured to the map. "Fort Marbella is the key." His index finger landed on the square positioned directly north of the capital. "The fort keeps spare horses for just such purposes. Corporal Leonid, I want you to go first. Leave as quickly as you can assemble your squad. Ride with the utmost haste, replace your mounts at the fort, and proceed northwest to Trepas Gulch." His finger traced a path to the series of squiggly lines near the border with Akenberg. "The canyon is directly between Cormona and Neublusten, and is central to our trap. Nicolas has only two choices: take the time to go around, or go through."

Gornada's finger tapped the location for emphasis. "If they go around, we'll catch them in open territory, where fresh mounts play to our advantage. If they go through, we bottle them up."

"Aren't there three canyons?" Corporal Pavel asked.

"At the southern end, yes. But these three canyons merge into one. If they go through, we don't yet know which one they'll take. But we do know where they'll come out." Gornada motioned toward the northern tip of the canyon on the map.

He held Leonid's eyes for this last command, measuring the younger soldier's understanding and resolve. "Your job is to plug the bottle—at the top, here. Force them to slow their march, to dismount, while we come up from behind with the main force." Seeing the enthusiasm register in the corporal's face, recalling the boy's brash tendency to zealously exceed his duties, Gornada issued a warning. "We want them trapped, not dead. Be careful not to risk a full engagement. You'll have only your squad, so find good defensible ground and make them come to you. Then pull back, if necessary. Remember, we'll not be far behind."

Then he faced the others. "The rest of you prepare the troopers to ride out by midday. Have any of the wounded recovered sufficiently to ride again?"

"Aye, Captain," Burro said. "Three more since yesterday. Another four or five may be ready by the morrow."

Gornada shook his head. "We cannot wait. Three more makes fifty-one. That will suffice. We need only convince young Prince Nicolas that his situation is too hopeless to fight." *And I have some ideas how to accomplish that.*

"Well, then, any last questions? No? Now see to the arrangements. Corporal Leonid, one further word with you."

Once they were alone, Gornada could at last share some more personal thoughts. "Leon, there is likely to be war between the kingdoms. Already the king prepares to form three armies: northern, central, and southern. And he has requested that I lead the last."

"A general? Father will be so proud. I'll follow you anywhere, of course." The corporal's easy grin was contagious, and Gornada could not resist his own.

He reached out, placing a hand on Leonid's shoulder. "Thank you, but I have a different thought in mind. The Guard will need a new captain."

The pleasure on that young face just about made the war worthwhile. The sight reminded Gornada of earlier times, when the boy had distinguished himself in training and received his invitation to join the guards. Yet even the joy of that moment could not rise to the clear pride of this one, only possible due to hostility and strife. How strange that brutal conflict could lead to these most rewarding of occasions.

It was Gornada's satisfaction to make this announcement, but the lad had certainly earned whatever laurels came his way. Leonid was as brave and capable as any man or woman in the Royal Guard. Perhaps a little overeager to prove himself, but Gornada remembered an age when others had thought the same of him. Time and experience would temper valor with discretion, as always.

But these promotions were of the future, and there was still business to take care of in the present. "We'll discuss it further after this expedition. Say nothing to your father just yet. If I know him, he'll boast to half of the countryside. The rumors of war will already be starting. We must not contribute to them."

"Of course, Captain." Leonid unsuccessfully attempted to temper his smile. He lowered his voice. "Thank you, Uncle."

"You've earned it, Nephew. Now move out."

On the subject of kin, Gornada watched a pair of newcomers enter the chamber as Leonid hurried out—Prince Tobias, alongside his radiant sister Letitia. It was not unusual to see them together. The two had always been close, but the stress of the recent battle and aftermath had made them inseparable. The crucible of rebellion and death could do that to people.

It was unusual to see them in the headquarters, however. As Anton's only son and daughter, they were naturally allowed to venture wherever they wished, but their appearance here and now piqued the captain's curiosity.

"Toby, Leti…to what do I owe the pleasure?" With no one else present, their speech could be friendly and familiar, free of the stifling restraints of imperial etiquette. That was for the best, for these two were as much like family as the departed corporal. Since his arrival in Cormona many years earlier, they had been surrogate children for his own. As it was, he missed Diego, Delila, and Iasha painfully. But his heartache would have been far worse without the king's children to take their place, and he believed they felt much the same about his replacement for their busy father.

Toby cleared his throat, a sign of awkwardness. "Fair morn, Uncle. We hear you are in charge of pursuing Nico...Prince Nicolas, that is."

"Indeed. Fear not, we'll have him and his company within a tenday."

The two siblings exchanged a glance, then looked back at Gornada with unexpected expressions. He read concern on the boy's face, outright distress on the girl's. Something deeper was at play here, he realized.

"I trust your judgment, of course," Toby continued. "But would you mind explaining your plan to me?"

The captain smiled. It was good that the prince take an interest in martial affairs. He was nearing that age when greater and greater responsibilities would fall on those lanky shoulders. Perhaps a newfound attitude had joined the fresh growth of beard and recent burst of height which catapulted the young prince into adulthood.

Gornada motioned the lad over to the map. "How well do you know northern Asturia, My Prince?"

"Not as well as I should."

"The land to the north is flat and barren, all the way to Trepas Canyon, here. Without distinguishing landmarks for anyone but locals. The Akenbergers will stay on the road. Not only is it their fastest route, but they risk getting lost without it..."

He provided a brief summation of the plan, conveying the full confidence he felt. Toby nodded at all the salient points, absorbing the details with impressive comprehension. Perhaps they would make an officer of him yet.

"I see. Thank you, Uncle. And how do you expect this situation to resolve?"

"Peacefully, if the Akenbergers behave rationally. Which I expect from Prince Nicolas."

"You think Nico will come back willingly?"

Again with the familiarity. Gornada was reminded that Tobias had trained for a short time under the Akenberger's tutelage. Such behavior should never have been allowed to happen. But circumstances after the battle had been...extraordinary.

"Prince Nicolas is a reasonable man. When he sees the futility of his position, I believe he will surrender."

Tobias was not so certain. "I will remind you that he is a Swordthane, Captain. His instincts are to fight."

And if he does, whose side are you on, young prince? But that question could not be asked of the king's own son, and Gornada felt treasonous for even thinking it. The lad had simply asked a question; there was no reason to suspect his loyalties were conflicted.

Nevertheless, Gornada hardened his tone. "We are prepared for that possibility. One way or the other, the traitors are coming back. That much is certain."

Conflicting emotions were clearly playing out inside the boy's heart as well as on the youthful face. Yet the captain was unconcerned. In time, adulation for a childhood hero would fade, replaced by love and loyalty for one's own. If and when conflict between the kingdoms broke out in earnest, the prince would be cured of any lingering doubts. War did that to people, for better or worse.

Sympathetic to the prince's confusion, Gornada changed the subject. He placed a hand on the lad's shoulder. "How fares the training, My Prince?"

Toby immediately flushed with excitement. "Oh! Thank you for reminding me, Uncle. I have a favor to ask."

"Indeed?" Gornada raised an eyebrow.

"Yes. As you know, Master Silgo was killed in the fighting. Prince Nicolas was training me for a time after that, but..."

"You need a new trainer. Of course. I'll see that someone—"

"Actually, Uncle, Leti thought you might train me personally." His tone was hopeful, but uncertain.

The thought of working with such an ungainly disciple was not particularly appealing. But at least Toby did not lack enthusiasm, and that was half the battle when it came to training. Gornada had seen more than a few soldiers achieve heights they had no business reaching simply through effort and determination, and had seen far more never realize their potential because of the lack of those qualities. In any case, training Toby would necessarily be only for a short time, until command of the southern army was officially announced. He smiled warmly, pleased by the new direction of the conversation.

"It would be an honor, My Prince."

The answering grin made the inconvenience more palatable. It was a good note to end on, and Gornada was relieved when Tobias bowed and took his leave.

That left only the captain and the princess, who unexpectedly remained after the departure of her brother. There was a careworn expression on her otherwise lovely features. She reminded him of his eldest daughter, Delila, who had recently celebrated her eighteenth birthday in his absence. The remembrance reminded the captain that he owed her a gift upon his next return to lands and manor. Hopefully, once this mission was complete and before taking command of the army—

"Captain, please don't hurt him."

Well, at least he was not left guessing. There was no conflict here. It seemed that Tobias was not the only member of the royal family with an affection for the Akenberger. An infatuation could have been foreseen. The poor girl would likely spend a few angst-filled nights until her attentions found a new mark.

Just now, Gornada had not the patience to deal with childish emotions. She needed to understand there was far more at stake than her juvenile whims. "That's entirely up to him, Princess." He turned back to the map, putting his back to her. "Now, if you don't mind—"

Leti stepped toward him and grabbed his arm, tugging so that he was forced to face her again.

He glanced down. Her grip was tighter than he expected. Far tighter, the fingernails digging painfully into his arm. Gornada looked into her eyes, seeing an intensity that was less readily dismissed. He had misjudged the situation, but now things became clearer.

He considered her situation. Betrothed against her will to a man she had never met. A battle that her father survived only because of the prince's timely intervention. A ceremony honoring said prince...

Even Gornada himself had participated in the fervor of that joyous occasion. He recalled sharing a drink with the young Thane. Nicolas was a good man, so clearly ignorant of the intrigues of his scheming father. What a tremendous shame that circumstances had come to their current point.

Prince, Swordthane, reluctant hero. He would have been a perfect match for the beautiful Asturian princess. Was it any surprise she should feel this way?

"I like him, too, Leti. Prince Nicolas is an intelligent man. He won't fight against impossible odds."

"If he does?"

"My orders are to bring him back, My Princess."

"And if those orders are wrong? You know he isn't at fault."

"That isn't my place to decide."

"And when you do bring him back? What then?"

"The son of King Hermann will be treated well."

"Like the son of Duke Iago was, this morn?"

He had no answer for that. At last she released his arm, leaving pale white markings on his bronze skin. He disliked seeing her this way. "Your father is angry, Leti. He feels betrayed.

But that will pass. We will talk sense into him. You and I, together."

He was pleased to see his words have a comforting effect, as an engaging smile spread across her delicate features. Irresistible features, to be honest. The young noblemen would no doubt be lining up to steal her heart from the Akenberg prince.

Leti hopped onto her toes to squeeze him in a quick hug. "Thank you, Uncle. Bring him back safely. And yourself."

"Naturally."

1

ASTURIA

The Threeshields rode in a northwesterly direction, as they had continuously for three tiresome days. Behind them, the dust on the southeastern horizon revealed that their pursuers were getting closer. Faster than Prince Nicolas expected.

"How are they gaining so easily?"

"Fresh mounts," Corporal Mickens replied from a few yards behind. "It's the most likely explanation."

Nico flinched. In his exhaustion, he had not noticed the corporal riding so close. For that matter, Nico had not realized he voiced the question aloud. Sleep deprivation and fatigue combined to play disturbing tricks on the mind. This was the second time in recent days that Nico felt disconnected from normalcy. The first had been the morn of the battle that temporarily made him a hero, shortly before he became a traitor and fugitive. Or perhaps those events were one more trick of the mind, all merely a dream. It certainly seemed so now.

The first signs of pursuit had not appeared until that morn. Before then, he had allowed himself to believe King Anton would allow the Akenberg company to depart unimpeded. Now Nico not only knew better, but realized they had little chance of winning this race. A confrontation, whether bloody or peaceful, was inevitable.

Nico inadvertently slowed his pace to look back. His company reacted by slowing, as well. They stared at him with exhausted faces, silently pleading for rest, knowing that relief eluded them.

At least they had gotten some sleep these past few eves. He had not, for the quiet nights were even more of a torment than the laborious days. While they rode, his mind was distracted by planning, orders, and an uncertain future. But when he closed his eyes in the dark, all he could see was a sublimely innocent face and a joyful past, lost forever.

Mickens pulled up to ride alongside. "Commander?" He spoke quietly enough to keep their discussion personal.

"Yes, Corporal?"

"We need to discuss a plan," he said disconsolately. "For when they catch us."

Nico nodded. He did not like the idea of making these decisions while his mind was functioning so poorly, but circumstances gave him no alternative. *I don't have a choice*, he had repeated silently many times. Leti's words were true about a lot of things.

He stared ahead, to more of the same barren plain. Stretching endlessly, or so it appeared. He knew there was a change in the flat, desolate landscape eventually, though.

"Corporal, do you remember the canyon we came through on the way south?"

"Aye, Commander."

"How far are we, would you guess?"

"Half a day's ride or so. We could get there by nightfall, if we don't break, and if we're not stopped first. But the canyon presents a problem of its own."

Indeed. He did not know whether it was an obstacle or an opportunity, but at least the feature provided an objective.

"Let's pick up the pace a little," he called, spurring his mount into a gallop. He expected to hear groans behind him, but did not.

Never a good sign when soldiers were too tired to complain.

Westward, the sun began to set before Nico took stock again. Despite the company's exertions, their pursuers had managed to close the distance to within a few leagues. Ahead loomed the change in the terrain that he had been looking for. The mouth of a canyon began a slow descent between rocky walls, wide enough for eight horses to ride abreast.

The labored breathing of the destriers revealed how tired they were. Heads down, nostrils flaring, pungent froth forming around the tack—all signs that worried Nico.

The Threeshields themselves were just as bad, if not worse. Most had not spoken for hours, and few had any water remaining in their canteens. Poor Private Rinnick, who had enjoyed barely a single night of rest for more than a tenday, appeared asleep in the saddle. And Conley, who had taken a slash at the Battle of Cormona, clutched her side as if the wound had reopened. Her balance appeared so unstable that he worried she might fall from her mount.

"We can stop here," he said as he tugged on the reins.

Hoofbeats approached from behind. "Commander, with respect, this is a bad place to camp," Mickens said.

"Pitch tents two hundred yards inside," Nico called out for all to hear. "Corporals, a word."

Once Ezra and Manus joined them, Nico asked for their thoughts without offering his own.

It was customary for the least senior to speak first, and so Manus offered the aggressive option. "We should fight them in the open, where we can maneuver."

"As can they," Nico replied.

"True enough. But what's the alternative? We cannot take away their strength without giving up our own."

"That's why we cannot risk open battle. We know not how badly they outnumber us, but we can be certain they do."

Ezra cleared his throat. "Do you think of surrender, Commander? To face Asturian judgment?"

Nico remembered Leti's final warning. *If you go, they will think that proof of your guilt.* He would certainly face imprisonment or execution. But he could likely spare the lives of his company with such a decision.

"The Threeshields do not surrender, Corporal. Not while I command. But we may find ourselves negotiating, and currently they have the position of strength. We must take it from them. Are there any suggestions to accomplish that?"

Their silence was discouraging, but not overwhelming. Now that they were discussing the problem aloud, Nico felt his mind sharpen, his focus narrowing. The doubts and lethargy were replaced by the anticipation of combat. This was a familiar friend that had served him well in his Proving and first battle. He would rely on the feeling once again to provide some miraculous insight.

"Ezra and Manus, see that everyone is fed and prepared for our next order. Corporal Mickens, ride with me, if you please."

Leading the way deeper into the canyon at a trot, Nico let his thoughts race ahead. The two of them were silent for five minutes, until the canyon widened and took a rounded turn directly north. If memory served him correctly, this stretch continued for two miles before a broad intersection. Beyond that, it narrowed and ascended to the end. They could not see the distant head from here, but Nico viewed it in his mind, closing his eyes to help the visualization.

"Your opinion, Corporal," he said at last. "If I were our pursuers, this would make a fine place for an ambush."

"Aye, Commander."

"If you were in command of their force—say, eighty troopers —how would you deploy for this ambush?"

While the scarred trooper considered, Nico studied the man. A homely face, made worse by the fresh growth of hair. No time for shaving since the flight from Cormona. But there was intelligence, or at least tactical savvy, behind those dull gray eyes. That had been apparent enough during the only battle they had fought together, defending King Anton outside the walls of Cormona. Now Nico was counting on that savvy again to influence his own formulations.

"I believe I would send two squads around," Mickens said at last. "Keep the main force looking as large as possible, so as not to give away the plan. Just in case the young, inexperienced Akenberg—your pardon, Commander…"

"Continue, Corporal."

"In case the young Akenberg prince lacks the experience to avoid the obvious ambush. Or is in too much of a hurry to care. Or—"

"Or is too overconfident to worry," Nico added. "That's much as I see it." He reflected for another moment. "If we move ahead, we are caught between the two. If we come out, their main force overwhelms us. If we stay put, we run out of supplies."

"Aye."

"All we need to do is disappear, or fly away."

"Aye, Commander," Mickens laughed.

Then it's decided. "All right, Corporal, let us head back."

The end of the sunset was lovely in more ways than one. On this occasion, the scintillating colors were less meaningful than the end of daylight. Few armies risked battle at night, which afforded Nico's company a modicum of relief. More importantly, however, maneuvers that were certain to be observed under the blazing sun could go unnoticed under cover of darkness.

Nico was unsurprised when their pursuers bivouacked a quarter-mile from the canyon entrance. He counted the tents with a growing sense of unease. There were enough to accommodate a hundred troopers or more. He did not think that so many had survived the Battle of Cormona, but here was evidence that their ranks had been replenished in the meantime.

Nor was he surprised to see them raise the standards of the Asturian Royal Guard, yet another shame in a growing list of them. The two units now opposing one another had so recently fought side-by-side, and the Asturians had even provided an official escort to the Threeshields after Duke Iago's defeat.

But there was reason for optimism, as well. Captain Gornada was that unit's commander, and Nico knew him to be a reasonable officer. Both commanders would seek a peaceful resolution to the confrontation. Or at least the most peaceful resolution that accomplished their aims.

The prince ducked inside his tent for a moment of rest. A moment was all he would get, and he intended to maximize every second. He stretched out on the bedroll, closed his eyes, and heard the flap of the tent open behind him.

"Commander, you wished to see me?"

Nico took a deep breath and sat up. "Yes, Lima, come in. I hope you've eaten already."

"Aye, Commander. Such as it was."

"Good. You're in for a long night. As are we all." He sighed, considering where to begin. "I need you to take a message to Captain Gornada."

Even in the dim lighting, he could see her slender frame stiffen. "What message?" she asked.

"Tell him I am willing to parley in the morn." She flinched in disapproval as Nico continued. "The captain and one escort only, at dawn. Sound demanding. Be belligerent. These are easy concessions for him to make, and we want him thinking about our attitude rather than what card we have up our sleeve. Is that clear?"

Her face was in shadow, but he detected the hint of a grin. "So we *have* a card up our sleeve?"

Nico was being cryptic, he knew. It was time to dump the rest of the burden on her capable shoulders. "We do. For that reason, you have one additional order to carry out. One extraordinarily dangerous order."

Even the shadows could not obscure the excitement in her face. One-handed, unable to fight with the others, she sought other ways to contribute to the company. He was pleased to be able to afford her just such an opportunity.

"We're leaving you alone, all night, to keep the fires going. Be seen moving between them. Laugh out loud. Ride to the entrance and back a few times."

"You want the Asturians to think we're all camped here."

"Yes. It means leaving some of our supplies behind. Tents, standards, and the like. But we can survive for a few days without them until we reach Akenberg. I hope to be well out of the canyon before the Asturians realize."

"And if they already block the north?"

"We'll have the entire company. If the surprise doesn't scare them off, the lack of support from their main force will."

Lima sniffed. "So you're leaving me behind, then?"

Nico was ready for the question, and wanted to convey his strength of conviction. "I wouldn't lose you for the kingdom, Private. Keep two horses, and move out before dawn. Follow the road and ride like your life depends on it. I would not ask you to do this if I didn't think you had the resourcefulness to escape and catch up."

He very much hoped he was right.

Change of plans.

For the third night in a row, Nico did not sleep a wink. Yet as the sun crept over the horizon far to the east of the canyon's southern entrance, he did not feel tired in the slightest. Two things kept him energized—the remnants of battlelust, and a boiling anger.

As light of morn illuminated the Asturian camp, Nico recounted the tents. The same number as the eve before. Based on what they had learned in the intervening hours, the Akenbergers were not the only ones up to a little deception.

He watched two figures approaching on horseback from the Asturian camp—Captain Gornada and one other. Coming for a parley that would not happen, or at least not in the manner expected. Nico was in no mood for negotiation; he was simply of a mind to castigate and withdraw.

It was a terrible risk to proceed with the meeting, as his corporals had warned. And not only them. Upon their unexpected return to camp, even weary Lima had expressed her displeasure at the change of orders. And when she asked the reason why, the only answer he could provide sounded hollow to his own ears. *Because it's right.* As if he could know that for sure.

Forcing his anger down and his breathing steady, Nico walked into the midst of his own bivouac. A few of the soldiers looked at him, curiously or expectantly, as he moved among them, looking for one who was as angry as himself.

Never as garrulous as the other twin, Pim had withdrawn further into himself since his brother Mip's death in a field hospital after the Battle of Cormona. And so he was alone now as the commander approached. Not inattentive to duty, however, and he straightened as Nico motioned toward the crossbow stowed on his destrier.

"Corporal Ezra tells me you are the best in his squadron with that weapon. Is this true?"

"Aye, Commander."

"Show me."

A look of confusion passed over Pim's sad face.

"Quickly, Private."

The youth hurriedly pulled the crossbow from its strap and loaded a bolt, then glanced at the narrow sunbeam entering the canyon's mouth. "There," he said. "See the rattlesnake on the flat rock yonder?"

"What snake?" Nico asked.

For a response, the crossbow fired with a loud twang. Nico watched as the bolt splintered into several pieces on a large rock in the distance, as did the small crowd that had quickly gathered around the exhibition. One trooper, a red-haired veteran named Mira, was already on horseback and headed toward the point of impact. She twisted in the saddle until horizontal, reached down, and lifted a long thin object from the sunlit stone. The snake's body continued to coil and writhe in her hand as she returned with it.

Nico admonished her. "By Theus, Private Mira, please put down that snake before it strikes you."

She smirked. "It's headless." She held the twitching body up.

Proof enough that Pim was capable, but did he have steel in him? Enough for Nico to entrust his life?

"Private Pim, I need someone to keep watch during the parley. I believed they were honorable, but after last night I don't know what to expect. Tell me true, are you up to it?"

The twin sneered. "Let them try something."

There is the steel I was looking for. Perhaps more than I wanted.

"Corporal Manus, you will wait for my signal. Private Pim, come." Nico mounted smoothly and set off for the entrance at a trot, eager to get this unpleasantness over with.

Gornada was already waiting, still on horseback, at the mouth of the canyon. So was his companion, the Swordthane Zenza, a particularly arrogant and hostile rival of Nico's. As the two Akenbergers approached, the captain took several paces forward.

Nico nodded for Pim to stop, then proceeded alone until ten yards from his counterpart.

"A pleasure to see you again, Prince Nicolas."

Nico raised his hand, palm out, putting an end to the formalities. He felt the inner rage building up again, and fought to control his emotions.

"Spare me the empty words, Captain, and I'll do you the same service. I'm not here to negotiate, nor to list grievances, of which there are many. Consider this meeting a courtesy that I already regret."

"Prince Nicolas, you are in no position to behave—"

"Your numbers are not nearly so overwhelming as you pretend, Captain, nor your position as advantageous as you believe. We depart as soon as this parley is concluded. If you follow us, prepare for a battle that you can ill afford."

Always the proper officer, Gornada's demeanor was unaffected. "The king orders me to bring you back. It is not my place to overrule—"

"The same king that my brother died protecting?" yelled Pim. "We saved his kingdom, and this is how he repays us?"

Gornada could not deny the justice of Pim's statement, nor the pain in his tone, and to his credit he did not try. Turning instead to Nico, he continued to make his case. "Prince, you must realize that we cannot let you go. You cannot outrun us, you're in unfamiliar territory, and your way ahead is blocked. Consider your position carefully. We have no desire for bloodshed here—"

"Perhaps you should have told your troops," Nico spat back. "Corporal Manus," he called.

At the prearranged signal, Manus rode forward from the cluster of Akenbergers, flanked by two horses and leading three more. Each held a body garbed in Asturian livery. The dead had been treated as respectfully as the Threeshields could manage, the blood wiped from faces and limbs, the stains on their tabards blending imperceptibly into the dark red cloth. But pale skin and lifeless stares revealed a gruesome end.

"One more is wounded. He couldn't be moved, so we are guarding him at the north end." *And what stories he told us.* "The others fled," Nico continued. "But not before these attacked, firing on us, ignoring our warnings and the odds against them. Two of my troopers wounded, one killed. Completely needlessly." He slowed his speech to avoid slurring the words so angrily spilling from his mouth.

Gornada had gone as pale as the corpses. He looked as though he had been struck. "Leon," he gasped.

The captain's obvious distress was lamentable, but entirely his own fault, so far as Nico was concerned. The midnight combat had been brief but bloody, the arrogant Asturian corporal yelling insults until the moment Manus silenced him with a sword thrust.

"You can see my reason for doubting you," Nico continued. "One unnecessary death is intolerable. Don't make the same mistake—"

"Ah!" The captain screamed, his face twisted in hatred. He looked at Nico, his feet kicking his warhorse forward, hand flying toward the sword on his hip. Then a feathered quarrel appeared in the center of his tabard, the olive tree sprouting a new branch. The captain's eyes widened in surprise, the look of hatred disappearing, replaced by confusion. His hand slipped away from the hilt, leaving the blade in its sheath.

Dumbfounded, Nico stared in amazement at the captain. Gornada opened his mouth, wanting to say something, then tipped sideways and fell from the saddle.

Calm yourself. Nico took a few deep breaths as he gathered his thoughts. *What's done is done.* There was no more time for arguing or fighting. This situation needed to be resolved before it escalated even further.

Manus and two other Threeshields surrounded Zenza. The

soldier made no move toward his weapon, but glared at Nico with unbridled hatred. Clearly he expected to meet his end, and faced it with the steely resolve expected of a Swordthane.

A quick glance at the Asturian camp showed activity. How long before they reacted, and a full-scale battle erupted?

"Private Zenza," Nico began. "You witnessed what happened here. The captain attempted to attack me under a flag of parley, just as your troopers attempted to ambush us in the canyon. Then, as now, we merely defend ourselves. This does not need to be war between our kingdoms—"

"Is that how you see it?" Zenza interrupted. "It's not how I do."

"I'm warning you... Do not start a war with deceit, Private."

Zenza spat on the ground, the spittle landing disturbing close to the body of the dead captain. "Kill me or let me go... *Thane.*"

"Corporal Manus, let the private go." *Why do I do this?*

"If we let him go, he'll tell any story he wants to King Anton," Manus said calmly. It was not a protest, simply a consideration, much the way Renard used to speak to Nico. How much he missed that gruff old bastard's counsel now.

"If he lies to King Anton, then he's in the wrong. Let him go." *Because it's right.*

"We will leave the captain's body here, along with the other dead. You may return for them as soon as we depart."

Zenza grinned as the Threeshields pulled away from him, his eyes never wandering from Nico's. "The next time we see one another, be prepared to fight," the other Swordthane warned. "I look forward to ending your delusions." Then he laughed, turned his horse, and set off at a gallop.

Nico felt the urge to cry, or scream, or do anything to release the frustration and anger that overwhelmed him. As an officer, he could do none of these things. But neither was he in the mood for discussion. "Mount," he ordered. He set off as abruptly as the other Swordthane had, in the opposite direction.

. . .

By that eve it was clear that the pursuit was over. Most likely, the loss of their leader and collapse of their plans put the Asturians in a state of confusion.

The terrain was breaking at last, the dusty plains of Asturia blending into gently rolling Akenberg ridges. Where exactly the official border lay, Nico did not know or care. The important thing was that they would be home within a few more days. And then a whole new series of problems would overwhelm him.

Nico allowed the company to stop early to set up camp. They all needed rest, most especially himself. Ever since the anger and excitement of the two confrontations faded, he had spent the afternoon struggling not to fall asleep in the saddle.

Now he isolated himself in his tent while the others ate. He desperately wanted to climb into the bedroll and let oblivion pull him down, but there was one more duty to perform first. Discipline was the sinew that held a fighting force together. He had himself to blame as much as anyone, but that did not absolve the others of guilt.

The tent flap opened. "You wished to see me, Commander?"

"Yes, Pim. Come in."

The young man looked nervous, like a child about to be admonished by a parent. Nico had to remind himself that the soldier before him was slightly older than he.

"That was poorly done, Private. Far better to have disarmed or wounded him." *Anything but killing him.* "I know you were defending me, and that I put you in a difficult position with little instruction. This is not an official censure, and I will put nothing of this conversation in my reports.

"But we need to be better, you and I. We cannot allow anger and vengeance to cloud our thoughts, for our actions have greater consequences than we know. I expect more discretion from you in the future. Is that clear?"

Pim stared at his boots. "Aye, Commander. I'm sorry."

"You will learn from this experience, Private." *As will I.*

Pim nodded. "Am I dismissed?"

"Not yet. There is one more thing. I am reassigning you from Corporal Ezra's squadron, Private Pim."

The shoulders shook once as the trooper struggled to retain his composure. Nico was impressed. This encounter had been difficult for the prince, and he was the one doing the reprimanding, not the one receiving. Thankfully, the rest of this should go much easier.

"Yes. You know of my brother's death, which makes me heir in a time of war. I expect to command the remnants of Prince Markolas' army, and I need loyal, capable soldiers to come with me.

"You have much more to contribute to Akenberg, Private. Let us hope this war ends quickly. But as long as it continues, I want you at my side. We have both lost a brother. We understand and need each other."

"Aye, Commander." The response was purely reflexive, born from years of unquestioningly following orders. But the sole tear rolling down the private's cheek revealed the turmoil inside.

Nico stepped closer, putting a hand on the lad's shoulder. They may be close to the same age, but a world separated them in every other way. He squeezed once, then stepped away.

"Now you're dismissed."

Pim nodded and turned, then wiped his face once before leaving the tent.

Nico sank into the folding chair, laid his head in his hands and closed his eyes. For the moment, there were no more decisions to be made, no more orders to give. He was alone with the thought he had avoided all day.

Leti, can you forgive me?

Just a few days earlier, Rinnick had carried a message of war between Akenberg and her two northern neighbors, Lorester and Daphina. Now, war with Asturia as well was a foregone conclusion. Three kingdoms against one, and that one had already suffered a catastrophic defeat.

The death of Prince Markolas meant this burden was Nico's to carry. His father was old and frail, and could not reasonably be expected to lead the kingdom through a difficult war. The responsibility fell to the new heir who, in time, would be king himself—if his homeland survived that long.

Yet all Nico could bring himself to care about was her. He had promised that they would never be enemies. Somehow, somewhere, he had become a liar and fool.

This line of thinking would trouble his sleep, and he wished for distraction. The sounds of a cavalry camp at night surrounded him. The clink of field utensils on plates, cursing and complaining, and laughter. A great deal of laughter, born from the release of tension of the past four days.

Stepping outside, he watched them for a minute. The familiar circle was forming, a hand of cards about to begin. Once, Nico would have been tempted to join, but he no longer felt the desire for games.

There were four players, and a small crowd of observers. Beyond, the troopers sat or stood alone or in pairs, telling jokes and stories.

This was his new family, but Nico could not bring himself to mingle. Instead, his eyes were drawn up the slope to the hill's rounded apogee. Not high, but enough to give a decent view.

He ascended slowly, enjoying that there was no particular hurry for a change. At the summit, he stared southward. Asturia had given hospitality and hostility, love and perfidy. How much had he learned about life in a few short tendays? How hardened was his heart?

"Leti, I miss you already." *And I'm sorry.*

He turned around, facing north. Ahead lay Neublusten, a majestic mountain, a peaceful lake. And war.

He did not notice the four troopers standing outside his tent until he was nearly upon them. Private Lima and the three corporals, waiting expectantly. Nico felt a moment of confusion, trying to remember whether he had summoned them. His mind was still muddled, so anything was possible.

Then Mickens clarified that they wished an audience. Nico nodded and led the way in. There was barely enough room for them all, and only two chairs. Since they would need to stand, Nico considered doing likewise, then realized that a blowing leaf might knock him over. He did not know what they wanted, but knew he should take it sitting down.

Once situated, he looked them over in earnest. He prided himself on reading people like books, and so his curiosity was piqued. They were excited about something.

"What is it?" he asked. He glanced from one face to the next, wondering which of them would speak.

Manus stepped forward, an awkward grin forming on his rugged face. That black beard had grown even thicker in the days since the hurried flight from Cormona, giving him the appearance of a wild animal. Once, Nico had felt a hint of uneasiness about the older veteran. Now that they knew each other better, Nico respected the man's honest, unfiltered opinions.

"The company discussed it, Commander. No one opposed, and we feel it's our right to do."

A sense of dread began creeping in. "Do what?"

Lima came forward with something in her single hand. A folded cloth, which she handed to the commander. Nico opened it, expecting to find something inside. But there was nothing, so he examined the cloth itself.

It appeared to be a miniature version of a battle standard like the ones outside his tent. But this one was not a design he recognized. It bore a resemblance to the Threeshields' crest, featuring the white mountain inside a shield on a background of indigo. But here was a sword added on one side and a crown on the other. Nico knew the emblem of every major unit in the Akenberg army, yet was unaware of this one.

"Whose is this?" he asked.

"The Princeshields," Manus replied.

"Who are the Princeshields?"

"We are."

Nico looked up. The elder corporal's face, normally quite dour, appeared uncharacteristically nervous as he cleared his throat. "The Threeshields have never been led by a prince. Or a Swordthane. We wish…to recognize that."

Nico stared. Manus shuffled his feet, back and forth, awaiting a response. The others looked just as antsy.

"You're sure of this?"

White teeth appeared in the midst of the ugly beard. "Aye, we are. With your permission, of course. But I figure you'll have a mutiny if you say nay."

Nico looked down. "Fine. Now leave me," he ordered with uncharacteristic abruptness, waiting for them to depart before rubbing his eyes.

2

BELOW

One-hundred steps beneath Neverdawn, the slowly winding stairway came to an end. Jak was already disoriented, and could only guess in which direction the rough passageway before them headed. It was wide enough to allow two abreast, with floor and walls shaped and smoothed by human—or inhuman—hands.

"Come on, you've got to see this," Riff exclaimed, leading the way down the corridor. He held the only lit torch, so the other three were forced to follow at the same excited pace.

"Where's Kluber?" Calla asked. Jak had been wondering the same thing. He had sent the two down with only a single torch, which meant the older boy was without a light source. Unless he had developed magical vision all of a sudden, he would be blind.

"You'll see."

The passageway curved left, then began a gradual descent, leveled off, and curved left again. Jak opened his mouth to inquire how much farther they were going, then closed it again as the silhouette of a figure formed in the blackness ahead.

Kluber stood where the passage ended, opening onto an impossible sight.

"Careful," he warned as they fanned out, staring down from the ledge into the enormous cavern stretching out below, illuminated in a faint blue glow. The far side was barely visible, but Jak formed an impression of an imperfect circle miles wide and thousands of feet high. The outline was natural, given the rough walls and immense stalactites jutting down from above. But the contents were clearly not. Stone buildings in varying states of decay dotted the cavern floor. Most were low, single-story structures, but a few stretched high above the others with looming grandiosity. Only a second glance revealed that many of these spires and monoliths suffered from the same wretched condition as their smaller brethren. In fact, the longer one stared, the more the whole place seemed poised to crumble into dust at the faintest touch.

It was a dead city, one the companions had no choice but to enter.

The streets below were dimly visible from the same glow that highlighted the cavern's perimeter, the source of which remained unclear. A hazy mist hung over the city, obscuring details from this distance, but one obvious feature was a long stretch of darkness just beyond the buildings, so black that it looked like a wall of pure evil.

"A lake," Kluber said, reading their thoughts. "It has to be."

That was exactly right. A tremendous underground body of water. Perhaps what had carved out this underworld to begin with.

Calla tapped Jak's shoulder. "The legends we read spoke of these places, but said they were all sealed off." She spoke quietly, as if worried the noise would carry to the city below and bring forth more demons like those that feasted on the village high above.

"Apparently not entirely."

"Would you two care to enlighten the rest of us?" Kluber asked in irritation.

"I wish we could," Calla responded. "We don't really know any more than you."

Aye, we do, Jak thought. *We know that this city was built by and for devils, that it is one of many, and that our kind don't belong here.*

"We need to find a way out," he said.

"Can't we explore a little?" Riff asked.

Jak closed his eyes. *Please, Tempus, give me the strength to guide us through.*

"Kluber, have you gone any farther?"

"A bit." He pointed one long arm along the side of the cavern. "This ledge leads to some more steps. I didn't go down yet."

"Are there any other options?"

"None that I saw."

"Okay, I guess we're going down, then. Single-file, nice and slowly. Riff, why don't you lead the way?"

The ledge was wide at the overlook, but narrowed considerably by the time they reached the first group of stairs. Those steps led to a lower ledge beneath the first, which in turn culminated in another set. It soon was apparent that the way into the cavern was a series of such switchbacks set into the side, part natural and part crafted. Jak hoped the trail they walked led all the way to the bottom, but his optimism diminished after a half-dozen turns.

"Riff, why are you stopping?" Calla asked.

"Because the ledge is gone," came the reply.

They huddled closer, and Jak saw that the other thrall was right. The ledge before them became steps, descending for only a few yards. There they had collapsed, leaving a gap far too wide to jump across.

"How do we get over?" Kleo asked.

"Do we get over?" Kluber replied.

The only other option was to go back. "We'll find a way," Jak said. He looked back, wondering whether they had missed anything. He did not see how that was possible, however. There had been no turnoffs, and the nearest supplies were all the way back up in the basement of the shrine, and that had been overrun by ravenous demons.

"Riff! What are you doing?" Calla cried out.

"What does it look like?" The boy was already mostly off the bottom step, grasping some unseen handhold along the cavern's side. Jak sucked in his breath as he watched Riff pick his remaining foot from the pathway and slide it around on the rough wall, seeking some projection to place his weight on. Finding one, he shifted his body, and the thick sole of the boot clumsily slipped off. The hands retained their hold, however, and Jak was able to resume breathing once the young climber found a more reliable foothold.

"Riff, get back here!" Calla stamped her foot once, emphatically. Jak wished she would not do that. The narrow stone felt insecure enough already, and just before them was evidence that it could crumble away.

He placed his hand on her shoulder. "It's all right. He knows what he's doing."

Kluber seemed to concur with Calla, however. "Riff, I'm ordering you... Come back before you fall to your fool death."

Ignoring his master, Riff worked his way to another handhold. He was nearly halfway across the gap. There he stopped and spent a long moment looking around. Using his left hand for support, he vigorously wiped his right on his breeches. Then he switched hands to wipe the left.

"What's wrong?" Kleo asked.

"The stone's wet."

Jak closed his eyes.

When he reopened them, Riff was leaning left, stretching out as far as his arm could go. He swung the hand down, brushing against a projection but unable to grasp it. He attempted it a second time, and again the fingers brushed rock without catching. Then Riff let go with his right hand, extending his reach as his body went into free-fall. This time the fingers found purchase, and he suspended his sidelong drift long enough for his right hand to join the left. Then his left foot began searching for a corresponding perch.

"Halfway there," Kleo yelled supportively.

"Only halfway?" Riff replied. "Shit."

Jak decided not to continue watching. He stared down at the blurry blue city, the blackened lake, the gigantic spiked columns of rock hanging from the ceiling, and anywhere else that did not have a fragile boy clinging to life by a few wet fingers. Then he heard a solid thump and multiple sighs of relief.

"Wait there," Riff called out, completely unnecessarily. "I'll see if I can find anything ahead."

"My back itches," Kleo said. She awkwardly reached behind herself to scratch.

"Be careful," Jak warned. "We should probably sit while we wait. I'm sure everyone can use a little rest."

He and Kluber sat with their backs to the side of the cavern. Kleo did likewise, using the rough stone to scratch the itch that bothered her. Calla, on the other hand, sat on the edge with her legs draped over the void. She appeared to be deep in thought. Her brow furrowed, and he did not have to guess what she was thinking of. A few hours earlier, she had believed she was getting married. Now her betrothed was likely dead, along with her father and everyone else in the village.

"Do you figure he'll find anything?" Kluber asked.

Not really, Jak thought. "Aye, I think so," he said aloud.

"Me, too," Kleo added, smiling at one boy then the other. "We wouldn't have made it this far just to be stuck here."

"Hey, everyone!" came Riff's excited yell from the distance. "You won't believe what I found!" His words were echoed by a loud scraping noise.

"A man-made bridge," Kluber said.

"How did you know?" Riff laughed. He lifted one end of the long wooden platform he had been dragging up the steps.

Jak wondered the same thing. He looked at the older boy, studying the expressionless face. Jak had always known that Kluber, and most everyone else, was smarter than he, but rarely had he felt the difference so keenly.

Kluber merely shook his head as he stood. "Here, Riff, slide it over. Careful, now. We don't want to drop it."

The platform reached across the gap with a few feet to spare on either end. Clearly, it had been fashioned for this very purpose. They were in luck that it had lasted for as long as it had.

Kluber held the upper end as each person crossed. Then Jak added his strength to Riff's at the lower end as Kluber took his turn.

"Should we leave it in place?" Kleo asked.

"Let's pull it down and rest it against the side," Jak suggested.

"There's a place for it below," Riff interjected. "Sort of a storeroom, with a hook."

"Okay." Jak saw no reason why it would matter where they left it. They were never coming back this way.

They soon saw the storeroom in question. It was little more than an enclosure at the location of a switchback. The steps led right to its edge, where a doorway framed this upper entrance. Jak was about to follow Calla through when he felt Kluber tap his shoulder, then point to the top of the aperture, where rusted iron spikes pointed down.

"A portcullis," Kluber said.

"A what?" Kleo asked.

"Like a gate that drops down," the magistrate's son explained. "This is a guard room, not a storeroom."

"Why? A place like this would be impossible to attack," Riff said.

"That's why they didn't," Jak added. "Supposedly, our forefathers just buried the exits so the Chekiks couldn't escape."

"The Chekican Communion?" Kluber asked. "So *that's* who built this." He peered out at the open cavern and ruined city. "How many years ago, I wonder?"

"Thousands," Calla said. "It's creepy."

"It's amazing," Riff corrected.

They were both right, so far as Jak was concerned. There was a time when he would have been just as excited as the other thrall. Eager to explore. He and Kevik would escape from the house for a day, get themselves lost, miss a meal or three, find a way back and return, scraped and bruised yet happy and fulfilled.

No longer. Now his existence was all about survival. His own and those with him. Two in particular. To one he owed fealty, to the other something more.

"Let's keep going," Kleo said.

"Aye, let's," Calla agreed.

The lower they descended, the more they could make out the buildings below. One emerged as the largest of them all, or at least of those in sight. It was not tall like some of the others, but quite wide, rectangular and well-preserved. It sat adjacent to a broad open plaza, to which several wide avenues led, and beside a particularly tall, askew monolith.

Jak's eyes were continually drawn toward the enormous structure, despite the uneasy sensation the sight of it evoked. And he was not the only one, for he saw Riff frequently steal glances in the same direction.

"What's that?" Calla asked.

Jak assumed she meant the building, then followed the point of her finger to a different location, where a thin curved line traced through the opaque void below. Each of its ends was obscured in mist, giving it the appearance of floating, as if a god had written in the sky.

As they continued downward, the line became more distinct.

A long, slender arch stretched from this side of the cavern out to a half-crumbled tower overlooking the city.

"What is it?" Calla asked again.

"A bridge," Kluber replied.

"Please tell me we're not going to have to cross that," Kleo begged. "It barely looks wide enough to stand on."

Kluber shrugged.

"Hard to tell how wide it is from this vantage," Jak said. "Or how high. It's probably not as bad as it looks from here."

"Maybe we won't even need to use it," Calla suggested hopefully.

A few minutes later, it was clear that they would. The switchback stairs led directly to the near side of the curved bridge. At the same time, Jak noticed that the fogginess became thicker as the fivesome moved lower. Even the tower across the way was blurry, the buildings and streets below nearly invisible.

They had reached the tip of the city, that much was clear. Perhaps it was for the best that they not be able to see just how far below the ground lay. He was already a bit unsettled by the bridge itself. Somehow, now that they stood on the precipice, the path looked even narrower than it had from above. Nearly as bad, there appeared to be nothing supporting the ancient, three-inch thick stone. All around them thicker, wider structures had crumbled. What were the chances this would bear their weight without collapsing?

Yet it would do no good to voice these concerns. They had no choice but to keep going.

He noted that most of the others avoided looking over the edge. That was good. "Don't look down and you'll be fine," he emphasized, then considered adding that the bridge was not terribly high, or perhaps over water. Something to soften their unease.

Riff peeked over. "Won't matter," he said. "Can't see the ground anyway." Then he hocked up some spittle and let it drop into the void, cocking an ear to wait for the sound of impact that never came.

Jak closed his eyes.

The best way to do this was to not think about it, of that he was sure. *Focus on a point in the distance and walk quickly.* He decided to set the example, reopened his eyes, and prepared to take that first step onto the platform.

"My back itches," Kleo said. "Jak, do you mind?" She turned for him.

"Riff, will you take the lead?" he asked as he moved behind her.

Kleo fidgeted as they watched the others cross, Calla following Riff then Kluber after her. Only when the third shape dissolved into the mist did Kleo speak again, in a hushed whisper.

"I don't think I can do it," she said. "My legs won't listen to my head."

"You can do this, Kleo," he assured her. "Pretend you're crossing Washer's Creek back home. That's a narrow bridge, like this one. Just put one foot in front of the other—"

"Nay, Jak, you aren't hearing me. My legs won't listen to my head. They won't move."

Jak nodded, finally understanding.

"We're all over," Kluber called from the opposite side.

"Just a minute, I'm working out a cramp," Jak yelled back.

"Do you think you can crawl?" he asked at last.

"I don't want..." A pleading quality had entered her tone. "Jak, I'm slowing everyone down. Go tell them to keep going." She wiped at her eye.

"Jak, what are you doing?"

He was already on his hands and knees, and had moved several feet onto the bridge. "This is easy, Kleo. You can definitely do this. Come on."

He knew the girl was following by the sound her bracelet of tiny gemstones made as it scraped on the rock. Within several uncomfortable minutes—after covering the distance of only a half-dozen full strides—his hands were cold and wet from the moisture on the stone, and an irresistible look down was making his balance swim uncannily like one of Kevik's practice sword blows to the head. Had he been able to simply walk across, he would be safe by now.

"What's wrong?" Kleo asked from behind. She was doing her best to keep pace with him.

"Nothing," he replied. "Want me to go faster?"

"Gods, nay!" she exclaimed. "Maybe a little bit slower, though?"

"Okay." He wiped a hand on his shirt before reaching out again. His palm was raw, and he felt an uneven knob of stone break the skin as he pressed down. "Be careful here, the surface gets a little rough."

The soreness in that palm became irritating, so Jak favored his undamaged left hand. He found himself pulling slightly left and correcting his direction after every few paces.

Now that they were on the descending half of the bridge, Jak saw the tower entrance in the distance ahead. The terminus of the bridge widened into a semicircular platform, upon which stood the other three companions, watching.

"You can do it, you two!" Calla yelled out supportively.

Jak felt embarrassed, prostrate as he was while she watched. He looked up at her and the other boys, hoping not to see amusement in their faces.

His left hand missed its target, coming down awkwardly on the edge of the bridge, and he found himself falling face-first into the malignant stone. His jaw slammed into the rock, his teeth bit hard into his tongue, and a taste of blood filled his mouth.

"Jak, are you all right?" Calla called.

He closed his eyes. "Fine!" he yelled back as cheerfully as he could manage. "Just showing off."

Kleo giggled behind him, and he smiled at the sound. That

made it worthwhile, quite frankly. They were on the last stretch, and she was going to make it. A little blood and embarrassment was a small price to pay.

The reminder that this was a city of the dead came in the tower. Inside the structure, the bluish glow from outside was blocked from sight. By the time Kleo stepped from the bridge into the rounded interior, Kluber already had a torch lit and held high. Jak regretted the need, for they had only a dozen between them, and no idea how many they might need in the hours ahead.

Yet there was no choice. The floor was littered with small, hazardous obstacles—most likely the remnants of decayed furniture and decoration. A circular stairway without a railing led down to another darkened chamber.

"Riff, lead the way, if you don't mind." Jak spoke barely above a whisper, unable to shake the sense of being among spirits better left undisturbed.

Riff took a cautious step toward the top of the stairs, then another over a pile of broken stones. His foot came down with a crunching sound, and he froze in place while Kluber swung the torch around and squatted.

"What is that?" Calla asked.

"A skeleton," Kluber answered.

"Are you sure?"

He nodded. "I've seen them before. After the shrine burns the bodies." He ran the torch in a line, exposing a stretch of what certainly looked like bones, although Jak had never seen them together like this. Then the light caught a skull, and they all flinched. Everyone had seen skulls before, of animals if not people.

Jak was surprised by his own revulsion. One would have guessed that after the horrors of the night before, they would be inured to death by now. He suddenly disliked the idea of an open wound allowing the evil that lurked here to creep inside his blood.

"Is it human or Chekik?" Kleo asked.

"Who can say?" Kluber stood up. "There's more on the stairs. Come on, let's get moving. Watch your step. Kleo, give me your hand."

As the others timidly moved forward, Jak took a moment to tear a strip of cloth from the tail of his shirt with which to wrap his bleeding hand. He tied it securely, then spat a hunk of blood and saliva from his aching mouth.

"Gross," Calla said. He had not noticed her waiting for him.

He looked at her confusedly as she stepped forward wearing a faint smile—or, at least, an easing of the lines of worry. Below, the light from the torch was quickly diminishing, bathing her features in shadow. Without sight to advise him, Jak was left wondering what she wanted.

She leaned close. "That was nice, what you did," she whispered. Then leaned closer yet to kiss his cheek.

He half-expected her to laugh and turn away, hurrying to catch up to the others. But she did not. Instead, she stood still, staring into his eyes. Waiting.

Jak wished he knew what she was waiting for. He felt a dozen impulses at once, so many that they got in each other's way. He picked one. "We should catch up before we lose the light," he suggested.

Calla nodded, then turned away at last. Jak followed behind.

"It's just like foxfire," Riff said.

"Foxfire comes from trees, though," Jak said. "And is green, not blue."

The glow of the dead city came from prolific small mushrooms growing on and around every natural surface in sight, but was oddly absent from the cut stone used for buildings and avenues.

Foxfire was the inexplicable light emanated by a mossy fungus that grew in the dead trees of Shady Glen's copious woods. Many nights, he and Kevik found themselves out after dark without a light of their own, reliant upon the supernatural greenish substance to illuminate their way home.

"I've heard of such things," Calla said. "Plants and animals that look the same but live in completely different environments. Related, like crows and nightingales, but diverse." She looked at Jak, hurt creeping into her eyes. "Da taught me about them." She sat on a crumbled stone and began to cry.

Jak sat beside her and draped an arm around her shoulders, wishing he could speak some magical words that would take away her grief. There were so many things in the world that he would change, if only he had the knowledge and power.

"We'll call this rockfire, then," Kluber said, oblivious to Calla's distress. Or choosing to give her and Jak a moment alone. "Kleo, Riff, let's see what's inside."

They had exited the tower onto a wide roadway between two rows of buildings. From their vantage point, the sides and ceiling of the cavern were invisible. Yet it was not only the blue hues and ruined architecture that prevented them from feeling they were inside a normal city aboveground. With the exception of a faint trickling and their own muted voices, the silence was unnervingly absolute.

Jak rubbed her back until the others disappeared inside the nearest intact building, a low squat structure with a colonnade of carved pillars in front of a wide arching entranceway. He did not like the party separating like this, but was reluctant to force Calla to move before she was ready. Having lost both her father and betrothed in a single grisly night was beyond Jak's comprehension. He wondered how the girl could even still function.

She took his hand with the two of hers, squeezing his fingers. "I couldn't do it, if not for you," she said, as if reading his thoughts. She held his eyes with her own, reflected stars of blue obscuring the green he knew so well.

Jak looked away from their intensity. He opened his mouth, could think of nothing to say, then closed it again.

She squeezed his hand once more, then stood. "I'm okay now, I think. Let's catch up to the others."

The building was clearly a vast library, or at least once had been. Now the books were rotted into nothing more than isolated patches of stiff leather on broken wood shelves. Jak could see four immense rooms, each the size of the Archives in Everdawn. The amount of wisdom once stored in this place was awesome to contemplate.

They found the others in the fourth chamber, examining a stone portal sealed shut. Covered in cryptic writing, its very method of opening a mystery—it had no doorknob, only three holes of various shapes spaced a man's hand apart: a circle, a crescent, and a six-pointed cross.

"See how there isn't as much dust and dirt here?" Kluber pointed out. "Could it be a magical door?"

"Until yesterday, I would have said that's impossible," Jak replied. "Today, I don't know. I don't know anything." He turned away. Regrettably, whatever lay beyond would have to stay forgotten.

"Come on," he said. "We need to find a way out."

"Can't we take an hour to explore?" Riff asked.

Feeling like a disapproving parent, Jak shook his head. "Our priorities are escape and food, in that order." He looked around to see if anyone disagreed.

"My back itches," Kleo said.

"Come on," Jak said again, before she could order him into more frivolous scratching. He led the way back out to the street. "This way."

"But that big one is over there," Riff said.

"That's further into the city. We want to find the way out."

Riff hung his head, but followed the others without another word. Soon he was back in front, leading the way, staring at each new discovery with longing.

The streets were cluttered with rubble, although never enough to block passage entirely. Smaller alleyways led off between buildings, but the group of refugees stuck to the widest thoroughfare, which seemed the least likely to get them lost.

Calla stopped abruptly. "Did you hear something? *I* think I heard something."

They had been through a lot, and it was only natural for their minds to assume the worst. Jak's own had played tricks on him at least a dozen times already. "You're hearing our echoes. No one has lived here for hundreds of years."

Kleo put her hand on Calla's arm. "I thought I heard it, too."

Jak looked at Kluber for reassurance. Their eyes met, but the older boy remained silent.

"Riff!" Jak called out. "Don't get so far ahead."

The farther they moved away from the library, the worse the condition of the buildings around them. The structures also became smaller and fewer in number, which hinted that the group was nearing the city's outer edge.

"Do you hear that?" Kleo asked. Jak stopped, and the others followed suit.

"It might be running water," Calla said hopefully. If so, it would be the first good news they had received in a while. Jak became aware of how desperately thirsty he was, and they all moved forward again with a greater spring in their strides.

They heard the stream's steady current long before seeing it. The buildings were now behind them, and the high cavern walls closed in not far ahead.

The water could not have been more than a few inches deep, its banks about six feet apart. What once was a bridge had collapsed, and the stream wove between large, well-worn stones with musical trickling.

Riff was first to refresh himself, dipping one cupped hand into the cold water and lifting it to his mouth. The others followed his example, and smiles quickly spread from face to face. Jak marveled at how such a simple thing could bring cheer in the midst of tragedy.

"Look, a lizard," Kluber exclaimed as he pointed.

Kleo jumped into his arms, and he laughed.

Jak frowned. Her abnormal fear for the scaly beasts was well known and frequently poked fun at, but though the mood had noticeably lightened, this was still no time for jokes. "There's no lizard, Kleo," he said disapprovingly.

"I wish there were," Riff said. "We could catch and eat it. I'm starving."

"We'll worry about food once we get out." The prospect of escaping this underworld was sustenance enough for Jak. He urged them forward, seeing how on the far side the trail continued in the opposite direction of the current.

Riff jumped from stone to stone as he crossed. Jak followed with lopes rather than leaps. "It's not slippery," he announced, reaching back to help Calla steady herself on the first block.

They stopped a minute later. The stream bubbled forth from a low tunnel in the side of the cavern where the trail abruptly ended. The current was deeper and slower here, but no more than a foot of clearance above meant that further progress would require crawling through the water. There was no passageway fit for travel. They would have to look elsewhere.

He would not allow his discouragement to show, however. "Let's follow the side for a while," he suggested. "Maybe we'll come across a new tunnel."

Movement off the trail was slower and more hazardous as they maneuvered around obstructing stalagmites and over uneven footing. The disappointment of the stream made the light-hearted conversation taper off to quiet sullenness. Jak almost wished Kluber would pull another prank on Kleo. Or, better yet, on him.

Riff was wandering farther and farther away. Now they saw him come back, looking dejected. "It's getting too rough ahead. We need to go back to the city."

Jak sighed. "All right. Don't worry, there's still a lot of cavern left to search. We'll find a way."

All the cheerful optimism—even Riff's—was noticeably absent as they made their way back to the buildings. Soon another wide avenue led them toward familiar surroundings. Just ahead, the plaza and great unknown edifice waited in silent malignance.

"Well, Riff, I guess you're going to get your wish, after all."

"What's that?"

"To explore the city."

Riff smiled without cheer. "I'd rather have food."

"Maybe we'll find some," Calla said.

Kluber snorted.

We're going to need to, Jak thought. *Along with a place to sleep.* The notion of spending a night inside this vast, morbid mausoleum held no appeal at all, but none of them had slept in more than a full day, and his leg muscles were cramping from strain. He was certain the others felt the fatigue, too.

"What's that ahead?" Kleo asked.

Jak squinted. There was definitely a shape in the twisting fog where the plaza formed a large open area between buildings. As they drew nearer, the shape crystallized into the outline of charred poles standing above a pile of wood. The setup was all too similar to the ritual pyres back home, where the acolyte of Tempus disposed of the dead. Which meant the hints of white just now becoming visible could be only one thing.

No one spoke as they approached the blackened remnants of wood and the thin skeleton half-covered in soot. The skull remained attached to the body, but sagged toward the cold stone floor. Jak was relieved the empty eye sockets did not stare back.

The crooked monolith loomed ominously on the far side of the plaza, a thin trail of cloud obscuring its peak. From this close proximity, Jak wondered how the entire unbalanced column remained upright. He also pondered what purpose it served. Was it a monument, the leftover remnant of some larger design, or simply a beacon of death?

Kleo coughed, then covered her mouth as if wishing she could arrest the sound.

No one else moved, and Jak's senses became alert to the slightest disruption. He thought of the girls' earlier reports of noises, and knew the others did, too.

Silence surrounded them, but for the gentle lapping of lake waters on shore, close yet invisible in the darkness. Not even the sound of their breathing was audible, and Jak wondered whether their exhausted hearts had all simultaneously ceased beating.

Then Kluber stepped closer, bent down, and rubbed his fingers through the pile of ashes beneath the skeleton. Then nodded. "Still warm," he said softly.

A sickening chill ran through Jak's body, the terrifying implication obvious to even his stupid mind.

"My back itches," Kleo complained. Everyone ignored her.

"I guess we're not alone, after all," Riff said.

3

VILNIA

The caravan was not much—eight oxen drawing four overloaded wagons, carrying a modest load of Vilnian tin and Oster fur. Four harpa traders, two women, two men, a driver for each wagon. A pair of skinny, antagonistic black dogs alternately running underfoot or curling up to sleep on the rear of the wagons, barking passers-by off, as if the precious cargo were royal gold and they were the emperor's own mastiffs. And one understrength squad of soldiers, seven misfit privates and one tyrannical corporal.

Nay, the caravan was not much, and rolling alone through the unpopulated frontier between Vilnia and Gothenberg was enough to give anyone an overwhelming sense of isolation.

For Yohan, however, the caravan was more than he wanted. There were conversations at every turn, often when he did not want them, his own sullen reticence never seeming to discourage the natural prolixity of others. The unending, meaningless banter often drove him away from the camp, seeking quiet solitude a few minutes at a time.

This was one of those moments. He sat on a boulder, plate of warm beans in hand, staring east at the distant mountains. The

Stormeres. He had spent half a lifetime on those hostile peaks, alone and yet not alone, preserving an unconscious then unfriendly woman who had come to mean more to him than anything else in the world. A princess whom he would still die to protect, despite the pain of abandonment.

Yohan was strangely transfixed by those mountains, and not only because they accounted for the sum total of his time with her. He had been tested there, and was satisfied with the outcome. He had learned much of himself, and of others. The experience put things into perspective.

These beans, for example. These beans were rubbish. Yohan could tell Brody made them, for they were as overcooked as they were underflavored. And yet Yohan welcomed each unpalatable spoonful, a far cry better than the intolerable hunger he had known.

A tiger, of all things, had saved them. At the time, it had not seemed as crazy as it did on reflection. Now Yohan was convinced that tiger was his own personal guardian, that its spirit had somehow passed into his own. He felt compelled to return to Sky's Pass, simply to thank the beast properly.

It was comforting, knowing the mountains were nearby. Morn to eve, eternally watching over him. The caravan remained a respectful distance away, sticking to the flatland where the nominal speed of the oxen could be maximized. But Yohan felt with an uncanny certainty that he would someday find himself back amongst the frigid, rocky ridges.

"There you are, Brother. Is there room for me?"

"There's always room for you, Brother." He inched over on the boulder.

Brody sighed as he sat. "How are the beans?"

"They're wonderful."

"Thanks, Brother. I made them."

"Well done. Perhaps you should take my next turn cooking."

Brody laughed. "What sort of a flat do you take me for?"

"A rather large one, to be honest."

Another laugh. "I appreciate your honesty, Yohan. Someday you're going to give me a compliment, and I'll know it's true."

Yohan focused on finishing the beans, allowing his companion to do the talking. The other soldier never ran short on words.

"Kelsey says there is a Proving coming up in Threefork."

Yohan's mouth was full, but he looked at his companion with a raised eyebrow.

"I know, you never want to take these rumors too seriously. But it would be interesting."

Yohan swallowed. "You mean to watch."

"I mean to compete."

In the five days they had known one another, Yohan had learned to recognize when his friend was joking. This was not one of those occasions.

"You want to be a Swordthane?"

Brody appeared surprised by the question. "Doesn't everyone?"

"Not I."

Brody narrowed his eyes. "Nay, I don't suppose you do. Perhaps that's your problem, Brother. You don't want anything. Or at least you don't *know* what you want."

Yohan looked away, discomfited.

Brody laughed. "I'm being unfair. Forgive me, Brother. You do want *something*, I know." He waited expectantly, but Yohan said nothing, hoping the other soldier would move on to whatever new subject his whims willed.

"I ask myself, 'Why is Yohan sad? Does he grieve for his comrades lost on patrol? Is he guilty that he alone survived?'

"But of course he was not truly alone. There was one other, and together they spent tendays fighting the evils of the barbarians, the mountains, the winter. Surely, they were… thrust together by circumstance. But the two of them were as different as night and day. Is such a thing possible? Nay, of course not."

Brody laughed again at the absurdity, and Yohan was relieved that his friend's playful musings were reaching an end.

Brody stroked his stubbled cheeks thoughtfully. "Then I consider that the princess is as beautiful as she is cold. And that my friend Yohan is not without a certain rugged handsomeness. And some women are sadly into that sort of—"

"Do you ever stop to breathe?"

Brody clapped a hand on Yohan's shoulder. "You'll find another, Brother. Then all will be well."

He turned his gaze toward the camp.

"Why don't you try talking up the short one? She's unbelievably cute…maybe not so stunning as the other, but she seems to like you, though gods know why."

Yohan wanted only for the subject to change. "All right. I'll try."

Brody's head swung back to face Yohan, the guileless brown eyes studying closely. "Well, that was easy," he said suspiciously.

"There is much to admire of these harpa."

Brody smiled. "You've never spoken truer words, my friend. I am pleased to hear you say so."

The woman in question was Meadow, the youngest of the traders. It was true that she smiled an inordinate amount when interacting with Yohan, but the culture of her people was confusingly difficult to understand, and he did not know how to distinguish everyday cheerfulness from genuine interest. Nor had he much reason to care. His mind admitted that Brody was right in needing to find another, but that was not the same as compelling the heart.

She might be someone he could fall for in time, however. She was as short as any adult he had known, reaching only the midpoint of his chest, but her soft features were a pleasure to view and her disposition as congenial as could be imagined. She used bright red wooden pins to rearrange her bountiful blonde hair, somehow failing to keep it from falling into her eyes no matter how often she adjusted them. The constant brushing back of hanging locks was as much a part of her as that easy laugh.

Her full name was Fairmeadow Sonnet. The name alone made her intriguing, and their first conversation had been about the harpa's strange naming conventions. Yohan had also quickly learned that they were a matriarchal people where women outranked men, and that they did not recognize the same gods as the rest of the empire. These traditions alone explained why the harpa were treated as second-class members of imperial society, with no homeland of their own, no privileges to participate in government, nor even an allowance to carry weapons. This last made clear the need for military escort, for the caravan was otherwise incapable of defending itself.

The little he had heard of the harpa prior to this trip branded them as dishonest thieves. That reputation did not comport with what he had learned in just a few days of personal exposure. Indeed, he found himself in admiration of these four.

The older woman, and thus the leader of the caravan, was an industrious sort named Summersong Maple. She could not have been far into her twenties, but she commanded the other three with a confident tenderness normally associated with aging mothers. Where Meadow was cute, Summer was an exotic beauty, with sharp features and dark hair. The confident, cheerful way she carried herself reminded Yohan of the best officers he had served under. Not tall, but self-assured to the point of intimidation. Yohan noticed how the other soldiers avoided looking her way, afraid of getting caught.

Her mate was a reserved young man named Patrik. Yohan did not know whether the same laws of marriage applied to their people and so avoided using the term husband, but their close association was clear to all. Every order from Summer was delivered with a warm smile, and received with the same.

Witnessing that relationship forced Yohan to recall his own contentious behavior with Jena, and wonder how things may have turned out differently if they had treated one another with greater respect.

The last, and eldest, trader was a large man who went by the name Silvo. Thick and heavy, as ugly as the women were pretty, Silvo kept his reddish cheeks clean-shaven, although a little facial hair would distract from the oversized nose and uneven blue eyes. Appearances aside, the man had a magnetic personality that was hard to resist. A storyteller and jokester, his deep voice was a main attraction of the caravan's fun-filled nights.

Along with the music. And the dancing. These were the true gifts of the harpa, the things Yohan most admired about them, and knew he would never forget.

These things touched him in much the same way as the tiger had, forever altering him. With every reason to resent their lot, these people embraced it instead. They celebrated life with an enthusiasm that shamed his own petty unhappiness. He had much to learn from them, yet was too daunted to begin.

"They're doing the *sadida* tonight," Brody said excitedly. "Come on, they're starting soon." He grabbed Yohan's arm as he stood. As if Yohan needed encouragement. He would not miss this for all the wine in Liniza. They hurried back toward the wagons.

Sunset blazing behind him, an audience of soldiers before, Patrik clapped out a steady beat with his hands. A small wooden fiddle rested in his lap, for later.

After a few moments, Silvo added his own clapping, turning his hands one way then another as his foot kept time. Yohan watched Ledo and Bostik tapping their own feet in rhythm, unconsciously, their eyes riveted to the two stationary dancers standing with bowed heads and outstretched arms.

As one, Silvo began singing and the women began moving, waving their limbs and twirling their bodies to each nonsensical syllable. The broad, forced smile on Silvo's face was part of the show, and he appeared so strained to maintain it that Yohan thought the portly man might fall from his seat. But his exertions were nothing compared to Meadow and Summer, whose movements alternated between precise and frenetic. Both wore their hair loose, creating long light and dark blurs that mixed with the drifting sparks of the campfire. The two began in parallel but soon flowed in wholly unique patterns, leading the viewer to assume the motions were improvised. Then, with no cue or forewarning, their dancing would become synchronized again. They fluidly moved in and out of these two styles, and all the while the two men propelled them onward with the music, both clapping and one singing.

Then Patrik raised the fiddle to his chin, nodded once, and brought the bow to strings. Soon Silvo joined him, and the musicians stood together. They began to career about as chaotically as the dancers, stamping their feet and swinging their shoulders wildly as they played, kicking up small clouds of brown dirt, handheld bows gliding with dazzling rapidity, eyes closed and faces twisted in manic exaltation. Yohan wondered how they managed not to trip and fall or stumble into one another, but the rhythmic rapture guided their feet as well as their hands.

Most of the soldiers were clapping along, and many were tapping their toes. Yohan looked down and realized he was one of them. He stopped, forcing himself into the soldier's stance. His feet resisted for a moment, then obeyed.

The music and dancing ended abruptly, replaced by cheering and laughter. Performers and audience began to mix. Yohan watched Kelsey place her hand on Patrik's arm to get his attention. Her words were inaudible, but the trader nodded and the two of them stepped away from the crowd to begin dancing together. Summer and Bostik joined them, and Yohan saw an intimate glance pass between the two lovers before giving full attention to their respective partners. Clearly, they would have preferred to be with each other, but the spirit of the harpa compelled them to share their joy with others.

Silvo showed some of the soldiers how to set a beat with their hands, then added his fiddle to the medley with another gregarious smile.

"Soldier Yohan, will you dance with me?"

Somehow, Meadow had approached without his noticing. Either she was born to sneak, or easy living was weakening his perception.

"Perhaps another time," he replied.

She smiled. "All right, then."

Brody joined them. "Yohan is shy like a bird, Fairmeadow. Give him time to get used to you, then he'll sing like a lark. In the meantime, dance with me." He led her away with a laugh, leaving Yohan alone to ponder his indecision.

"Private Yohan?" came a harsh voice.

He turned to face the newcomer. "Aye, Corporal?"

Mercer's face was a perpetual unhealthy red, visible even in the firelight. "As you aren't dancing, how about doing something useful?" While he spoke, bits of the Naru tobacco he frequently chewed dribbled over his lower lip. "One of those mongrels is set up in my tent like it's his own personal castle. Lure it out or kill it."

Yohan could hear the cur growling as he neared the tent. He glanced around for the other, saw it observing him from a safe distance. He had no idea what the harpa named these two— probably Happygrin and Sunshineheart, or some such nonsense —but the soldiers had taken to calling them Spite and Malice. Malice was the bitch he could see watching him, which meant Spite was the mean male whose silhouette Yohan could see through the tent's thin siding.

With music in the background, Yohan sat cross-legged in front of the open flap, letting the dogs see that he meant no harm. He had no fear, either, and relied upon their ability to sense that. There was no hurry. The dancing would continue for hours, and Yohan could not return to it tonight. He found it confusing. Emotion-stirring, when his emotions had no desire to be stirred.

If he had any sort of singing voice, he might have tried a tune. Instead, he decided to tell the dogs a story. He considered other animals he had known, and thought of two in particular.

"Have I ever told you of how beasts saved my life?" The response was increased growling, and not just from inside. Malice had moved closer, her teeth bared in a sneer, a scar running across one eye. He looked at her, smiled sadly, then stared down at his hands. "One was a horse, Ofero." His voice caught on the name, and for the first time in days saw the same mental image that he had carried in his mind for so long. It was the model for a piece of sculpture he had whittled. A crude, cheap, useless gesture.

"The other was a white mountain tiger. A magnificent creature, really. It gave us food when we were dying." He paused. "It gave me hope when I was lost. Let me tell you about it…"

The story was as much for his own sake as theirs. He needed to relive this one last time before he could move on, and he lost himself in the telling, losing track of the minutes, not knowing when the first dog placed her head on his thigh, when he began to stroke the thin black fur, when the other joined them, when it licked the tears from his cheek. He knew only when he was done. The purging complete, he was ready to move forward.

Yohan would have rejoined the dancing then, but he heard them finish in a final crescendo of cheering. That was all right. There was always the morrow, and he felt as content as he was capable of.

.   .   .

"You need to see this," Brody said. "Meadow is telling fortunes."

"Does that sound like the sort of thing that would interest me?" Yohan asked. "I thought you knew me better than that."

Brody grinned. "Shut up and come along."

The harpa already had her first dupe lined up. Ledo stood before her, watching as she shuffled a deck of cards with one hand while straightening the corners of a blanket on the ground. She was sitting cross-legged, Spite and Malice resting comfortably on either side. Spite lifted his head at the approach of newcomers, then stood up and paced over to Yohan, who squatted to scratch behind a crooked ear.

He met Meadow's eyes. Lovely, astonished eyes. Then he noticed the other soldiers staring at him, as well. He shrugged. "Animals like me. Don't ask me why."

Meadow looked down at her work, flipping over cards from the deck and laying them on the blanket. A momentary flush of red appeared on her pale neck, but faded by the third card.

"Why three?" Ledo asked as he sat across from her.

"Each man walks three paths at once," she replied.

"Each man?" Ledo asked.

"Aye. Each woman walks two. Women are not so confused as men."

"Ain't that the truth." He leaned forward, eagerly anticipating the first card. "So, let's see it."

"Not so fast," Meadow corrected. "First, a question. What does Soldier Ledo seek more than anything?"

He considered. "Does happiness work?"

She smiled. "Truly. Nothing more pure beneath the moon and stars." She reached to the first card, paused for dramatic effect, then flipped it over. "A black map. Interesting."

"Absolutely fascinating," Ledo said flatly. "Do you want to tell me what it means?"

"The map represents exploration. Curiosity. Discovery. But

the black means it is unwanted. An exploration forced upon you, not a discovery of choice."

Ledo stroked his chin. "If you say so. How about number two?"

She flipped the second card. "The blue scroll. Knowledge. Understanding." She smiled at the dim-witted soldier. "This jibes nicely with the first card. I told you it worked."

He scratched his temple. "And the third?"

She turned over the last one. "Red plague. Sickness. Disease. But not yours. Someone close to you."

Brody took an exaggerated step away from the man. Yohan smiled at the humor, but neither Ledo nor Meadow seemed to notice.

Ledo looked like he had swallowed an entire lemon. "Your pardon, Sister, but that hardly seems like me," he said at last.

Meadow looked as confused as the soldier. "The cards are correct, but I sense the truth in your words." Her brow furrowed in thought. "I wonder if you are a conduit for another…"

"A what?"

Then she scooped the deck of cards back into her hands. "It's nothing. Sometimes the cards attune themselves to the wrong person. Allow me to try again," she requested.

"Nay. But mayhap one of these other flats will take a chance." He stood up.

Meadow looked imploringly at Yohan. He hesitated, torn between helping her and resisting the superstitious nonsense.

"Happily," Brody said, then filled Ledo's place as quickly as the other abandoned it. He flashed a warm smile at the girl. She returned it, glanced once more at Yohan, then focused on laying three more cards.

"And what does Soldier Brody seek more than anything?" she asked.

For once, the garrulous private remained silent. Contemplative, or hesitant.

To be a Swordthane. But he dares not say that aloud, for fear of ridicule. "Glory," Yohan volunteered.

Brody nodded. "That will do."

Three cards later, and this reveal was even more dubious than the last. The happy soldier stared down at his own fortune, then laughed. "You see that, Yohan? There's glory for you. I'm going to be king."

The blue battle standard symbolized victory. The black dagger meant betrayal. And the blue crown was obvious.

Yohan would have felt better for his friend, if not for the look of horror on Meadow's face. An expression that said she had lost all faith in her own abilities. He felt a surge of sympathy for her, and could think of only one way to help.

"Read mine next, Sister?"

She looked at him, startled. So did Brody. "Are you sure?" they asked in unison.

Yohan nudged his friend aside and sat, facing her. "Please?"

She watched the cards as she shuffled with both hands. Her hair drooped in front of her eyes, hiding them from his sight. But not her smile.

"Now, what does Soldier Yohan seek more than anything?"

He had been considering this for the last minute, but still did not have a good answer.

A purpose. I had one, and now it's gone.

He shook his head. "Nothing, really."

"Love," Brody said.

Yohan glared at his friend, who clapped him on the shoulder.

Meadow looked at him quizzically. "Love, is it?"

He nodded and watched as she flipped the first card—a blue lyre.

"Happiness," Meadow said, and grinned.

"Where did Ledo get to?" Brody asked. He raised his voice, calling out to the emptiness. "Hey, Ledo! Yohan got your happiness." Then he laughed and slapped his friend's back merrily.

"Can we continue?" Yohan asked.

Meadow concealed her smirk and reached for the second, again pausing for effect before turning it over.

"A heart," Brody said enthusiastically. Yohan felt the grip on his shoulder tighten. The other soldier was genuinely excited about this turn of events.

"A heart," Meadow confirmed. "Love." She was smiling at him, apparently as satisfied with the results as his friend.

Yohan could not help himself. "It's black," he said. "Unwanted, you told Ledo."

Her smile faded a bit, but not entirely. "It could simply mean unexpected. One does not often find love where they look for it."

I cannot argue with that.

"And the last card?" *If I get my purpose, then I'll believe.*

Meadow was hesitant to finish the fortune. She knew better than he that the promise of the moment could be dispelled in an instant. Her hand paused, not for effect, over the final card. He watched her face instead of the card as she turned it, knowing that her reaction would tell him more than the picture it depicted. She drew her hand back, and closed her eyes.

"Another dagger," Brody said. "What did that mean?"

"Betrayal," Yohan said. "Red. By someone close to me." He picked up the card for closer study.

Meadow reached out to touch his hand. "Not betrayal *by* someone close to you. Betrayal *of* someone close to you."

Brody laughed. "It'd better not be me, Brother." Then he winked at Meadow. "Thank you for your time, Sister. Your lovely, lovely time."

Silvo's full name was Silverson Goldthrush, as Yohan learned while the two of them prepared the eve meal.

"An impressive name, for an impressive musician. I am happy for the opportunity to tell you how much I enjoyed the *sadida*."

Silvo chuckled. "You've been learning flattery from Soldier Brody, I see." He pulled his hands from a pot of water and shook them dry. "Come. These tubers can wait a few minutes. Allow me to show you something, Soldier Yohan." He led the way to the sleeping area, where the personal effects of the harpa were stowed in various bags and crates of different sizes. Silvo went directly to one mahogany box with ornate fastenings and bent over it.

Yohan's attention was struck by something else, however. "Is that a bow?" he asked.

Silvo straightened and turned, eyes darting between Yohan and the curve of wood lying partially concealed beneath a loose pile of colorful garments. "Nay... That is to say, aye. We use them sometimes to hunt rabbits and small beasts for food. Come, Soldier Yohan, allow me to show you a miracle of the heavens." He turned back to the box.

Yohan had grown up in Nurosterlend, rich in elms, yews, ash, and hazels. His home, a small village named Parca, specialized in producing arrows of fir. He knew a hunting bow when he saw one, yet had never seen one such as this. Even unstrung and only half-visible, this one was clearly thicker and longer than those familiar to him.

Yet Silvo was clearly uncomfortable with the subject, and Yohan had no desire to irritate the pleasant trader. In any case, both men were distracted by the object the harpa then lifted from a bed of straw.

It was an instrument Yohan had not yet seen used in the nighttime amusements—an elegant polished lute, exquisitely crafted, far more valuable than the campfire fiddles. Silvo plucked the strings once, smiled gloriously at the single note, then prepared to stow it back in its crate.

"May I?" Yohan asked.

Silvo was openly reluctant to hand it over, but the good manners of the harpa compelled him to. Yohan made certain to treat it with as much care and respect as his rough hands would allow. Even so, the friendly man's anxious fidgeting became oppressively pronounced, so Yohan handed it back without the full examination he would have liked.

"When will we get to hear this?" he asked.

"Perhaps never," Silvo replied. Then laughed. "Perhaps tonight. I play only when the craving becomes irresistible."

There was no music that night, however.

Kelsey spotted the flames first, when they were nothing but a pale red glow on the darkening horizon. She pointed them out to Yohan, her arm aiming due south, farther along the rudimentary road used by caravans and naught else.

He nodded. "That's fire, all right. At least one. We'll see them more clearly after sunset." Behind them, the sounds of camp prevented anyone from overhearing.

"What should I do?"

It seemed obvious. This was not their decision. "The corporal needs to know."

She shook her head in agreement, but made no move toward his tent.

Yohan studied her. "You want me to tell him?"

"Would you? I don't much like…" Her voice trailed away.

Yohan patted her shoulder. He took a step, then reconsidered, looking back at Kelsey. "Tell the harpa." Then he made his way to their superior.

"Corporal Mercer?"

"What now?" came the reply.

"Something you need to hear, Corporal." Yohan waited.

The irritated face stuck out of the tent, the cheek puffed full of tobacco. "Come in, Private."

Mercer took one of the two chairs. Yohan waited to be offered the other.

"Private, don't just stand there. Give me this report."

"Fires, Corporal. Due south, along the road. Perhaps five miles, perhaps closer."

Mercer leaned forward. "Shit."

"Aye, Corporal."

Mercer glared at him. Then clucked his tongue inside his cheek. "I suppose we should check them out. It might be just a few travelers."

"This is not a campfire, Corporal. The only people who use this road are caravans and bandits. If it's a caravan, it's burning. If it's anyone else, there's enough of them that they don't mind calling attention to themselves."

"That's enough, Private. This is not your decision, it's mine."

"Nay, Corporal, it's mine," called a voice from outside. The flap pulled open, and Summer entered the tent. Behind her walked Malice, sniffing at the edge of the tent disapprovingly before following.

"Sister," Mercer said hurriedly, an obsequious tone replacing his former irritation. "Please, have a seat."

"Nay, thank you, Corporal." She remained standing, scanning the surroundings.

Yohan felt something against his leg, looked down, and watched Malice tap him a second time with her paw. He smiled, crouched, and scratched beneath her submissive neck while she panted. "I'm happy to see you, too, Malice."

He looked at the others and noticed Summer glaring at him with a curious expression—an unsettling alloy of puzzlement and annoyance. As their eyes met, he suddenly felt guilty, as if the dogs were harpa property and he a thief. He considered uttering a banal pleasantry about the affectionate mutt, then realized he did not even know what name the harpa had given her.

"Sister, I believe we should investigate these fires," Mercer began.

Summer faced the man. "My people have learned to avoid fights wherever possible, Corporal." The indignation had left her tone, but not the authority.

"Aye, but I have an obligation to defend Vilnia."

"Must I remind you, Corporal, that your soldiers are here to protect my caravan until we reach Threefork. There you may ask to be released from your duty, if you wish. But not before."

Malice barked once, and both others turned to face Yohan.

Summer frowned. "Soldier, do you have anything to add?"

"Aye, do you…Soldier?" Mercer asked.

Yohan cleared his throat. "Nay. That was the dog."

Slowly, Summer's lips turned upward. Although Mercer continued to scowl, her frown became a grin, bringing an infusion of mirth to dispel much of the gloom in the air.

She turned back. "Corporal, please tell your troops to pack up again. We'll head west overnight. We can reach a secondary road by midday of the morrow. One delay is nothing compared to the safety of this caravan. Is that clear?"

Summer brushed by Yohan on her way out. She leaned close to his ear for just a second, her whisper barely audible. "Her name is Lullaby."

4

BELOW

The last hours of wakefulness brought worry to Jak and his companions. The discovery of the skeleton and the dawning realizations that followed started a series of disappointments.

Once again, fear served as a powerful motivator. Sheer exhaustion became frantic energy. They hurried to search for an exit, driven by fear and desperation, until hope was replaced by panic—then, at last, acceptance.

Two tunnels led away from the grand cavern, but both were ultimately blocked by immense rockfalls. The first was a letdown, the second a revelation. If there really was an escape, grasping about in the semi-dark was not the way to find it. The cavern was simply too huge for random, directionless exploration. Jak clung to the notion that there was another, better way to look, all the while pushing back against the idea that really disturbed him—that the old legend was right, every way out was buried, and the five refugees trapped.

He was the last to accept it. When the others begged for rest, Jak pushed them on, pretending not to feel the fatigue, hunger, and disappointment they did. But the combination of their pleas and his own sore muscles finally wore him down. He reluctantly acquiesced to a "rest" back within the lighted confines of the dead city's haunting streets. Avoiding the words *camp* and *sleep* helped trick his tired mind into believing the stoppage was only temporary, a postponement rather than a cessation.

But the decision to stop, even momentarily, was an undeniable defeat. Jak felt a profound sense of disaster befalling them in this place. His responsibility was to get them all out safely and as soon as possible, and every minute trapped below was an admission of failure, a tacit consent that the looming doom was preordained.

And so with Calla's head on his leg and his own on a rock, a young scared thrall went to sleep, worried they might never awaken. Yet they did, one by one, each face wearing a unique mask of turmoil highlighted in eerie blue. Each had lost loved ones, each bore their own individual griefs, and the list of horrors they faced continued to grow.

Food became the new priority. Kluber and Riff wished to search the ancient city for some. Jak felt an inherent revulsion toward the buildings in general—and to one in particular—but allowed inspection of the smallest along the ruined perimeter. Kluber argued that the larger, intact structures closer to the city center were more likely to have useful supplies, but he argued alone, quietly, and in vain.

While the others hunted, dispatched in different directions, Jak stayed alone in the street, staring at the distant monolith's visible peak, thankful that he was unable to see the massive building beyond. Due to its size, probably a palace, a place where ghosts of dead kings ruled on, ordering the execution of any living soul that dared violate their sacrosanct realm. He was growing more and more certain that within was the source of the ominous dread afflicting his mind, draining his spirit.

Each of the other four returned, empty-handed and long-faced, their efforts useless.

"Let's search the undamaged houses now," suggested Riff. "Especially the big one in the middle." He grinned as he pointed, looking forward to the opportunity to fulfill a desire he had felt from the first sighting. Clearly, the oppression of the underworld had less effect on the other thrall, for he still seemed to be enjoying the adventure. Neither hardship nor danger dampened the boy's spirits.

"Nay," Jak directed. "Let's check the lake. Perhaps something edible grows near the water." Riff shrugged and led the way.

The totality of the blackness that was the lake was disconcerting and disorienting, and only a quiet lapping assured them they were not walking directly into a sinister void. How strange then that this lightless abyss soon provided a form of salvation.

The rockfire fungus thinned near the water's edge, so the companions lit one of their few remaining torches. Soon they would have another item to add to their tally of scarce commodities. As the tallest of the group, Kluber held the torch high to maximize the flickering glow. The stronger source literally made the rockfire pale in comparison, and their eyes quickly became dependent on the flame's illumination. Similarly, its heat saturated and soothed their bodies with a warmth they had not known was missing until this restoration. Bodies and spirits were drawn to the precious beacon, however fleeting. Of the five, only Riff remained willing to wander out of its beneficent radiance.

The young thrall was singing in a low hum, occasionally scooping up a loose stone to toss into the lake. As Riff's silhouette faded into the darkness, Jak resisted the temptation to call the other boy back. Before today, Jak would have eagerly started a game to determine who could throw farthest, but now he thought only of danger and preservation—a shepherd tending to flock, or a father to vulnerable children. Yet Jak held his tongue.

Better that one of them feel some slight amusement than his own dour mood spread to all.

He tried not to think of the unfairness. Riff's master was in the group, as was Jak's. Yet the burden of care and supervision had fallen on just one of them. He had taken on this role the moment he punched Kluber in Calla's home, and so the blame was Jak's alone. But knowing that did not preclude him from envying the other thrall. How nice it would be to feel no responsibilities for the others, to worry about only oneself.

That assessment was not entirely fair, he knew, for Riff had contributed more to their collective survival than all the rest put together. How many times would the group have died if not for their youngest member?

They heard a splash, different from the sound of the stone tosses. Jak looked up, worried that Riff had somehow fallen in. But instead the youth was on his knee at the water's edge, splashing the surface with one excited hand. "Everyone, come here!" he yelled.

They obeyed, and Kluber held the torch out to get a better look at what Riff was doing. His hand wiped clear an area of the thin layer of algae that lay on top, causing cascading concentric circles to recede into the distance. Otherwise, Jak saw nothing.

"What is it?" he asked at last.

Riff stopped brushing long enough to look up. "I saw a fish."

They stared at him in skeptical silence. He felt the weight of their doubt and looked down. "Well, I heard a fish. It was a 'plop' sound, and when I looked there was a ripple." He pointed a short distance from the shore, as if that would help.

Kluber coughed. "Of course there are ripples now, Riff," he said sternly. "You're pounding the water like it's wash day."

"Well, listen!" Riff pleaded. "Maybe we'll hear it again."

"We're not going to hear anything now," Jak said coolly. "If there was a fish, all the noise we're making scared it away." He stared out at the water, wondering how seriously to take the other thrall's claim.

Plop.

Jak closed his eyes, took a deep breath to steady his suddenly shaking body, and spoke quietly. "I just saw one, too." Smaller than a man's hand, it had reflected the light from the torch with a pale iridescence. Under normal circumstances, such a paltry catch would quickly be tossed back, but now Jak's mouth salivated at the thought of a single bite.

Nevertheless, he could not feel hopeful. There should have been exaltation, for this discovery meant their most immediate need might be satisfied. But his sense of gloom only intensified. Surely, something so dark and sinister as this lake could not yield anything but more death and despair.

Kluber clapped Riff on the back. "Well done, you clod." The youngster grinned, blushed, and turned away. He began walking again, this time away from the shoreline.

"Where are you going?" Jak called abruptly.

Riff turned back. "Looking around. Maybe one of these houses nearby has something we can use to catch—"

But Jak was shaking his head. "We'll figure something out with what we have." He could discern Kluber frowning. "We should stay away from the intact buildings."

"You don't think it's worth searching them?"

Jak grimaced. "I really think we should avoid the places that may be occupied. Whatever lives here, we don't want them to know about us."

Kluber's face morphed into a look of sympathy that was worse than the frown. "We have to put survival first, Jak."

He was right, of course, but still Jak hesitated. The decision hung in the air, already decided but for simple acknowledgment. Yet he could not bring himself to agree. Deep inside his heart, he knew that this path led to tragedy. But there was no logical vocalization he could give to his thoughts, and the weight of their stares bore him down heavily. He looked down and weakly nodded.

Kluber put a hand on Jak's shoulder. "Just these. We won't go near the big ones close to the plaza, all right?" Then he turned to the others and began to direct them into action.

Jak found himself lightheaded, perhaps from hunger, and found a place to sit. The reality of the situation was finally sinking in with the power of a thunderstorm. Jak had led this small band from one disaster to another, and the likelihood of survival was as bleak as a winter night. Their friends were dead, their families were dead, the world above a nightmare and the one below a living hell. If Kevik had been with them, perhaps they would have stood a chance. As it was, Jak gave his friends hope without substance. Why they followed a dimwitted, uneducated thrall at all was a mystery that he had purposefully put off pondering until now.

Kluber would have been the better leader, but Jak had stolen that role. Clearly, now was the time to relinquish the responsibility.

He lost track of time in these unwelcome thoughts, until Calla pulled him away with a warm smile.

"Guess what Riff found," she said.

"A sea dragon in the middle of the lake?" The quip was an attempt at humor, but he immediately regretted saying it. He had no desire to contaminate the others with his own melancholy doubts.

"No, Silly. A dock. And a boat. And in the boat, a fishing pole."

Jak nodded, feigning enthusiasm. "Great." *It's just a matter of time, now.*

She stared at him a moment, her smile slipping a bit. "You aren't pleased?"

"I am. Just...tired."

"I'm going to look for something to use as kindling. Come with me?"

He shook his head. "Sorry, I need to rest another minute."

Jak relived that expression of disappointment in his mind's eye countless times in the days that followed.

Kindling, more poles and line, a net, mysterious light-emitting lures—they discovered all this and more in one large structure near the dock. The others showed these things to Jak with hopeful smiles that he did his best to emulate. With some success, for the prospect of imminent food made his stomach jump and his misgivings recede.

He walked in silent step beside Kleo. Ahead Riff led the way toward another unexplored structure—a low, wide edifice that reminded Jak of the library they had already discovered.

"Is something wrong, Jak?" She spoke in a tentative voice, so unlike the harsh taskmaster he had grown up with. He wondered how she coped with the loss of her entire family. For that matter, he wondered whether she considered *him* family. In the absence of all others, she may have looked to him as a surrogate brother.

"I'm fine," he assured her, pondering how they might resume a hint of their former relationship. Before, he had never enjoyed being imperiously bossed around. Now the idea was downright comforting. "How is your back? Anything I can do?"

"It feels a bit better now. I'm sure Kluber is happier about that than I. He must have scratched it for me a hundred times last night."

"I'm sure he doesn't mind. He clearly cares about you."

Kleo winced, then nodded. "I suppose so."

The discomfort was obvious, so Jak sought to put her mind at ease. "He does. He's a good man, Kleo. Smart. A reliable leader." Realizing he may have been seeking to reassure himself, Jak turned the topic back to her. "He knows he's lucky to have you."

The look she flashed him contained a hint of the old Kleo— quick to anger or annoyance. Then she began walking faster and reached the building ahead of Riff. She lit a torch and disappeared through the immense open portal.

The exterior may have been intact, but the interior was in shambles. Fragments of hardwood and stone abounded, the decayed remnants of furniture and shelving. Scattered about were more skeletons, in greater numbers than seen previously. On the far side of a grand foyer, Kleo inspected the contents of several decomposed chests.

"Find anything, Kleo?" Riff called.

"I did!" she replied happily, if distractedly, her spirits already recovered from whatever irritation Jak had inflicted.

The two young men approached the chest she was eagerly rummaging through. Jewelry.

"At a time like this, Kleo?"

The pique returned. "Hush, you."

No help at all, Riff joined her. Jak watched that boyish grin widen as he held up a whistle carved from alabaster and shaped like a snake. He blew on it once, creating an unpleasant shriek.

Jak turned away. He wanted to stop them, to point out how trinkets were of little value now. But he was through giving orders. He headed back toward the entrance. Stopping once, he glanced back, hoping they had followed of their own volition. But both continued to poke through the useless ornaments, and neither so much as raised their heads to watch him leave.

Returning to the makeshift camp, he saw Calla preparing a small cooking fire. Hopeful that he might get a few minutes to make up for his sour mood from earlier, he headed directly toward her. "Anything I can do to help?" he asked cheerfully.

"Aye!" Kluber called out, just then returning from a moderately successful outing. His right hand carried the pole, his left a pair of small unidentifiable fish hooked by the mouth on his index and middle fingers. "You can clean these."

"With what?"

Kluber smiled. Placing the fish near Calla's fire, he drew out a miniature knife. "Found it with the poles and lures," he said.

Jak glanced once at Calla, but her eyes and thoughts were with the burgeoning flames. He took the knife and slid the first fish into position.

The shrill shriek of Riff's whistle broke the silence. He and Kleo rejoined them, looking as content with the rewards of their efforts as Kluber with his.

While he worked, Jak glanced around from face to face. The smiles and occasional laughter were contagious, and soon he participated in the ease and merriment without feeling guilty. His fears from before waned, the cloud of doom pushed away in the warmth of the fire and the sumptuous aroma of two meager fish roasting. By the time they all closed their eyes to a second night of subterranean sleep, an aura of sanguinity brought pleasant dreams. And when they woke many hours later, Riff was gone.

"Where could he be?" Calla asked.

Kluber shrugged.

"Maybe he went fishing," Kleo suggested. "Morn is a good time to catch them, from what I hear." She looked at Jak. "That's what Kevik always told me."

"The boat's still here," Calla said. "But I suppose he might have found a spot on the shore." She raised her hand to her eyes as she stared into the distance, as if that could help her see farther.

"He's exploring," Jak said, with a finality that no one argued. "He knew I didn't like it, so he did it in secret."

"If he wanted it to be secret, he'd be back by now," Calla stated.

"He's still a bit childish," Kleo said. "He probably found something and lost track of time."

Kluber frowned, looking as worried as Jak had ever seen him.

"He's smarter than you give him credit for. Something went wrong."

The concern spread from his face to Kleo's. "What do we do, Jak?"

Why are you asking me? "He's Kluber's thrall. We should—"

"He's more than my thrall, Jak. He's my *friend.*"

Jak looked down, embarrassed. The admission made sense, of course. Reflecting on his own complicated friendship with Kevik, he should have known that Riff and Kluber would have a similar bond, even if it manifested differently.

"He'll be back," Calla offered hopefully.

Kluber shook his head. "We need to look for him."

Reluctant to start an argument, Jak hesitated to point out the obvious. Thankfully, Kleo did so for him. "What if he comes back on his own and no one is here?"

"Maybe two stay while two search," Jak suggested. The others looked at him, making him uncomfortable. "It's an option. I don't think anyone should go anywhere alone from now on."

Kluber nodded. "You and I can go first."

"So we just wait here?" Kleo asked in annoyance.

"Nay, you can fish up today's supper."

Jak considered, reluctant to contribute further. But he could see discontent on the faces of both girls. "We're running low on torches. Maybe you can figure out a way to make more from the supply of wood." They nodded and got to their feet.

Eager to get started, Jak and Kluber searched the buildings nearest the lake first, then began to head back into the city proper. They moved house-to-house, calling quietly into the dark interior of each without penetrating deep within. They carried one torch each, but did not light them, knowing the absence of visibility limited Riff as much as it did them. The young thrall had taken none of their remaining supply for himself, so it stood to reason he would not leave the shadowy fringes of the ubiquitous blue glow.

There was little conversation between the two of them, but strain and worry showed in Kluber's face and heavy breathing. Jak wished he could say something to comfort his companion— to assure him that the boy would wander back safely with news of another discovery—but the earlier sense of doom repossessed his thoughts, and he searched with little hope of success.

They returned for a silent, dispirited meal before resuming the hunt. Once they left the listening range of the girls, Kluber voiced his thoughts. "Jak, we both know where he went. The rest is just wasting time."

"All right."

They knew the lake curved inward at some point, for they had heard its soft rippling in the distance when last deep in the city. But they elected to stick to the streets they knew, taking nearly twenty minutes to reach the area of the library, plaza, and monolith. As before, wisps of mist hung in the air, partially concealing the columned portico of the imposing building across the square. Even before the discovery of the skeleton—and the fresh ashes—Jak had been wary of this location. Now it positively terrified him.

Once again he pondered what function this place served. In his experience, the ritual of burning the dead was associated with the followers of Tempus, the god of fire. The shrine in Everdawn had cremated everyone who died in Shady Glen as a sacrificial offering to Tempus. To protect their souls, as Jak had learned from Disciple Lukas just before the end.

The skeleton indicated that a similar ritual existed down here, as well. Did that mean the building before them was a massive shrine of Tempus? A temple? That all the dead were burned here, just as they were above?

His mind made a simple correction. The shrine had *not* burned everyone who died in the Glen. He and Kevik had hidden a body to conceal a murder. Gallo's soul lacked protection, and the demons had come shortly thereafter. Jak had assumed those creatures had followed Rufus and the sword he took from the mountains, but now he realized there was another connection. The destruction of his home may not have been entirely the Third's fault. *It may have been mine.*

"Are you all right?"

Jak shook his head to clear the disturbing thoughts. An important objective required his focus. "Do you see an entrance?"

Kluber shook his head. "Come on, let's look for one."

He led the way to the near side, where smooth-cut stones formed a long exterior wall decorated with a carved frieze along the top, the monstrosities depicted there blessedly shrouded in the dim light.

A few minutes of inspection yielded the outlines of a square portal in the center. Like the mysteriously sealed door in the library, this one showed no practical manner of opening.

"Does it have holes like the other, Kluber?"

"Aye, three. But in this light, I can't make out what they are."

They spent the better part of an hour searching the building's perimeter for another method of entry, to no avail. Ultimately, they found themselves back in the plaza, staring at the menacing structure with a mix of emotions.

"We're not getting in," Kluber admitted at last, the defeat in his voice palpable.

Seeking to be reassuring, Jak voiced the silver lining. "If we can't get in, neither could Riff. He must be somewhere else, after all." That point made, Jak became anxious to leave at once.

His companion, however, continued to scan the area, reluctant to give up just yet.

"Jak," he asked curiously a minute later. "Does that monolith look straight to you?"

Sure enough, from this angle the unbalanced spire no longer appeared askew.

Except that the change was not only from this angle, as a

quick triangulation proved. Jak's blood suddenly ran cold. "Kluber, let's get back."

"Aye. Let's."

The two of them hurried from the plaza at a pace nearer an ignominious run than a composed walk. They returned to the camp for a final eve meal and another false night of sleep. The physical exertions of the day paled in comparison to the mental, and Jak found the latter more demanding, sliding deep into oblivion the moment after closing his eyes.

Riff did not return by the next morn, and a second day's hunting yielded no better results than the first. Nor was Jak able to engage Calla in a discussion that felt more essential—more imperative—with each passing hour. Some dynamic in their relations had changed, but exactly how he was unable to say. There were plenty of opportunities for conversation, of course, but at every attempt she threw up a wall of polite resistance that left him wondering whether she held him responsible for all she had lost. If so, he could not blame her, but he desperately hoped to make amends.

Not until the third morn since Riff's disappearance did Jak find her willing to accept company. She sat apart from the others, arms wrapped around her knees, staring out at the watery blackness. He approached her tentatively, worried that she might decide now was a good time to take a lakeside walk—or worse, shoo him away. But she remained in place as he sat beside her, and they silently contemplated the soft rippling together for several long minutes.

"I think the color is changing," she said at last.

"The color?"

"Of the rockfire. It was pure blue when we first saw it. It has a hint of green now. I wonder why." The sentence trailed away like her thoughts, which clearly were not entirely on the fungus. Jak said nothing, hoping she would speak whatever was really on her mind. There were so many possibilities—a wedding halted most cruelly, a father dead, a betrothed lost. Any one of them would have undone most people.

When she finally spoke again, it was not at all what he expected. "I never thought I would hate this dress so much," she said. Jak had become so inured to seeing her in the dirty, tattered peach gown that he no longer noticed. This reminder made him realize how horribly uncomfortable she must have been these last harrowing days.

"I thought it was so beautiful that day," she continued. "Everyone was smiling, saying how nice it looked, how happy they were for me, how radiant I was. Now look at me."

"You're still radiant to me."

The smile of appreciation she flashed was the first sign in days of the old, easy-spirited Calla. Seeing it was a powerful reminder of how much he had missed such simple gestures. However insignificant, that smile was a welcome respite from an otherwise dismal existence, and he loved her for it. Jak felt the instinctive compulsion to tell her so. He barely opened his mouth when the screeching began.

The two of them rushed back to the morn's small cooking fire, where Kluber knelt beside Kleo, holding her shoulder as she writhed in distress. "It burns!" she sobbed between piteous shrill shrieks. "It burns, it burns, it *buuurns…*"

"I know, I know," Kluber repeated calmly. His hand rubbed her shoulder, her neck, her back. Then it stopped suddenly and withdrew, as if directly feeling the burning she described.

Kleo noticed the gesture. "What's wrong?" she pleaded.

"Nothing." But he would not return her gaze, looking instead at Jak and Calla. The young men's eyes met, a reluctant question forming in one pair, a hesitant nod coming in response.

Calla knelt beside Kleo, stroking her hair, soothing her agitation. "*Shh.* Hold still. We're just going to take a look."

Jak moved closer as Kluber untied the dress at the back and opened it from the neck downward. Sweat and grime made the garment stick to her skin, so he patiently peeled the fabric back as collectedly as her twisting movements allowed. The delicate smooth curve of her spine appeared, running down the elegant back, soft pale skin faintly reflecting the strange composite glow of firelight and fungus. Except where it did not.

Her lower back was covered in scales. Indistinct in color but dark and flaky, and definitely not skin. Kleo was as pretty as young women came, yet Jak fought not to recoil in disgust. He forced himself to maintain the poise of his two companions, who looked from affliction to face with sympathy and compassion.

"What is it?" Kleo asked.

"It's nothing," Kluber said. "A tender spot where it's raw."

Calla gently ran the backs of her fingers over Kleo's moist temple. "It's just a rash. Nothing to worry about."

"Well, it hurts like the devil."

Jak watched as Kluber covered the corrupted area back up and retied the dress. Then the two of them left the poor girl in Calla's capable hands and wandered a distance away to talk. Yet there was little to say. The search for Riff needed to continue, but now they admitted to an even greater incentive to escape these diabolic caverns and get Kleo back to the real world, to a city if possible, and into proper care.

The boat gave them another option to consider. The far side of the gigantic cavern was far too shrouded in shadow to discern from this distance, but someone in the dinghy could investigate the opposite shoreline up close. The effort would take all day, but such a search might reveal an exit from this dismal place after all —if Riff were found, or if they decided to leave him behind.

As they discussed options, Jak became aware of a confusion of authority. Ever since the decision had been made to search rather than avoid the less damaged regions of the city, Jak believed the responsibility was no longer his. Only now did he realize his assumption that Kluber had taken over was just that—an assumption, implied but unspoken. And, apparently, unshared.

"I think Kleo needs help soon. But I don't want to abandon Riff, wherever he's got to." Kluber trailed off questioningly, awaiting a response that Jak was uneager to proffer. He wondered why the more educated, more intelligent, more capable older boy so much as cared for his opinion. Had one punch really drained all the conceit and pomposity from the magistrate's son? However necessary it had been at the time, Jak now regretted that act.

"I don't know. I really don't. Honestly, if you wanted to take charge for a time, I wouldn't protest."

Kluber stiffened. "I couldn't do that, Jak. If we lost one or the other because of a decision I make…well, I don't think I could live with that. My conscience, I mean."

"And you think I can?"

The narrow shoulders shrugged. "I think I'd be dead if you hadn't taken charge up there. You got us this far. That's good enough for me."

I hope you remember those words the next time something goes wrong. "All right. Calla can look after Kleo for now. You and I will keep looking for Riff the rest of today. Maybe we'll get lucky and he'll wander back on his own. One way or another, we can reassess in the eve."

Those plans changed as soon as they returned to the girls, however. For whatever reason, Kleo rediscovered her former bossiness and desired Jak to stay with her. Understanding as always, Calla simply smiled unperturbedly and made him promise to take good care of the acerbic patient. The reason for the request never became clear, for his mistress soon fell into a disturbed sleep while he tended the meager fire.

They were running low on firewood and would soon need to collect more from the supply Riff had found. Jak wondered whether the disappearance was at all related to that discovery. Might he have tried taking something else, and the owners caught him stealing? Who were the owners, anyway? And where were they?

Near the city center, most likely. The large edifice there, the plaza, and the monolith still discomfited Jak. That location was the epicenter of the fears plaguing his troubled mind. Just because he and Kluber were unable to get in did not mean it was necessarily unoccupied. Perhaps its residents simply fashioned a method to keep intruders out.

The same could be said for the library, or at least its inner sanctum. The sealed portal there certainly appeared similar in design to the grand building's mystifying entrance. *Figure one of them out, and gain access to both...*

"You're always so lost in thought, Jak. What about?"

Kleo was wide awake, sitting up, showing nary a trace of her earlier ordeal. Either sleep and time had inured her to the soreness, or her back had finished whatever transformation was happening. In either case, he welcomed a change of subject.

"Any idea what a circle, a crescent, and a six-pointed star have in common?" He chuckled at the way he had formed that sentence, much like a bad joke his friend Kurtis had told at the last festival. *What do the farm girls and cowshit have in common? The older they get, the easier they are to pick up.* Like much of the bawdy talk he heard, Jak had not really understood the humor. But Kevik had laughed so hard, he nearly spit mead from his mouth.

Jak's heart constricted painfully. How he missed his friend and wished he were here. Kevik the Courageous would never have hesitated to lead, the way Kluber had, and Jak would not be suffering this hopeless, irrepressible burden.

The sudden, intense sadness distracted him from Kleo's altered expression. Now he took notice, and recognized that emotion from long, repeated exposure. For most of his life, it had been her most prominent attribute. Irritation.

"I know you don't approve, but I don't see the harm."

The comment was as out-of-place as her countenance.

Despite all that had happened, Jak was suddenly the housethrall again, desperate to please an unhappy mistress. "W-what?"

Her eyes narrowed as she glared. Then she turned to rummage through a small pocket on her dress, so discreetly woven that he had never known of its existence. She withdrew a thin circular band of indiscernible metal, the diameter of a large man's fist, with three small carven stones spaced evenly around like charms. Too small to make out from even a few feet away, but he did not need to see them to know what they were.

"Kleo…where?"

"The jewelry. I thought it was a bracelet, but it's too big for me. Most of the other pieces were too far deteriorated, but this one stood out." She stared at him, the annoyance fading, their roles reversing. "May I keep it, Jak?"

He gaped, first at the item, then at the girl holding it. Rarely had his thoughts raced so chaotically as they did now. He had to find out if the object was the key, and he had to find out now.

A brief pause to collect his wits. "Are you fit to walk?" he asked at last.

She nodded, but her face held a question. "Aye, but—"

"Come on. I'll explain on the way."

He dragged her by the hand until she finally matched his hurried pace. His explanation was as rushed as their feet.

"Jak, shouldn't we wait for the others at the camp?"

"We're just going to try this and come right back. We'll be there when they return."

The urge for haste exceeded that for caution, and they covered the distance to the inner district much faster than he and Kluber had a few days prior. Jak lit a torch and led the way into the library, through the spartan, ruined chambers to the doorway in question, then paused in a moment of indecision. What if he was wrong? Could he take another disappointment?

"Aren't you going to try it?" Kleo whispered expectantly. The edge in her voice rekindled his excitement at the prospect of solving a deep mystery. Perhaps because he knew how his own meager intellect compared to others, Jak always took pride in figuring out difficult puzzles. He lifted Kleo's discovery, matched the three charms to their respective holes, and pushed them in. There was a clicking sound as some unseen mechanism triggered, then a smooth rumble as the heavy stone door slid open on its own, propelled by some unfathomable power.

The two of them exchanged a look of amazement. Then Jak held the torch out, and they stared into an immense octagonal chamber filled with more bookshelves—not merely lining the walls, but row upon row throughout, with barely room to walk between. And on every shelf sat whole, undamaged books. Somehow, the hermetic sanctum prevented their decay.

This place put the Archives in Everdawn to shame. There Jak could have spent years reading everything—were he capable of reading, of course. Here he could spend lifetimes.

"Jak!" Kleo hissed in a harsher whisper. "Jak!"

He stopped, only now realizing he had walked in. He was standing in a narrow lane between two of the heavy hardwood rows, his feet carefully spread so as not to step on the volumes stacked on the floor. Glancing back, he noted a curious look of apprehension on his companion's comely face. "Come on in," he said in a conversational tone. "There's nothing to fear."

Reluctantly, she joined him, and they moved slowly throughout the library within a library. He stopped at a series of particularly large tomes and held the torch up to the words exquisitely scrawled on their broad spines. "What are these?"

She shook her head. "That's not a language I recognize."

Disappointed, he moved on. Three more times he stopped at something notably interesting or compelling, and each time she shook her head.

The flush of excitement was beginning to wane when they reached the end of the row. Jak turned up the next, then felt her fingers grab his arm. She pointed. "There."

He held the torch out where she indicated as she moved closer to one of the smaller, less imposing bookshelves. She pulled one book off, looked at the cover, then flipped it open to the middle of its delicate thin pages. She looked up enthusiastically. "Carthic. I don't know it well, but enough to read some. This is about plants."

"Are all these Carthic?"

She quickly scanned along the row. "Aye." She continued to the next section. "Come on, Jak!"

Now she led and he followed. "Dauphi!" she exclaimed. "I don't know it much at all, but I'm sure these are Dauphi." She absentmindedly pulled him closer as she approached a third section, the smallest yet with the least impressive books they had seen. She picked one up and inspected it, then smiled at him so beautifully that the underworld brightened. Her finger gently tapped the cover. "Imperial."

There is a lesson in the story of the Chekiks, for the race that enslaved the hratha were once slaves themselves. Subjugation, maltreatment, and suffering inevitably lead to determination, violence, and independence.

The inhuman beasts we know today started as a pacifistic society on the eastern fringes of the continent. Then the burgeoning Azilian Empire swept over the land, dominating those it had use for and slaying the rest. The tall and weak Chekiks were made into teachers and scribes. Over time servility became zeal, humility became ferocity, and erudition became power.

Recognizing that the Azilians found strength in their barbaric gods, the Chekiks discovered deities of their own. The Nine Devils taught their new worshipers how to fight with such cruelty that even their savage overlords learned to flee and submit rather than suffer the brutal consequences of defeat. Of those who fought, the lucky were those who died in battle, for the taken faced a far more terrible fate. Prisoners watched as the Chekiks devoured their comrades alive, slowly and tortuously, tormented screams pleasing the gluttons like wine and seasoning. And each onlooker knowing their own turn would come.

The Azilians were dispersed and eradicated, effectively annihilated from existence everywhere but these fragile pages of history. Even their warlike gods were thrown down by The Nine Devils, who became the new rulers of the otherworlds above and below, spreading their evil traditions with each new land the relentless Chekiks conquered. Their malignant liturgies grow more twisted and craven with each passing year, and will continue to do so until this world is consumed, or they themselves cast aside and replaced by a stronger pantheon of a new people.

The Chekican Communion has existed for a dozen generations and may thrive for a dozen more, but its end will surely come as its beginning—at the hands of those made slaves. The hratha lineage will surely become the masters. And will find its own victims to subjugate and mistreat. Such is the circle of time.

Kleo was capable, but stylistically far less emotional and emphatic as she read. Her voice spoke the words in a near monotone, so very unlike the way the words jumped off the page when Calla had gone with him to the Archives. Jak had always thought reading was reading, but as with so many things lately, he was discovering a new level of complexity. The world was never as simple as it appeared.

Nevertheless, he was thrilled at the turn of events. Never had he better understood Riff's constant urge to explore. This discovery—solving one puzzle of many—only piqued his appetite to learn more. Terrible as this underground cavern was, desperate as the five of them were to escape, leaving this place and all these books behind would be very difficult indeed.

"Here they are!" Kluber's astonished voice echoed inside the enclosed space. Jak and Kleo looked up in surprise as their companions entered.

"You two figured out the door!" Kluber exclaimed in wonder. "How did you do it?"

The question was aimed at Jak, but he ignored it for the moment. His gaze was drawn to Calla, her every motion and reaction registering in his mind with perfect clarity. She took in the scene with one quick view, her eyes moving from him to Kleo and the book she held. A gleam flashed in her eyes, a wave of resentment rolling across her amiable features. Then the look disappeared just as abruptly. She smiled at Kleo. "I'm glad you're feeling better." Then she turned and walked out.

Kluber placed a hand on Jak's shoulder. "You have to tell me everything. On the way back. I'm starving."

The banter during supper was noticeably more convivial and less restrained than usual. Jak allowed Kleo to recount the events leading to the unexpected reunion in the library. She fielded questions happily, the return of pleasure to her face giving satisfaction to those who had worried about her.

As promised, he and Kluber reassessed their plans afterward. The ugly affliction on Kleo's back was still a concern, but at least was not inflicting any overtly deleterious effect on the girl. Riff remained the higher priority, and they elected to spend at least another day searching for him. Jak tried not to believe that the reason he agreed to the plan so readily was in order to spend more time with the books. But he did know that in the morn he would suggest they relocate their camp to the library.

When they finally lay down to sleep, the mood was as light-hearted and optimistic as any since their harried flight from the demons above.

Jak awoke to the shaking of his shoulder. He opened his eyes and found a momentary relief in the sight of Calla. But the worry in her face quickly washed away that spontaneous hope. The doubts flooded back in one tremendous wave.

"Something's happening," she said.

Jak nodded and sat up. Kluber and Kleo were already standing, both staring into the distance. Toward the city center.

Nothing out of the ordinary was visible, but they all felt the pull.

Barely speaking, the foursome hurried as one toward a location that they were coming to know all too well. Kleo was the first to see the bright blue spot standing out from the hazy greenish rockfire. She pointed it out, the speed of their steps taking on a new urgency, and one by one the others saw it, too.

A radiance like flames, alike in every way but color. Even as Jak squinted to make out the details, the effulgence receded. They ran the rest of the way, along a wide avenue surrounded by collapsed structures and ancient ghosts and anguished fears. Yet the closer they came, the dimmer the beacon. The blue flames were dying out.

They stopped on the edge of the plaza, not far from where they had stood days before. A new skeleton had replaced the previous, and a fresh pile of soot and ash.

"This one is smaller," Kleo said.

"Perhaps it's a woman," Calla suggested.

Jak waited for Kluber, but the taller boy was riveted to his spot, silent and uneasy.

So the reluctant leader of the refugees approached the remains. Bending down to feel through the warm ashes, his fingers brushed over an object. He lifted a whistle shaped like a snake, patches of ash dulling the luster of white alabaster.

Kluber kneeled, head bowed in distress, and Calla placed a comforting hand on his back. The soft sobbing was the only sound in the world.

Desolate days, as if from a nightmare. Jak prayed they would soon end.

5

VILNIAN BORDER

Golden days, as if from a dream. Yohan hoped they would never end.

Not since the carefree years of his childhood in Parca had he so enjoyed the steady passage of time, from warming morn sunrise to the cool anticipation of sunset, and all the hours in between. His fellow soldiers were good companions, the harpa even better, and though still lacking a salve for the raw wound in his heart, Yohan could not recall ever feeling so at peace with his own existence.

The caravan enjoyed the last of three days camped on the banks of the Valena River, still north of the dividing line between Vilnia and Gothenberg. Farther to the south, he could make out the rounded peaks of the Triumph Mountains, a range that sliced eastward through the Gothic plains to merge with the greater Stormeres. The wagons would follow a trail straight through a break in the mountains ahead, a cut faintly visible from this distance.

The river provided a source of rest and resupply for the traders. As unhurried in these activities as they were in all things, the harpa used the river for restocking the water barrels, washing their abundant—and abundantly chromatic—clothing, and invigorating their bodies with brief swims in the frigid current. The Vilnians often observed—but did not join, due to strict orders from Corporal Mercer.

Not without reason. The first eve on the water's edge caused no small commotion among the soldiers. The first time they had seen Silvo bathe in the nude led to hushed whispers and ribald anticipation that Meadow and Summer would follow suit. But then the two comely women and the handsome Patrik came out in discreet garments cut similarly to smallclothes, but designed for submersion.

Nevertheless, although not entirely naked, their lithe bodies were visible and appealing enough that the men gawked like boys before looking away in embarrassment. Yohan was not an exception. He had gazed upon the bare skin and plentiful curves of a princess, but that had been under such dire circumstances that it had not seemed remotely sensuous. These two, on the other hand, might have been seductive nymphs luring the soldiers to a watery grave. Not that they flaunted their bodies—well, perhaps Meadow was a bit deliberately provocative—but the combination of skin and splashing, laughter and longing made him as uncomfortable as the other men.

These glimpses brought an added excitement to the customary eve-time revelries, when the two dancers wore full dresses that covered these same bodies, yet everyone knowing what lay beneath. Innocent frolicking by day, impassioned exhibitionism by night—an undeniable appeal to this lifestyle of a people he had grown up believing were liars and thieves.

Yohan was never an active participant in the dancing, but always an avid observer and even an enthusiastic clapper. An Oster in the Vilnian army, long used to being treated as an outsider by his comrades, he had spent years building a protective layer of disinterest and separation. A layer that he could now feel crumbling, piece by piece, although he was unsure that he wanted it to.

Currently, the caravan's established roles were reversed. After a tenday of the harpa entertaining their Vilnian escort, now was an opportunity for the soldiers to perform for the traders. Six contestants in a test of endurance.

Assuming the basic combat stance—knees flexed, right foot a single pace back—Yohan extended his left arm in a straight line at chin level. His eyes naturally gravitated along this axis, and he became only tangentially aware of the crowd all around. At a signal, he drew his sword and raised it to the same level as his arm, holding it horizontal and unmoving. The weapon felt light and comfortable, his wrist strong—but he knew that would change.

As the blades lifted, two more spectators joined the others. Lullaby and Pleasance moved about the camp as if its owners, haughty and aloof as lords in their manor, but today they were willing to slum with the peasants to observe this unfamiliar disruption to the daily rituals.

Meadow began counting. "One for Mother, Two for Sister, Three for Lover, Four. Five for trader, Six for jongleur, Se'en for soldier, Eight…"

Yohan had executed this training exercise many times in the early days. Holding this position for extended periods strengthened the muscles of the shoulder and arm, while repeated thrusting developed hand-eye coordination.

On this occasion, they were simply holding still. That was the entire competition. The sword had to be kept at the height of the outstretched arm for as long as possible. Whoever maintained the posture last would be the winner.

Yohan believed Bostik had the advantage. His personal weapon was a hand-and-a-half sword, longer and heavier than the standard imperial longsword, meaning his muscles had grown accustomed to a greater burden. His own sword would have precluded him from this event, of course, but Kelsey had lent him hers rather than take part. No one blamed her—although frequently more nimble than men, women did have a disadvantage in tests of strength. Yet to the astonishment of some —and evident delight of Meadow and Summer—freckled Krisa had joined the contest. Her thin, wiry frame was not particularly intimidating, but Yohan had watched her practice enough to know that she concealed a toughness and steely resolve.

At one-hundred he could feel the pressure in his arm mount. At two, a steady throbbing, not painful but persistent. At three, someone had replaced the blood in his arm with liquid fire. Disappointing and instructive, for at one time he would have gotten to five-hundred before feeling this effect. Clearly, he was out of practice and understrength—a dangerous condition when one's livelihood is war.

Not that he was the only one. Duffey, Ledo, and Krisa had dropped their swords by this point. Only three competitors remained. And Brody's arm was visibly shaking—not excessively, but even the minutest amount was perceptible to a veteran of as many fights as Yohan.

As a distraction from the discomfort, he allowed his mind to wander. He pondered the didactic nature of fights, and the relative merits of practice duels versus earnest battle. Most soldiers naturally saw far more of the former, but Yohan reckoned that each of the latter was ten times the value. Immediate peril clarified the senses. This shiver in Brody's blade would have gone unnoticed if Yohan had not learned to detect the slightest movement as tell-tale signs of attack or vulnerability.

He expected Brody's sword to drop at any moment now, and was surprised when Bostik resigned next. The point of his weapon stabbed into the earth, allowing the big man to rest his right arm on the pommel while his left hand slapped repeatedly against his temple in frustration. Brody laughed before bringing his eyes into focus on Yohan's, a sly smile creeping onto his lips. "I can do this all day, Brother."

"So can I."

Brody's smile slipped, and a look of determination replaced the amusement. Always outgoing and engaging, the garrulous private's emotions were simple enough to read—he was desperate to win. Yohan was reminded of his friend's spoken ambition to become a Swordthane, and his unspoken desire to find esteem—in himself, and in others.

Yohan's eyes shifted from his opponent to those who watched. "Four-hundred... One for Mother, Two for Sister, Three for Lover, Four. Five for..."

He focused on Brody's blade, the quivering more pronounced. It could not stay up much longer.

Yohan gritted his teeth, groaned, felt the intensifying pain in his own arm, and let his sword drop with a grunt.

Lullaby barked once in annoyance. Bostik pounded his head once more for good measure, while beside him Kelsey muttered an oath. Corporal Mercer snorted and turned back toward his tent.

"Ha-ha!" Brody cried, then slapped his living hand onto Yohan's shoulder while the dead one hung limp and useless. Both of their swords now lay on the ground between their feet. "Close. You nearly had me."

"I'm out of shape," Yohan admitted. He began working the muscles of his sore forearm with the fingers of his left hand. Brody gave him one more pat, then turned away to share his exaltation with the lovely judge.

"Well proven, Soldier Brody," Meadow said.

"It was the music of your voice that kept me strong." He laughed, and so did she.

Yohan gave his arm one last rub, then retrieved his sword from the ground. As he sheathed it and looked up, his gaze landed on the duo of Summer and Patrik standing not far away.

There was a wistful look on the young man's face, as if he were contemplating life as a soldier. *Keep your own*, Yohan thought. *This one pales in comparison.* Then he noticed Summer looking at him, a bemused smile barely apparent. He raised a questioning eyebrow, but she simply shook her head. "A valiant defeat, Soldier Yohan."

She was mocking him, but playfully. He did not mind, and merely nodded. Her smile increased, then she tucked her arm inside Patrik's and led her betrothed away.

Brody bent down to pick up his own sword. It was barely off the ground before his arm gave out and it tumbled back. He switched to his left and awkwardly managed to return it to its sheath without slicing himself in the process. Now he and Yohan were the only two remaining. "I don't know about you, but I'm ready for some supper. Then music and dancing."

As the sun began to set in the west, Yohan glanced back and forth from its brilliant reds and oranges to the bleak blacks and whites of the Stormeres to the east. Both were beautiful in their own ways. He had a sense that one was his past, the other his future, but was unclear which was which.

"Did you leave your coin purse in the mountains?"

His eyes shifted to the newcomer. Summer plopped a full basket of clothing on the riverbank. He saw the rainbow of colors and recognized the outfits she and Meadow often wore while dancing. They appeared comparatively dull now, but how vividly they came to life as they whirled in the night.

Physically shaking his head to clear a confused mind, Yohan replied to her inquiry. "Your pardon, Sister?"

She laughed, and he realized she was only teasing. Her eyes focused on the first garment that she lifted and shook, then dipped in the water. "I've never seen anyone stare at the Stormeres with such longing."

Eager to change the subject, he watched her shake a second garment—the bejeweled teal dress she had worn the previous eve. The harpa had concluded with a particularly spirited song accompanied by unforgettable dancing, the fiddlers walking in circles as the dancers flitted back and forth in an ember-wisped haze, at times reaching a tempo so frenetic, he had grown exhausted just watching.

"I think last night's performance was my favorite so far."

She smiled, still not looking at him. "You liked that, did you? The *ngoro*. A difficult dance, but I always feel cleaner afterward."

"Cleaner? It reminded me of a battle."

She smirked. "Nay. The *ngoro* is actually an ablution. To lose oneself in the movements—and those so rapid, so violent, that all cares are cast off. It is a washing of worries, of foolish desires." She lifted her eyes to his. "Meadow requested it."

He looked away from her gaze, saying nothing. Yohan did not care to speak until the right words came to him. Considering himself no great thinker, that meant he was often silent.

Summer chuckled—a rich, pleasant sound. She was quick to amusement, a trait he admired but sadly lacked. He glanced back, saw she was once again focused on the washing.

He watched her work. In a way, it was as peacefully reassuring as staring at the mountains, although he could not explain why in either case.

"You should be flattered, Soldier Yohan. Meadow is not used to such frustration." Another chuckle. "She believed you might prefer the company of men. Soldier Brody assures her this is not the case, that she simply must be patient with you." Summer paused to flick her long black hair back over a shoulder, then resumed soaking the dresses. "An odd thing for him to do, considering he fancies her for himself."

She paused again, this time staring toward the setting sun. "I will never understand why people behave in a manner so clearly against their own interest. Yet I see it often enough." Amused by the contradictory nature of men, she laughed louder still. But not without a hint of sadness—the first time Yohan could recall associating that emotion with the harpa leader.

"In any case, I told her it is far more likely your heart is simply elsewhere."

"Is she angry at me?"

"By the moon and stars, nay." Summer's smile grew wider. "She believes a restless heart only makes the fruits of love all the sweeter."

Now that's an interesting thought. Yohan wished he had believed that a tenday ago.

"You sound skeptical," he said aloud, as much to deflect his thoughts as to continue the discussion.

"I believe that when love is before you, you have an obligation to take it. I have the joy of many blessings, but the greatest is to live and work each day beside my life's companion. My pleasure could hardly be enhanced if I had to pursue him, or forced him to pursue me. Would that everyone lived by such simple rules."

The conversation was beginning to feel a bit like a lecture, her self-assurance oppressive.

"We aren't all so fortunate to choose who we fall in love with, Sister." He stood up. "Your pardon...the corporal expects me back."

She stared at him with unreadable eyes. "Of course, Soldier. Do not let me stop you."

As point men, Yohan and Bostik walked together a few hundred yards ahead of the caravan. The Valena River was now two days behind them, the Triumphs two days ahead. Already the ground was growing rocky and uneven. More challenging for the wagons, which meant the turtle's pace would slow even more. Yohan did not mind in the slightest.

"I have a favor to ask of you, Comrade."

Mildly interested, Yohan examined his companion. If he did not know better, he would guess the big brute of a man was embarrassed. "Aye?"

"Will you couple with Sister Meadow already? Some of us need that to happen before...other things can."

Yohan was not sure what he had expected, but certainly not this. "I don't follow."

"It's Kelsey and Krisa. You're too poxing dumb to notice, but they both fancy you and ignore the rest of us. And it's driving us mad."

Yohan could not help grinning, both at his partner's discomfort and his own blind stupidity. Once again out of his element, he simply allowed Bostik to continue.

"There's something about that Krisa. Maybe it's the freckles. Maybe it's watching those two sirens dance night after night. And seeing them bathe like that... By the Devil, a man's got to find some relief."

"And you think Meadow—"

"We figure that takes you out of the fight. Your pardon, Comrade. No offense meant."

"No offense taken. I'm not sure that I can help you, though—"

"Great Theus!" Bostik exclaimed. "Do you see that?"

Yohan did. Crossing over a minor ridge, they looked down a modest slope where the shoddy road traced a path through a wide depression, necessarily weaving between outbursts of broken rock and spartan patches of prickly shrubs. Midway between the height where the two soldiers stood and the next distant ridge lay a scene of carnage.

A single glance revealed at least a half-dozen bodies scattered amongst the burnt husks of harpa wagons. There were certain to be more, but the point men had a duty to report back before investigating the battlefield.

Although there were no signs of any immediate threat, Corporal Mercer ordered the squad into combat formation as they collectively descended on the grisly site. A cursory inspection yielded a final tally of eleven. Three harpa, two men and a woman, dressed in the style of colorful outfits used for dancing and merriment. Five soldiers—three women, two men—with Asturian colors over simple chain. Each kingdom provided security for the caravans, who were prohibited from defending themselves. The splintered barrels of wine, olives, and palm oranges indicated that this group had come from Cormona, which had such luxuries in abundance.

The harpa outfits indicated the caravan had been at rest. Reveling. The attack had been unexpected—but the defenders still managed to kill at least three.

Barbarian tribesmen, not unlike those from Yohan's recent experience. Big, bearded, and adorned in a hodgepodge of stolen gear from vanquished foes. The survivors had removed their weapons, but their armor was imperial make, and their pockets full of the knick-knacks so common amongst soldiers. A toy skylark carved from fir brought to mind memories of Yohan's home province of Nurosterlend.

Blade wounds caused the deaths of all the defenders and one of the barbarians. Curiously, however, thick arrows killed the two other attackers, a pair remaining lodged in the chest of each. Crossbows were the missile weapon of choice by the Vilnian army, but Yohan wondered whether bows were more common in other kingdoms.

"Damned brigands," Brody cursed. "This never would have happened while Eberhart ruled."

"Aye," Bostik agreed. "We need a new emperor. Badly." He kicked a fragment of shattered crate in disgust.

As the reports filtered back to Corporal Mercer, he in turn relayed them to the four harpa, who observed the scene and investigations in clear distress.

"Well, Sister, as you're making decisions for the caravan...we now know the brigands are active in this region. Do we turn back, or continue?"

Summer faced him resolutely. "We continue, Corporal. The prospect of danger is why you are with us. For the harpa, trading is life." She paused for emphasis. "*This* is what we do."

Mercer replied with a polite bow. "Of course, Sister." Turning to the squad, he issued the appropriate orders. "Ledo, Duffey…scout the vicinity to one mile. Bostik, Krisa…find out if there is anything salvageable. Kelsey, Brody, Yohan…bury the dead."

As Yohan approached the corporal a discreet distance from the others, Mercer narrowed his eyes suspiciously. "Private, don't you have duty to attend?"

"Aye, Corporal. I felt there was something you should hear first, however."

"And?"

"About these brigands…" He paused, considering how best to relay what he knew. And what he suspected.

"Well, Private, stop shirking your work. Spit it out and get back to it."

Yohan stiffened, and delivered the blow. To the Devil with consideration. "They likely aren't brigands, Corporal. In fact, they're certainly not. Vilnia—and now Gothenberg, apparently— are being invaded."

"Invaded?" Mercer spat a glob of tobacco juice onto the ground. "By the tribes? What horseshit are you selling me?"

"By the tribes, aye. And the Chekiks." Yohan watched the man's red face turn green, from some combination of fear and the tobacco he had just swallowed. "I thought you should know. I'll return to my duty now, Corporal."

Each squad of Vilnian soldiers always carried a few hand shovels for such unwelcome work. Kelsey handed Yohan one as he joined them, noticing that Bostik and Krisa were helping— there was nothing remaining to salvage, that much had been immediately clear. Yohan thanked her, pushed the blade into the hard earth, and kicked.

This time their places were reversed. Yohan came upon Summer, watching the sunset alone from a rocky perch. The horizon blazed the deepest orange he had ever seen, illuminating the distant plains while the immediate surroundings stayed bathed in shadow. Her thin outline was a black silhouette painted against a radiant canvas, so striking that he was loath to disturb it.

She heard his footsteps and turned, the outline changing shape but the expression still lost to the shadows. "Soldier Yohan. You come to contemplate your mountains."

"Do I disturb you, Sister?"

"Nay. Join me." She shifted on her rock, making room for him. Yohan preferred to stand, however, and heard her sigh. That was the last sound for quite some time, as each respectfully allowed the other to reflect in silence. His initial reaction was to be pleased that his presence did not frighten her away, nor upset her thoughts. On further reflection, however, Summersong Maple did not seem the sort to let a quiet stranger bother her. She was as much a rock as the one she sat upon.

"Did you know them, Sister?"

Yohan felt a momentary panic, for he had spoken without conscious decision. Curiosity was a natural part of him, but to voice it was not. "Your pardon, Summer. I spoke without thinking."

Her head had snapped his way, but her tone remained friendly. "You do not give offense, Yohan. Nay, I did not know them. But they are still my sisters and brothers. All harpa are family."

"If you wish to mourn alone…"

"Nay, do not leave. My heart aches for those who died, aye, but I think more of those who did not." Her voice quivered, as subtly as Brody's sword had. "I'm sure you noted there were four wagons, and only three dead traders."

"Aye."

"I worry a sister is taken, and her fear brings me pain." The shape resumed peering into the distance. "Do you have any sisters, Yohan?"

"Nay."

A long pause as she waited for more. "Do you have *any* family, Yohan?"

"Nay."

The head turned again. He could feel her eyes watching him, though he could not see them within the black shadow. The effect was unnerving, so much was the unspoken side of conversation relied upon for context. But the sunset was already fading, and soon his disadvantage would fade with it.

Together they watched the final slivers of color disappear. Then, cautiously, he risked a continuation of the subject. "If all harpa are family, that explains why you use 'Brother' and 'Sister.' We use those terms, too, but not in the same way."

"Nay. You soldiers are a curious lot." She wiped her eye, and he wondered if a tear had broken through. If so, it was the last. "The titles are for formal conversation. For outsiders. Such pretensions fall away among those we are comfortable with. When the performance is unnecessary, the masks come off. We don't often use these titles alone, amongst our closest family."

"I imagine not."

To his immense relief, she gave the hint of a chuckle. "You speak as though you've thought about this, Yohan."

"Your names are extraordinary. Your full names, that is."

She laughed, this time without constraint. "Do you like them?"

"Aye. But I cannot imagine you use them often, either. My tongue still trips over them."

"True enough. We use shortened versions with those we

know and like. For others, the proper name must remain. There is a threshold that must be crossed, like two banks of a river."

"How do you know when to cross?"

She shrugged. "There are no rules, but one knows. You may not have noticed it, but we crossed in the midst of this conversation, Yohan."

"I hadn't. I hope I've not misstepped."

"Nay. We are not so burdened by formalities. You are here to protect us, after all." Her cheer steadily increased throughout the discussion, and now she seemed almost amused. Perhaps the harpa were incapable of extended periods without happiness.

How nice that must be. "Do your names have special significance then?"

"Always. And never. Harpa names are whimsical. Full of joy. As are we."

"What about your betrothed, Patrik? He is normal." Yohan regretted the word as soon as it came out.

Now visible in the twilight, Summer's face altered, the smile receding. "You'll need to ask him."

Fool. This is why you shouldn't speak to others.

"If you'll excuse me, Soldier Yohan, I must return."

He watched her stand, brush off the skirts of her dress, and walk back down the trail. He had spoken poorly, yet could not help believing this was overreaction on her part. Surely she could not think he believed they were all abnormal. Nor would she care if he did. Summer was the harpa leader, and he a single soldier whose opinion meant nothing.

Regardless, for the first time he found himself less concerned about the mountains in the east than he was about the people in his midst, and for that he was thankful.

The gap in the Triumphs opened before them. The road, such as it was, ran straight into the mile-wide opening. Yet progress was as slow as the ground was uneven. The oxen struggled with difficult footing on loose stones. Corporal Mercer did not like the dark sky with premonitions of rain. Yohan did not care for the myriad rock formations rising up to either side, giving ample cover for ambushers.

It would take at least a day to pass through the mountains. He was curious what the other side would hold, for this was his first time in Gothenberg, and his limited education had not extended to the geography of every kingdom.

The rain came, cold and uncomfortable. The chatter between the soldiers turned sour, as oaths and insults outnumbered friendly stories and jokes. Even the wagon drivers became more reserved than the norm, their goodwill and gay laughter absent. There was no revelry that night, and the caravan resumed as early in the morn as the oxen could be induced to move.

Yohan marched on the right flank, scanning each nook and cranny for signs of danger. One particularly large hillock worried him, and he held his breath as they traversed the semicircular stretch of trail beneath its bulk. He counted at least a dozen potential hiding places that could conceal two squads or more of enemy soldiers, brigands, or worse.

By midday the gentle descent of the road leveled off in the grassy Gothic plain, and they left the rocks behind. But not the unease, and although the good humor began to be restored throughout the procession, a palpable component of anxiety remained.

Therefore no one was surprised when the point men hurried back to the wagons with a warning. "Riders to the southeast," Duffey announced. "They saw us and galloped off." Everyone stared at Mercer, who stood as still and silent as a statue, tobacco juice leaking from his lip. He said nothing for a moment, then looked ahead to the front wagon.

"Stay here," he ordered.

Yohan and Brody followed a discreet distance behind as

Mercer approached Summer, who was already scrambling down from her seat. The leaders of the harpa and their Vilnian escort spoke quietly, leaving the others in doubt. Yohan wondered whether the two of them knew just how important this moment was, how their decisions might very well hold the power of survival or destruction. Then Mercer pointed ahead, to the south, and Summer nodded in response.

With feet moving before his mind told them to, Yohan walked himself into the discussion. Mercer flashed a look of disdain, Summer of curiosity.

"Go back to the others, Private. You'll hear your orders in a minute."

"Wait a moment, Corporal. Do you have something to say, Soldier Yohan?"

"Only a suggestion. We passed a hillock this morn that made good ground for defense." He looked at Mercer. "If you should decide to make use of it, Corporal." Yohan intended to make his tone deferential, yet found it difficult to put his heart into such useless gestures.

Summer looked from one soldier to the other. "Well, Corporal, does this alter your strategy?"

Mercer finished glaring at Yohan before replying. "Perhaps. We'll fortify a position and wait for one day. Probably a waste of time, but if you insist there is no hurry…"

"The caravan could stop for a tenday, Corporal." Summer's tone was far more assured than that of the man she spoke to. "I care not for delays. The welfare of my people and the protection of the wagons is all."

"Very well. Private Yohan, tell the others we turn back. For now."

They were on the hillock for less than an hour when Kelsey saw the riders again. The wagons finished moving into a circular pattern around the base of the hill where the cover was minimal. As each rolled into place, its oxen were unhitched and led up the steep slope.

Yohan was satisfied with the layout, considering the short time they had to work with. The wagons were positioned such that the gaps between were blocked by boulders and sheer rises everywhere but in two places. These two trails provided the only means up the hillock to the trader's stockpile of crates, barrels, and boxes. Paths where the defense would need to be focused.

Leaving the incessant growling of the corporal behind, Yohan and Brody walked the perimeter once, verifying that no one could easily find a way up behind the defenders.

Summer and Meadow had the same idea. The four met by the final wagon and shared a few hurried reassurances.

"The wagons are set. I think we're as secure as can be." The harpa leader's demeanor was calm, but strained. She looked tired.

"Are the soldiers ready?" her petite blonde companion asked. With the possibility of combat approaching, Meadow became as fragile as a toy doll.

"Always," Brody replied, grinning as broadly as ever.

Yohan noticed that Summer was watching him. She was trying to read his expression, he was sure of that—taking measure of his confidence, having already dismissed the bravado of his friend. "We're ready," he confirmed, then paused for emphasis. "This is what *we* do."

As soon as more shapes appeared on the horizon, Corporal Mercer went silent.

"Perhaps they're friendly," Kelsey suggested.

Ledo snorted. "Aye. They rode off to get their friends so we can all have one big celebration. Why don't you put on the tea?"

"Why don't you—"

"Ledo, see if the harpa can use a hand," Yohan said, interrupting the argument before it combusted. "Kelsey, you and

I will hold the left gap, here. Brody, you and Krisa can hold the right, aye?"

"Aye."

"I'll join them," volunteered Bostik. He looked at Yohan questioningly. "If that's all right."

"Fine. Where's Duffey? Duff, when Ledo is done helping them, you and he are the reserves, all right? If anyone gets by us, you take care of them."

"Devil's breath," Krisa exclaimed. "There's so many of them."

They followed her gaze toward the approaching figures, now less than a mile away. Yohan estimated two dozen, perhaps more. Three on horses—two in the lead, one in back. A tall figure dressed in white robes. The standard in his hand flapped in the breeze, the six-legged snake emblem unmistakable. Yohan had seen banners just like it—perhaps including this very one—at Sky's Pass, a few days and a lifetime ago.

Kelsey's voice was low and uncertain. "Is that—"

"Brody, get your group in position." A nod and the three of them moved away. "Kelsey, look at me. Stay behind this rock until they start coming up the slope. We don't know if they have crossbows, so don't expose yourself until you have to, got it?" She was staring at him, nodding. There was fear in her eyes, but nothing unmanageable. It would get bad, though—for her and the others—if things started to go poorly. They could all use a boost. Perhaps he could provide one with a simple show of confidence.

Near the base of the hillock, the attackers split into two sections. A group of ten or twelve formed below, at the point between the wagons that formed the left gap. Yohan could not concern himself with how many were hitting the right—these before him now were the priority.

Unhurriedly, he drew his sword and stood where they could see him. This was encouraging potshots, he knew, but did not see any crossbows amongst the enemy. Hoping to convey a message to anyone watching, Yohan stretched one arm casually, then the other, then flexed his neck and shoulders. Feeling better in mind and body, he swiped his boot across the dirt and stones. *This is the line you will not cross.*

They were coming up, passing between the wagons one at a time, widening to two where the trail allowed. They moved slowly, and his first thought was that they were being excessively cautious. Then he realized time had slowed down.

Raising the shield, Yohan charged forward. The two lead figures stopped to brace themselves for impact. Having been on the receiving end of a shield rush before, Yohan knew how unsettling it was to see one coming. He could crash directly into them, bowling one or both over—then get himself hacked to pieces by the next ones in line. Their momentum was already halted, which was the important thing.

The nearest tribesman held his axe before his chest like a barrier against the charge. It would have done little to secure him from the rush, and did even less to protect him from Yohan's sudden thrust. The big blue eyes widened as the man saw the attack coming, then the blade pierced through the neck and those same eyes went wild. The axe dropped as both hands clutched the wound, blood spouting from between the fingers as his body toppled into those behind.

The thrust had been the preferred option because it allowed Yohan to maintain enough balance to move right into another attack. He spun, momentarily putting back to the barbarians—a risky move against anyone but a surprised opponent—and used the added momentum to put more force behind his swing. The sword arced toward the second man in front, who had just enough time to block with his axe. With the extra inertia, the blade chopped through the wooden handle and into the shoulder. This tribesman was not dead, but would be out of the fight. Yohan could safely ignore him to concentrate on the next one coming up.

He hated fighting axemen, because those heavy blades could make short work of a shield. Fortunately, the higher ground made the incoming attacks slower and more awkward, easier to dodge completely. So long as he was willing to back up. He could do so only a few steps, however. There was a line he intended to protect, and not for show. The pathway up limited the attackers' maneuverability. Once they got past the line, however, they could spread out and overwhelm the defenders with numbers.

Yohan faked one more step backward then turned it into a lunge. The tribesman—correction, tribeswoman—before him attempted to dodge by backing up herself. The congestion behind her prevented that, and her stationary form became an easy target. As the blade entered her side, Yohan felt a familiar rush of panic. Swords that entered bodies often became stuck there, and a soldier without his weapon for even one second became a corpse.

He pulled it back out with palpable relief and kicked her back against the man behind, then turned his shield onto the downward swing of another. He attempted to guide the blade past rather than take it full on the boss, but the quickness of the strike prevented such subtleties of action. He felt the rough impact and heard the splintering of wood. One more block like that and the shield would be useless.

As much as he disliked fighting axes, there was an advantage to doing so. They were heavy and hard to control, and this barbarian had put a lot behind his swing. Now in the follow-through, his body was exposed. The thick fur armor provided limited protection at best against a sword, but the neck and head did not even have that. Angry at the damage to his invaluable shield, Yohan slashed left to right. The sword bounced off the curvature of the head, taking off a section of scalp and skull in the process.

He had hoped the accumulation of bodies would slow the advance of their comrades. Instead, the dead and wounded were unceremoniously tossed aside to make way for the next ranks. Now the attackers were getting more organized, no longer running ahead on pure bloodlust but using coordinated tactics. The next two advanced side-by-side, one axe swinging while the other stayed back, poised to take advantage of a counterattack. Their eyes were full of hatred, and completely focused on Yohan, so did not see Kelsey's blade until too late.

Her swing cut deep into the neck of one attacker. The high ground was proving exceptionally beneficial by the manner in which the most vulnerable portions of the enemy were also the most accessible. Hate-filled eyes snapped shut as though the man were falling asleep. The graceful way that his body fell, slowly and stiffly like a toppled tree, added to the effect. But that savage mind would never wake up.

Surprised, his companion half-turned toward the newcomer, finding himself outnumbered rather than the reverse. Trying to defend against two at the same time was the same as defending against none, and Yohan's thrust easily avoided the distracted defense to penetrate the side. Not a killing blow, but enough to twist the hips and bend the knees, allowing Kelsey to follow up with a stab to the chest. As she tried to withdraw the blade, however, it did not come out. The man crumpled, taking her weapon with him.

Kelsey stepped back with a frustrated yelp. Yohan put himself between her and the next two opponents, one wielding a giant mace. If there was one weapon Yohan hated more than an axe, it was this. The powerful iron head would not split a shield like the other, but could slowly batter one to pieces. Along with the arm holding it in the process. With his shield already damaged, Yohan feared a solid swing might numb his left arm, or even break it.

But there was no room to back up. He planted his back foot and lunged again, feinting a move on the axeman only to turn at the last second on the other. Both were ready to defend, and the long mace handle parried the attack. Yohan continued to press, taking a swing against the axeman again while shifting to the left in order not to make an easy target of himself. This attack was also deflected, but enough inertia remained to turn it into yet another slash at the maceman. There its momentum was stopped cold by a solid block.

Yohan felt the beads of sweat on his temple, and not just from the effort. He had to gain an advantage somehow, for he could not allow them even a moment to press the advance. With only a weaponless partner to defend his side and a half-broken shield to defend himself, this battle was on the brink of disaster.

The sword swung again to the left, then backswung to the right. He knew he was burning through a lot of energy, and had to make a breakthrough soon. He feinted at the maceman's head, then quickly slashed low at the axeman's leg. The aim was off but the surprise attack got through, and he felt the blade cut into the flesh of the hip. Then it struck bone and stopped, and Yohan tugged backward with all his remaining strength to free it. He had no choice in the matter, but already could see the heavy mace raising to take advantage. *There goes the shield,* he thought resignedly, raising it to take the blow. Better his arm than his skull.

An arrow appeared in the fur-covered chest. The mace remained suspended in the air at its highest point. Then a second arrow appeared beside the first. The mace dropped of its own accord, the man holding it suddenly slipping to a knee. Yohan righted himself and thrust at a downward angle where the shoulder met the neck. The body fell flat.

A horn blew in the distance. Yohan could not afford to look, but felt certain what it was. The retreat of the remaining barbarians confirmed it—they were being recalled. They had lost too many fighters without any appreciable gain. They would find easier prey elsewhere—or return to whatever base they operated from to lick their wounds. Either way, the caravan was safe for the time being.

Sweating in the cool air, shoulders heaving from strain, he looked at Kelsey. She stared back, wide-eyed. He slipped the splintered shield from his left arm in order to clasp her shoulder, giving and receiving reassurance. They caught their breath for a moment—he more so than she—and then heard the wailing.

Yohan had lost track of the fact that there was another gap, another point that had to be defended. All the attackers had withdrawn, but they had left their mark. As soon as he saw the many figures gathered in one spot—facing down in silent sorrow—he knew that meant one thing. Between the legs of the onlookers, he could see Krisa down on her knees. At first his heart felt relief—for although he hated something to have happened to her, at least she was alive.

Then he moved closer, saw that she was not the object of the group's concern. Rather, she was crying over the body of Bostik. Judging by the volume of tears, the big man had gotten through to her more than he knew.

The *mbe* was a song of grief.

Eyes closed, Patrik brought bow across string, creating a single haunting note. That one note hung in the air, long as life and sad as death, resonating in their hearts so painfully that one might pray for deafness. Yohan longed to see the bow move again, that more notes would come to drown out the first. If ever they needed harpa music, it was now.

He was not disappointed. The playing began slowly but gradually picked up speed, so that once Silvo joined in, the two fiddles created the familiar effects so common to their songs. Feet began to tap, heads to nod, and emotions to swim along invisible currents.

Summer and Meadow danced slowly, their beautiful features hidden behind thin scarf-like shrouds. Their arms and feet flowed with the music, gathering ethereal burdens then poignantly releasing them skyward, ascending to the heavens among a cloud of wafting notes.

Thus unladen, the dancers slipped off the shrouds. Their movements found a new, exultant life, as did the music.

Yohan watched the fat man play with particular attention and newfound appreciation. He had been the source of the arrows that felled the maceman, saving Yohan's arm and probably his life. These traders truly had many talents, not all of them obvious at first glance.

But this one was. Silvo played wonderfully, a tremendous smile encompassing the entire face, bright teeth shining in its homely center. Never had Yohan seen a man look so happy, and although much was performance, the emotion could not have been all acting.

The *mbe* was also a song of memory, and celebration in honor of lives lost and those who live on.

Silvo carried the tune alone while Patrik danced with Summer. Then Patrik returned the favor so Silvo could dance with Meadow. He was amazingly nimble afoot for such a disproportionate man. Then he released Meadow and went straight to Krisa. Her tears had largely dried, but the sorrow remained. She had little resistance to Silvo's blunt charisma, however, and soon he was swinging her around like a hapless damsel.

Yohan watched Brody approach Meadow. He could not hear the words, but he saw their effect. Soon the two of them were in the circle with Silvo and Krisa, making obvious attempts to avoid their swift, chaotic circumvolutions.

Somewhat more shyly, Kelsey and Ledo joined the growing crowd. Their slow motions did not match the speed of the music, but they were happy and that was more important than grace.

Happiness. It was a compelling emotion, but one that Yohan seldom allowed. He was afraid of it, even as it tugged at his heart and his head. And, surprisingly, his leg.

He looked down. No, that was not happiness, that was Lullaby. Behind her sat Pleasance, both looking at him expressively. Calling him a fool.

Yohan sighed. There was nothing good that could come of this, he knew. But he had felt the same about another notion recently, when he had forced a princess to call him by name. Despite subsequent events to the contrary, that decision felt good at the time. Just as this one did.

He stood and walked past the fire and dancers. "Sister, will you dance with me?"

Summer smiled and stood. She did not so much allow him to dance with her as guide him along. She placed his hands on her side and shoulder, then showed him the basic footwork necessary to not step on her or make a fool of himself.

"You learn quickly," she said.

"It's not unlike swordplay. Slower, perhaps."

She grinned. "This one is, but if you're ready for something faster—"

"Nay, please. I'm a baby learning to walk."

"Perhaps not a baby," she said. "More of a child." There was teasing in her words, but respect in her tone, and he appreciated that deeply. "You may make a fine dancer yet. You are not without grace."

"And you are not without secrets."

She stared up into his face, measuring his sincerity. "You did not think our people would accept being completely defenseless, did you? We make the best of what we are allowed."

"Those bows are allowed?"

"Nay."

Yohan had brought this up only because he wanted to make one thing clear. "We will not reveal your secrets."

She smiled, but the tightness in her face showed reservation. "I believe you won't. I am not without concern about your corporal, however."

Yohan had no response to this. He was not without concern, either. And so he changed the subject.

"I'm sorry I said 'normal.'"

Again she stared into his face, then laughed with genuine mirth. "Has that been bothering you? I took no offense."

"But the way you left—"

The amusement showed in her smile, her cheeks, and her eyes. All very appealing—he could see why other men might fall for her. "You misunderstand our ways, Soldier Yohan. Patrik's name is a soreness to us. An open wound that we pretend to ignore."

"His name isn't really Patrik, is it?"

She shook her head. "You are sharper than you appear, Soldier Yohan." She giggled. "Let us speak of happier things. Or better yet, let us speak not at all. The *mbe* will speak for us."

But the *mbe* was coming to an end. The music diminished, slowing to a soft and reticent rhythm. With no small disappointment, Yohan waited for it to taper off completely. To fade into nothingness, like so many hopes had.

Instead, the fiddle found a different pattern, born of more delicate emotions.

A new tempo meant new footwork. Summer looked down at their feet and placed her hands on his hips. She guided his movements, gently tracing a slow circle on the grassy earth until their positions were reversed from a moment earlier. His feet were used to the science of fighting, with its incessant forceful maneuvers. Thrust and move. Parry and move. Feint, slash, and *move*. Always moving. Even more so than with the previous song, this dancing felt uncomfortably deliberate, and instinct made his muscles impatient.

Sensing his discomfort, Summer slipped her thin arms further around his waist, holding him tightly and securely. From the corner of his eye, Yohan saw Brody drape his arms around Meadow, who rested her head against his chest. Now Yohan did likewise to Summer, and she responded the same. He imagined he could feel her breathing, eyes closed in carefree complacence.

He had needed a purpose. It was very comforting to know that he found one—to protect these people, and even to learn from them. He tightened his embrace of her slender shoulders, conveying an unspoken message of invulnerability. She sighed contentedly, a sound lovelier than the music.

6

NEUBLUSTEN

Nico had not expected a hero's welcome on his return to Neublusten, nor did he receive one. In fact, his return barely received any attention at all.

Cormona after the battle had been a city on edge, waiting for the death or recovery of their beloved king. A city that wanted to celebrate victory, but could not. Before the battle it had been a city of worries, fearful of the possibility of defeat.

Neublusten was different. This was a city in mourning, not only for their fallen prince but for themselves. Defeat was not a possibility—it had already come.

If the residents even knew the younger prince was home, they clearly did not expect his presence to make any difference.

Nowhere was the solemnity more apparent than in the barracks, which were not only morose but pitifully empty. Nico led the Princeshields into the military quarters with nary a comment from the few remaining troops stationed in the capital.

The circumstances were even bleaker than he had expected, and he craved updates on the events past and present more than a good washing or meal. Fortunately, he had personal access to the best source.

"Corporal Mickens, you will see to the supper and bunks for the company. Private Lima, please gather whatever news you can from anyone who remembers how to speak. Private Pim and I are going to have an audience with the king."

"Me, Commander?" Pim suddenly looked more frightened than he had before battle. "With the king?"

"Indeed." Nico set out, forcing the trooper to follow immediately to avoid insubordination.

Outside the barracks, Nico reassured the young man. "Don't worry, he won't even notice you're there. To my father, you're beneath notice... Your pardons."

Pim shook his head, the prospect of being insignificant more a relief than an insult.

As they entered the castle proper, one of the petty servants acknowledged the prince with a bow. It was the first sign of normalcy since their return, and Nico wished he could hug the man for it.

Ascending the steps to the upper level, a palpable anxiety began to build. Exhaustion and hunger disappeared completely, replaced by apprehension at the imminent reunion. Audiences with King Hermann generally consisted less of conversation than confrontation. That his older brother had been the more suitable heir was the dominant dynamic between king and prince, father and son.

A calming of the heart and mind was in order. Along the passage to the king's chambers, Nico paused to peer out the broad windows on the scenic outlook. A fresh breeze blew in at the same moment, carrying the scents of pine and juniper from his father's precious gardens. Nico soaked in sight and smell like meat and wine, then let out a contented sigh. "This view never fails to lift my spirits. What do you think, Pim?"

"I never really thought about it." He stood back from the window, as if worried he might fall out. Nico knew what the young man's discomfort stemmed from, however. As a thrall, and a fieldthrall at that, he had probably never been in a castle like this, let alone so near the royal quarters. This world did not belong to him.

Nico wanted to change that mindset, to convince the trooper that no one would accuse him of stealing just for looking out a window. The process would take time, however.

No better opportunity to start than now.

"Well, look at the lake. From here you can really see why it got its name."

"Why's that, Commander?"

"You don't know the story?" Nico was surprised, having assumed every child of Akenberg learned this basic lesson, one of the few he had retained from his early studies.

"I was a fieldthrall. You...probably don't want to assume I had the same education as you."

"Fair enough. Legend has it the first settlers to this region saw this lake in the distance, so placid and sparkling in the sun that they thought it was pure gemstone. They named it 'New Blue Stone.' The city and castle they built were originally named for their founders, but no one ever used that and the name is lost to time. Everyone preferred Neublusten."

"I can see why."

"Yes." Nico grinned, happy to see the private at last absorbed by the beauty of the view. "Sadly, we must hurry. Come on."

For the first time in his life, Nico did not request an audience from his father's chamberlain. They simply nodded to one another in silent acknowledgment, and the aged man opened the door.

Stepping inside, Nico paused. "Wait here," he whispered. Then he proceeded to the center of the room, where the king sat staring toward the open balcony, frail hand gently stroking the immense black head of his mastiff.

"Father."

Hermann slowly turned to face him. The tendays since their

last visit had not been kind to him, that much was obvious. The sorrows and misgivings of the entire city were concentrated here, in the anguished expression of this old man.

"Nicolas. You survive. One of my sons lives." The rest of the thought was clear enough. *Not the one I expected.*

"Yes, Father. My mission was on the brink of success when the news of Prince Markolas came." Seeing the body flinch at the name brought a sense of guilt. Nico would not mention it again.

"Tell me of your mission, Nicolas. Everything."

Nico did as he was told, providing every detail but one. Not far into the account, Hermann's eyes closed, and Nico believed his father had fallen asleep, until the first question interrupted the flow.

"And so you decided to involve yourself in Anton's personal vendetta?"

Nico did not hesitate. One thing he had learned growing up was that his father detested hesitation and second-guessing. "I did not see it that way. But yes."

The old lips curled into a smile. "Tell me of the battle."

This was not a memory that Nico liked to relive, and much of it was clouded in confusion. But he provided the best account he could, making sure to focus on the bravery and prowess of the Princeshields, for they had made his first action a success. At terrible cost.

"When I allowed Renard to go with you, I expected he would disabuse you of such foolishness."

Nico did not approve of any aspersions cast upon the great man, who had been an outstanding teacher and reliable friend. "Renard gave competent advice, but the decision was mine."

"No matter. He paid for his failings."

The same anger that Nico had known facing Gornada in the canyon rose within him again, requiring every ounce of discipline to restrain. He felt his muscles tighten and his temple pulse, but said nothing.

"You may continue your report, Nicolas."

There were more interruptions, but the gist came through eventually. The Asturians were certain to be furious, and may very well seek to take advantage of Akenberg's sudden weakness. Nico did not attempt to conceal his own blundering role in the regrettable turn of events, but neither did he hide the disapproval at what he had learned of imperial politics.

"You should have warned me, Father. You and Anton have a history that I was not aware of. A contentious history...and a contentious present. There were reports that Duke Iago's uprising was supplied—"

"You have much to learn about being a king, Nicolas. And precious little time to learn it—presuming, of course, that we remain lords of Akenberg beyond the coming dawn. We will discuss all things in time. Return to me in a few days, and we'll begin."

"Your pardons, Father, but this city, this castle... Things need to change. I wish to begin today."

"Very well, then begin acting as a prince. For once."

"I have your leave to do as I will?"

The lips curled into another smile. "Yes, Nicolas. Let's see what you can do."

They returned to the barracks, where Lima awaited. "I have news for you, Commander."

"Thank you, Lima, but not here. Come with me. Pim, Mickens, you as well."

He led them to the large building between the barracks and castle known as the Rechshtal. Its impressiveness stemmed neither from size nor ornament, but from purpose. This was the military headquarters for all of Akenberg, and Nico intended to make it his own.

General Koblenzar, a longtime ally and friend of King

Hermann's, was the current leader of all things martial, from the soldiers in the field to the ceremonial houseguard stationed in the throne room. He also had a particularly derogatory manner of speaking to those beneath him, and he clearly believed that included a second prince. Nico had never been comfortable in the haughty man's presence, and did not at all look forward to this meeting.

The headquarters was a second home for Koblenzar, and not because of an excessive workload or zeal for duty. Rather, he used the building as a convenient location for feasts, balls, and dalliances—often with the wives of officers he sent out on campaign, if rumor held true.

Currently, Nico found him seated in the spacious war room, deep in conversation with Captain Reikmann of the Royal Guard, another associate of King Hermann's since the early days. Beside them, two tankards rested on a massive table, where spillage of the red liquid within had stained the giant map pinned there. Their laughter was audible from outside the chamber, and continued well after the four newcomers arrived, followed by a pair of attendants who had unsuccessfully attempted to block entry.

Bewildered by the interruption, the general remained seated as he addressed the prince.

"Commander, have you come to report on your deployment? I hear you have sizable losses to explain. Or perhaps you have decided that the army is not the life for you, after all?" He smiled disdainfully and reached for his drink.

"Neither, actually. King Hermann just appointed me to overall command of Akenberg's forces. Thank you for your service, you are relieved of duty."

Koblenzar sat up abruptly, causing more wine to spill from the tankard. "What is this nonsense?"

"Ask him, if you wish. I have work to do." He turned to face his companions. "Pim, escort the general to the castle. He wishes to speak to the king. Mickens, have a seat. Lima, prepare your report." Then he faced Reikmann. "Captain, do you desire to keep your command?"

"Yes, My Prince."

"It's 'General,' now. Fine. You can stay. Add what you will to Lima's account, starting with the current status of your company. Then help me summon any officers stationed in Akenberg to give them new orders."

"Yes, General."

"This is a farce," Koblenzar said. "I'll be back in less than an hour to spank your spoiled ass. Keep away from me!" This last was directed at Pim, who had moved closer.

"Don't kill him, Pim," Nico said casually, hoping the news of Captain Gornada's fate had made it this far. "But do help him find the way out without stumbling." He grabbed the two tankards from the table and held them in the direction of the attendants. "You two, please take these. We won't be needing them, or any other drink, for quite some time."

The reports were entirely bad. The Battle of Allstatte had resulted in the nearly total annihilation of Prince Markolas' army —foolishly named "The Emperor's Army" just prior to its first and only engagement. Caught between the combined forces of Daphina and Lorester, most of the force was killed or captured. The odd group of stragglers shuffled back into Neublusten each day, but they were few in number and in no condition to return to action. Worse were the stories and rumors they spread among the residents of the city. The loss of the army was unfortunate enough, and repeated words of impending doom only reinforced the negativity. Only a victory—of any size or importance—would reverse the tide. That needed to be the highest priority.

Precious little remained with which to accomplish that victory, however. The bulk of the veterans had marched off to glory with the ill-fated prince. Those who remained had been hastily thrown together into a second army and sent northwest in an attempt to slow the Lorester advance. Fresh recruits were few and far between, which was understandable considering the bleak prospects. Reikmann reported that King Hermann had proposed conscription, but that Koblenzar talked him out of it in the belief that nonprofessionals took too long to train and were more trouble than they were worth.

"Everyone has to start somewhere," Nico said. "Not long ago, I was a nonprofessional." He did not add that people like Koblenzar still considered him one. He suspected that Reikmann did, too. "One learns quickly when one has no choice."

"Yes, My Prince. I mean, General."

"We need soldiers, and they aren't summoned from the mists. We need to find out what will encourage people to join. Failing that, we'll need to follow the king's suggestion, after all. All right, let's continue."

The news from abroad was not any more reassuring. While the Dauphi remained in place to complete the siege of Allstatte, the Loresters turned their focus on Neublusten itself. The Second Army stood in their way, but restricted itself to harassing attacks and minor skirmishes, with strict orders not to risk a full battle they were certain to lose. That seemed a reasonable strategy to Nico, though it did naught but delay the inevitable.

Meanwhile, their friends in Asturia were using the "Akenberg aggression" to unify the last of their dissenting factions. King Anton was reportedly raising a formidable army with the intent of finally concluding his longstanding grievance with Hermann.

Therefore, Akenberg was opposed by the full strength of three kingdoms, while being severely shorthanded herself. In a very short period of time, she had gone from the strongest of the twelve kingdoms to one of the weakest.

Not including Nico's self-promotion and Koblenzar's departure, there were three active generals in Akenberg service.

"General Freilenn commands the Second Army. General Cottzer was with the Emperor's Army when Markolas took over. He remained to advise the prince. Reports are that he was captured, but we don't know for certain. That leaves General Handersonn." Lima hesitated to go on.

"Tell me."

"Word is that he's a drunkard."

Captain Reikmann squirmed uncomfortably, but said nothing.

Nico turned to him. "Captain, I want your honest opinion. If we can keep him sober, is he competent?"

"I believe so, My Prince. I mean, General."

One thing that stood out during the discussion was the absence of any mention of surrender. The notion itself was so foreign, so anathema, to the Akenberg mind that it was beneath consideration even in these dire circumstances. Nico attributed this to his father's reign, comprising one success after another. Since his coronation, the kingdom had thrived and expanded, with nary a failure to contemplate. Hermann's acts were often a mystery to Nico, but not for one moment did he doubt their value. These achievements illustrated how he could never live up to his father's legacy. Akenberg would mourn the day it lost the great man.

Suddenly yawning, Nico rubbed his eyes. Mental exhaustion had finally caught up to the physical. "All right, that's enough for now. Let's all think things over this eve and resume in the morn."

Captain Reikmann coughed politely. "General, you asked to see the other officers."

Damn. "Yes. Thank you, Captain. Please bring them in." *I'll get to sleep eventually.*

Nico eschewed his royal bedroom for the officers' barracks adjacent the Rechshtal. Intending to set the example by starting at daybreak, he was mortified when the sounds of clattering equipment woke him in the midafternoon. He hurriedly splashed water from the basin onto his face, strapped on his sword belt, and rushed outside. Dazzling sunlight disoriented him.

Lima and Pim were waiting, silently amused by his mild discomfort. Beyond them, Nico saw a crowd filling the courtyard. The noise must have come from the pile of practice swords near where a score of young men and women were utterly failing to form a straight line.

"Today's new recruits," Lima informed him. "Hopefully, the first of many."

"How?" His eyes had adjusted to the light, but his mind remained discombobulated. Apparently, a half-day's sleep was not enough.

"Captain Reikmann," she replied. "He sensed that you favored decisive action, so he started spreading the word last night."

"What did he tell them?" Nico felt a growing sense of unease. Somehow, he knew he was not going to like the answer.

She straightened her back and deepened her voice, emulating a herald. "Fight beside the Swordthane. Victory is assured. Become heroes of Akenberg."

Nico clutched his head. The cobwebs were clearing, only for a dull pain to take their place.

"He asks that you inspect the recruits, General. He says it will help morale."

Nico nodded. "Lead the way."

They made a slow circuit behind then in front of the awkward line. He did not know what to look for, nor would he reprimand anyone on their first day. Instead, he merely stopped occasionally to inspect a face or request a name.

As he finished with the first group, a second lineup began forming on the other side of the courtyard.

He pulled Lima aside to whisper. "I don't need to inspect them, too, do I?"

"Aye, *General*." Her emphasis on the title he had given himself reminded Nico that he had asked for this. He nodded, and she led the way again.

Halfway through the line, a commotion occurred on the far end. Two soldiers pulled on one man, who resisted. "I wish to fight," he pleaded.

Nico's eyes narrowed as he approached. "What's going on?"

"This one shouldn't be here, General."

"Why is that?"

"He is one of the king's servants." The soldier tugged at the arm again, and again the man—not much more than a boy —resisted.

"Stop," Nico commanded, and both the tugging and the resisting immediately ceased.

Leaning forward, he examined the familiar features. "I know you." Ignoring the terror on the youth's face, Nico dug deep into his memory. "Kip, isn't it?"

"Aye, My Prince. That is to say, Yes, My Prince."

"General. And this isn't court…you can say 'aye' in the army."

"Aye, General." Kip studied his feet, his cheeks turning a pale red.

"You say you wish to fight, Thrall, but your posture admits defeat. Which is it?"

The body tightened. "I wish to fight, General."

"Then lift your head."

Already, the germ of an idea took root in Nico's cluttered mind. He looked at Lima, reminding himself to get her reaction as soon as possible.

"You can stay, Private." Nico turned to the two veterans. "He can stay. If anyone complains, send them to me."

"Your father—that is to say, the king—won't like it."

"You're right about that. Carry on."

. . .

The only surprising thing was that the summons did not come until the following day.

Nico stood before his father, studying the king while the king studied him in return. Anger had taken at least ten years off the venerable face. Now Hermann looked almost healthy enough to take command of the armies personally.

"I admit, it was promising to see the way you took charge from Koblenzar, but this... What the Devil do you think you're doing?"

Enlisting thralls who volunteer in exchange for an end to servitude. "Didn't you do something similar when you allowed thralls to serve as cavalry?"

"Only the very best, and only in small numbers. You just let anyone who can swing a hoe into the army."

I know. We've had hundreds of volunteers already. It's wonderful. "We need troops, Father."

"When you are king—*if* you become king—you will learn that you have to keep the nobles happy. Making them cook and clean for themselves does not make them happy."

"And they would be happier when the Loresters take their land away?"

Hermann sat back in his armchair. Nico assumed the man was too angry, too unaccustomed to the backtalk, to respond. Then, amazingly, the king began to laugh. Weakly, laced with coughing, but definitely laughing. "I am a fool. How could I have been so wrong?"

The frailty was back, and the self-deprecation difficult to hear. Nico stepped forward, compelled to reach out and comfort the weak man. "You're no fool, Father."

The hand was slapped back. "There is no time for that. Go on, then. Do as you will. Know that you will be judged by success or failure, not by good intentions."

I've already learned that. All too well. "Thank you, Father."

. . .

An hour of watching illuminated one incontrovertible fact. Four days of drilling had not appreciably improved the quality of the new recruits.

This courtyard—one of five throughout the city appropriated by the army—was filled by one hundred trainees. The instructors had formed them into two companies, assigned temporary corporals, and were attempting to move them as cohesive units. Sadly, the teams never managed more than a few turns without someone going in a wrong direction and colliding with a neighbor.

Disorder was happening again, right before Nico's eyes, and he was not surprised to see that the culprit was Kip. This was the third time in as many days that the thrall had blundered, leading Nico to wonder whether the castle staff had been taught left and right in reverse as some sort of practical joke.

At this rate, it might take a year for these soldiers to make an efficient fighting force. Maybe the Loresters would give him that long if he asked politely...

They all heard hoofbeats, and the added distraction caused even more disarray within the undisciplined troops. Nico turned away in disgust to watch the rider enter the courtyard, do a quick scan of the surroundings, then head directly for the prince. He smoothly dismounted and took a moment to catch his breath. "General Nicolas, a message from General Freilenn. The Second Army returns on the morrow."

Nico chewed his lip. The Second Army had orders to delay the Loresters as long as possible. He was hoping for at least another tenday. Had they already run out of time?

"Thank you, Private. Please tell General Freilenn to bivouac outside the city. The barracks grow full. Also, that I wish to see him personally. This eve, if possible."

"Yes, General." The messenger leapt back onto his mount and rode away.

Fast. Efficient. Professional. Clearly a young nobleman, or

possibly a relation of the General. Sons and nephews made popular choices as aides and officers.

The contrast with the rabble in the courtyard could be seen by a blind man.

He met with General Freilenn in an office of the Rechshtal. Younger than Koblenzar and Reikmann, but still far older than the prince, his was a face seen occasionally about Castle Neublusten but always on the fringes of importance. Nico did not believe they had ever formally been introduced, although they may well have spoken in passing at some event or another. And now they were discussing the existence of the kingdom itself.

"I was under orders not to engage in battle, General. That restricted my options severely."

"I understand." Nico had thoughtlessly allowed his disappointment to register in his tone, and the perceptive man grew defensive. "No one will accuse you of dereliction. It is the circumstances I regret, not your conduct." He rubbed his temples, wishing the pounding would recede, even if only for a moment. "We are now faced with a choice: battle or siege."

The broad shoulders stiffened. "The Second Army stands ready for either."

Nico sighed. He expected bravado, but preferred honesty. "I have no doubt about that. Tell me true, however—you've spent two tendays in the field. Marching, fighting. How long before the troops are…restored?"

Freilenn stared directly at Nico, evaluating. Not the answer, but the man before him. "Three days."

"How far behind are the Loresters?"

"One day."

"Lima?" She was behind him, he knew. She was always behind him.

"Aye, General?"

"Send word to the senior officers. Prepare the city for siege. All citizens, foodstuffs, and water inside the walls within two days. And send Mickens to me."

She left without a word, the most capable one-armed woman who ever lived.

"Well, General, we need to buy a day. I can give you one additional cavalry company. Understrength. Can you scrounge up enough fresh soldiers to punch the enemy one more time?"

"I believe so."

"Let's take a look at the map. See if we can figure something out."

The two generals found a modicum of comfort with one another, as one would propose an idea and the other found a way to reject it. Nico made it clear that he did not mind disagreement, but expected respect—not only in word, but in manner. He simply did not have time to find out the hard way which old soldiers held disdain for newcomers. To his credit, Freilenn gave the prince no particular cause for concern.

They were still brainstorming a short while later when Corporal Mickens stepped into the room. "General, you sent for me?"

"Yes. Congratulations, I'm promoting you to captain. You can worry about the uniform later. For the next two days, you and the Princeshields are under General Freilenn here. Understood?"

"A-aye, General."

"He'll send for you when he's ready. Make me proud."

"Aye, General." He stepped out as quickly as he had arrived. A capable corporal, but would he make a capable officer? They would know in a day or two.

An hour later, the outlines of a plan were agreed upon. Nico trusted Freilenn enough to adapt it to time and circumstance, as needed.

It was well after dark, and the General had a ride ahead of

him. Nico wished him luck and bid him goodbye. Then, as the hoofbeats faded, wondered whether they would see him again. If not, the time for all of them would be short, indeed.

"Father, you wished to see me?"

"Yes, Nicolas. Please come in." The king stood to clasp Nico's hand in both of his.

The excess of politeness triggered a warning within Nico's mind. He looked about the room as if expecting an ambush. Sure enough, there was another man present. A stranger, silently standing near the balcony, admiring the incomparable view.

Nico looked at his father, whose eyes flashed anger. The hands squeezed as hard as they were capable of, which was not enough to cause the slightest discomfort. But the message was clear. *Do not disappoint me.*

"Nicolas, it is my pleasure to introduce Arturo—the Third of Swords."

The room spun momentarily while Nico steadied himself. Lately his mind had been so preoccupied with such critical tasks that he had lost track of his place in the world. This meeting came not just as a surprise—it completely shattered his perspective.

Arturo casually approached the royal father and son. "Thank you, Hermann, but there is no need for formalities. Nicolas and I are family, too, of a sort."

"Well, you asked to see him. Perhaps now you will tell us what brings you here."

"Of course. I understand that you are at war, that the Lorester army is at your doorstep. I desire you to surrender."

Hermann snorted. "You've wasted your time, Thane."

"'Third.' I understand your reluctance, and that you would like to…throw me from your castle, but I ask your forbearance for just a minute. I've given this matter a great deal of consideration, and I think you will come to accept my suggestion."

"No. We don't have time for—"

"Father." Nico felt uneasy for interrupting, but had no choice. He shared a bond with this stranger, and that bond included courtesy and respect. "You may speak, Third. But please consider that every minute is valuable to us right now."

Arturo bowed. "Events unfold of which you have no awareness. I am here, in part, to rectify that.

"When Eberhart left, he warned of calamitous events. King Hermann, you were there, I believe. Surely you remember this.

"These events have now transpired. This civil war you find yourself in is but one danger threatening the empire, and the simplest to resolve.

"The Chekican Communion returns. We know Gothenberg has seen invaders already, and we fear Vilnia is about to, as well. I don't think I need to tell you of the horrors of the Chekiks, other than to remind you that they enslaved our people for generations. If the legends hold true, that was the least of their oppressions.

"And that is not all. In the north, from Falkenreach, we hear reports of demons. Not mother's tales to frighten children into obedience, but genuine beasts of evil and blood. Some say they are the devils themselves, coming to rejoin the Chekiks and restore the ancient ways.

"The empire desperately needs a new emperor, we all know this. Our leadership has discussed this situation thoroughly, and are unified on one course. Second Garrett served for years beside Eberhart. He seeks peace between the kingdoms so that these outside terrors can be pushed back."

"He seeks to become the new emperor himself," Hermann said.

"He does. Our continued existence requires it. Once unity is restored, those who sacrificed to achieve it will be compensated."

"If we give Allstatte to the Dauphi, and the north to the Loresters, he will restore them to us?"

"I cannot give specifics, of course, but all sacrifices will receive just compensation. It is far better than the loss of the empire entire."

"You know very well our enemies will never give back the land they steal from us."

"The land once stolen from them? These are minor disagreements. The Order of Swordthanes is not driven by petty politics and personal rivalries, not when there are greater matters to concern us. Your son understands this—do you not, Thane?"

Nico nodded. He studied the Third in detail. Handsome and dark-skinned—perhaps from Buldova, where the Naru influence was strongest. Not quite middle-aged, trim and tall, with absolute poise and precision of movement. Very much the ideal that Nico hoped to achieve one day.

"We reject your offer, Third," Hermann stated flatly.

"If we may, I'd like to hear the prince's thoughts."

"I'm still king."

"Yes… Nevertheless, Nicolas is heir. He must live with any decision made today. He is also a Thane himself, and I will surprise no one when I say that I am his Patron. He must obey me, or renounce the ethos of the Order."

"It is not the way of the Order to interfere in politics so directly."

"Not unless circumstances justify doing so. Eberhart understood this when he unified the twelve kingdoms. And so things now stand."

At the time of his Proving, Nico was merely an insignificant second prince without role or responsibility. He admired the Order, its traditions, and its values. Discipline. Prowess. Courage. Honor. Never did he imagine he would be forced to choose between it and his kingdom.

Seeing the conflict show in the prince's face, Arturo frowned sympathetically. "I put you in a difficult position, I know. I would give you time to consider, but as you yourselves admit...every minute is valuable right now."

Nico met his father's eyes. The warning was still there. What would happen to king and kingdom if they accepted the Third's offer? Would it really be so bad? Akenberg would lose land, but they were already the largest of the central kingdoms. They could survive a subtraction. The ignominy would be hard to take, but an overwhelming enemy was bearing down on them already, threatening annihilation. This offer spared them from that worst of all outcomes. And it was possible these other threats were real enough. If so, the Chekiks alone would require the combined might of the twelve kingdoms to resist, and even then the outcome was dubious at best. Demons. Devils... Arturo was right. A new emperor was needed now more than ever.

Nico could not abandon the Order. It had meant too much to him for too long.

He sighed. Hermann scowled, and Arturo smiled. "A Swordthane quickly makes the right choice. Yes?"

Nico nodded. "Tell me, Third, when was your last defense?"

The smile dropped. He glared back. "Nearly three years."

"It's an honor to challenge you."

It was the only way.

7

BELOW

The badger led Jak and Kevik on a wild chase through the forest, until they were hopelessly lost deep within the glen.

"But why are we chasing it?" Jak called to his best friend.

"Because it's running," Kevik yelled back.

"But why is it running?"

"Because we're chasing it."

At last they cornered the fearful creature amid a proliferation of leaves that filled a shallow depression. The badger stared back with blazing blue eyes, daring them to take one step closer. They did, its blue eyes flashed green, then it promptly dove beneath the sea of leaves.

"Where did it go?" asked Jak.

"Look," Kevik replied, brushing aside handfuls of debris. "A hole within the ground."

"Where does it lead?"

"I don't know. You should look."

"Why me?"

"You're the smaller. I can't fit in there."

Jak could see the logic in this, even if he did not like it. He approached the hole and peered inside. There was nothing but blackness. He leaned further.

"See if you can grab it," Kevik suggested.

Jak reached in with both arms. Then felt a kick from behind, and his body tumbled forward, clogging the hole perfectly. He frantically twisted this way and that, but his body was stuck around the hips, his arms helplessly pinned inside.

That was the worst—the uselessness of his arms. They were trapped, which prevented Jak from freeing himself, which prevented the use of his arms, which prevented Jak from freeing himself, which prevented the use of his arms...

And all the while Kevik laughed.

"Jak!"

Kleo was shaking him, her face looking down with fright and concern.

He gasped for breath, wondering when exactly hell had run out of air. He could not breathe at all, and glared at Kleo in panic. "H-help," he gasped. Although lying on his back, Jak felt that he was going to fall...down, down, even farther than they already were, deep into the earth where the cold stone would close in and swallow him.

Thankfully, his arms were free after all, and he clasped Kleo by the fragile shoulders. "Don't let me fall..."

She grabbed his forearm with both hands. "You're not falling, Jak. You had a nightmare."

Laughter. Where is that laughter coming from?

Slowly, he began to recover his wits. There was air—and he was not falling. But they were still trapped in hell.

He hurriedly looked around. He could see Kluber sitting up, watching. But the place where Calla slept was empty.

She was gone. Just like Riff.

"Calla," he croaked, his fingers pressing hard into Kleo's soft skin.

"She's fine," Kleo said soothingly. "She just...went for a walk."

Went for a walk? Down here? With all that has happened? Jak was about to rebuke the others for allowing such irresponsibility, until he realized what Kleo meant. Calla had simply gone to make water, of course—and Jak needed to get control of himself.

He nodded, released Kleo's shoulders at last, and felt her reluctantly let go. "I'm sorry," he said. *I'm sorry.* His chest heaved. A tear rolled down his cheek.

"We all are." She hugged him, and he closed his eyes again.

When he awoke a second time, Kluber and Kleo were missing.

He looked up at Calla, who sat nearby, staring into the pitiful flames of a puny fire, arms wrapped around her bare knees. The wedding gown was frayed and torn to the point of scarcely covering her thighs. She rocked, either to keep her muscles warm or with the nervous dread of their circumstances. Perhaps some combination of both.

"Fishing," she said.

He nodded, pushed himself up, and wandered a short distance away to take care of his own business. Upon his return, he tried to sit near enough to let her know he was open to conversation, but not so close as to irritate her further.

They had barely spoken for two days now.

Riff's death had hit them all hard, and the four survivors had simply gone about the motions of life through a full cycle of eating and sleeping—Jak no longer thought of days and nights, since there was no difference between the two in the down below, and no way to tell which it was up above.

Eventually, the shock wore off enough for his mind to start functioning again. Then the idea came to him that the library might provide a means of escape, if only they could find a map or text that described this world they were trapped in.

Kluber and Kleo were fishing at that time, as well. And so he asked Calla if she would read for him.

"Why don't you ask Kleo?" she snapped in reply. The words stung, but he could see in her face that the pain she felt exceeded his own. He had not known how to comfort her then, and did not know how to comfort her now, just as he had not known how to save his village from the demons or his friend from the pyre.

She stood, rubbed her dirty calves, and walked away. He wanted to stop her, if for no other reason than her own safety. But he was tired of giving orders, and tired of seeing them fail.

Losing track of time, he closed his eyes and allowed his mind to wander. He saw a badger go into a hole, and felt himself getting ready to dive in after it. His body began to stiffen in anticipation of this recurring panic attack...

"Jak! Jak!" Calla whispered harshly, and his eyes popped open.

"What is it?" He could see the excitement in her body, a tremulous mixture of hope and fear.

"I saw someone."

He stood up quickly. "Where?"

She led the way through a narrow alley to an open avenue. "There," she said, pointing to a small square house-like structure a block away. A nondescript building, wholly unremarkable except for being one of the few intact amid a string of crumbled rock piles.

"He came out of it and went that direction." She pointed toward the city center.

"He?"

Calla looked up at Jak in agitation. "I don't know. Could have been a she. I didn't get a chance to check. I hurried to tell you." She looked down, and her shoulders began to quiver.

He touched her gently. "Calla, you did great. Let's find the others. See if we can figure out a plan."

Basket in hand, the robed, hooded figure walked the dead avenues in silence, away from the grand structure and toward the foul-stenched building they thought of as the larder, where they had found the rack of dried fish, the casks of water, and the farm of shit-and-compost mushrooms. This was the second time in the four days since Calla's sighting they had watched him follow this same route, and the first since they laid the trap.

Kluber had the idea to use the net from the fishing supplies. He and Jak held it between them, stationed on their perch on the roof of an empty but intact house. They had carefully planned this location and the signals they would use in silence, one of which they had just received from Kleo from her position as spotter. Calla waited around the corner, makeshift club in hand should further subduing be necessary. Jak would have preferred Kluber have that job, but he worried that the older boy would take his anger out on their prey by beating him to death.

Three, two, one...

The figure was directly below. Jak nodded to Kluber, and they cast the net over the side. Then the older boy was immediately scrambling over the edge, dropping down beside the entangled prisoner. Calla came around the corner, swinging the club while Kluber lashed out with his feet, kicking and stomping.

Jak knew he should stop them, but he understood the urge that drove them to violence. This was the first opportunity to strike back, and they had a growing tally of frustrations to work out of their systems.

The man in the net grunted, but did not speak. Not even as they dragged him the length of three blocks to their camp, where Kluber kicked him one more time for good measure. Then the four of them slowly peeled away the net and stood around the prostrate form, each waiting for another to step forward and lower the hood. To reveal the face of evil.

Thin, feeble hands slowly reached up, the prisoner performing the task for himself. The four of them looked upon a white-bearded man, as old as any person Jak had ever seen. The delicate body kneeled before them, utterly powerless but firm and straight, the head unbowed and unmoving. Then, slowly, the man looked up to his captors, from face to face, lingering on each for a brief study. Jak felt a chill as those pale eyes evaluated and judged him.

The voice that spoke belied the fragility of the being. "You have questions." There was no reference to the assaults inflicted upon him. He might not have noticed.

Jak took a step back, suddenly afraid of that resoluteness. But Kluber reacted differently, stepping forward to kick the man again. The figure went down to the hard stone, then pushed himself back up without a word.

"Aye, we have questions," Kluber said with a grimace. "How would you like to *burn?*"

"My time will come soon enough. I do not fear the flames, although it is my sadness that my heart cannot embrace them. I feel I have more work to perform first."

This was not the answer any of them expected, and they were all restored to silence.

The man continued. "You have other questions, surely. Ask them of me. I will answer, without the violence. It is my life's work to teach."

"How dare you lecture us about violence," Calla rebutted. "You murdered our friend."

The old head shook negatively. "There was no murder. The boy gave his life willingly." He returned her hatred with sympathy. "He was a good young man...intelligent, unselfish, giving. He would have made a good disciple. We offered that option. But he chose sacrifice."

Calla covered her face, then turned away. Kleo quickly put her arm around her friend's shoulders, pulling her back. Jak watched the two of them retreat to the campfire's dimmest fringe. Then he looked back at the old man—saw that he, too, was watching the pair.

The man next looked at Kluber, perhaps assuming the tallest and oldest was their leader. But Kluber could no longer hold the man's penetrating gaze, and the pale eyes turned to Jak.

"So, there she is. The one for whom the boy sacrificed." There was a sadness in the voice, echoing their own in tone if not in magnitude. "He loved her. I believe he loved you all. He was committed to his choice, even at the end."

"Stop talking in riddles. We don't need more confusion."

"I do apologize. I know not where to begin, for I know not where you stand. What you have learned already, what you have gleaned, what you surmise." The man sighed. "You are confused, but you are no fool, Housethrall Jak. You understand more than you care to admit."

Jak flinched at the sound of his name. How had they so quickly lost the advantage over their prisoner? "What do you mean?"

"The girl is corrupt, just like her brother."

Before he realized he was doing it, Jak slapped the man. Then he quickly looked back in the direction of Calla and Kleo, and was thankful to see that their attention was elsewhere.

"She doesn't know, does she?"

Jak felt the tears coming on, but shook them away. He did not intend the gesture as an answer to the inquiry, but the old man took it as such.

"She could still be saved, of course. The corruption moves... unpredictably. And Versatz Tempus resists. But as in all things, sacrifice is necessary. And no longer have we the resources, not since your village was lost.

"She will not be the last. Nagnuaqua's strength returns. His taint touches us all, some more than others. He will consume the whole empire, should we not stop him—and of that, we are incapable. We can only hinder the spread."

Kluber spoke again at last. "Jak, don't listen to him. He's a manipulator. His words are poisonous." Jak stared back at his friend for a long moment, uncertain and afraid. Once again, Kluber had the right of things. Yet more than anything else, Jak craved knowledge. Day by day, his world was collapsing, his loved ones hurt, all because he did not know how to turn back the tide. He swore to make sense of it all, eventually.

But not now. Not here, not yet. With a final glance at the old man, Jak turned away to see if he could be any comfort to the girls.

He could not. In this, as in all things, Jak was relegated to observer. He had not the power to do anything but watch events unfold.

They fed the old man, but Kluber silenced him at every word. He was their captive, yet no one felt that he was under their control. Their fear of his authority was evident by their conspicuous avoidance of further conversation. No one so much as asked his name.

The four of them took turns guarding while the others performed the rituals of existence. Without purpose—the search for an exit called off, and for a lost companion no longer necessary—each of them found their own way to occupy time and suppress grief. The basics of survival kept them alive, but Jak could feel the reasons for living slipping away.

His turn having come, one by one the others abandoned the camp for their own personal sojourns of catharsis.

"Ask me your questions, Child. You are a thinker. This much the boy made clear." The man had discovered his voice now that Kluber was not there to stop him. "He said you are the smartest man he'd ever known... Before he met us, of course."

Jak shook his head. "I'm just a thrall. I can't even read."

"Don't confuse ignorance with imbecility, Child. I was once a thrall, as well."

"Don't call me 'Child.'"

"I do apologize, Housethrall Jak."

"Don't say my name, either."

"How do you prefer to be called, then?"

Jak closed his eyes, then rubbed them. He would lose any test of words and wills with their captive, this much he knew. But he wanted so badly to understand. "Who are you?"

"I am Disciple Hobbes, servant of Versatz Tempus."

"Your home is a temple, then?"

"It is far more, but you may call it that."

"How many of you are there?"

A sigh. "Not enough."

"What do you do, besides murder innocent boys?"

"We attend the shrines of the Glen. We teach those who would protect the souls of the ignorant. We protect the world from Versatz Yagos' touch."

"Please stop with the riddles. I'm not as smart as you think."

Hobbes smiled benevolently. "I taught your disciples, Bashir and Lukas. Did you not wonder where they came from?"

"*You* taught them?"

"Not I alone, but yes. Both were wise men, in their own way. I was particularly fond of your Lukas. He tried so hard with his lessons, but was as slow as anyone I've ever taught. We regretted sending him to you before he was ready, but his predecessor's death was imminent."

Jak remembered the sadness and horror of their flight from Everdawn. "He saved us. He was terrified, but he held the demons back while we escaped."

Hobbes nodded. "Yes. We felt his sacrifice. In the end, each of us finds out who we are. Some are prepared to give our lives to help those we love. Or even those we've never met." He looked at Jak penetratingly, his eyes evaluating once more. "Some are not."

Jak shifted uncomfortably. "What's wrong with Kleo?"

"She is corrupt, as I told you. It is not her fault, but the taint has chosen her. Perhaps because of her brother."

"She's getting better." Kleo had not complained of discomfort in days, and Calla reported that the "rash" had not grown larger.

"Since the boy's sacrifice, yes? He would be pleased to hear this."

"Stop talking like that. One of us is likely to punish you, and it won't be pretty."

"I think perhaps not. I am here to teach you. You desire knowledge, that much is clear. We give ours freely. Come with me, learn with us."

Jak shook his head vehemently. "Nay. Never."

"Think, Child. Your enemies are elsewhere. Not here."

"Prove it."

The old man stared back for a long moment, considering. Then he nodded, and raised his arms to the height of his shoulders.

Jak detected movement at the periphery of the flames. The others must be returning.

But it was not the others. It was a half-dozen robed figures, and they had him surrounded.

"Your friends are with us already, Jak. Do not worry, everyone is unharmed. We only wish to talk."

"Your words are poisonous." Kluber was right. Jak felt the recurring sense of doom as powerfully as ever. This would not end well, he was sure of that.

"The *world* is poisonous. We merely reveal the treatment." Hobbes stood, his frail old body no longer seeming as powerless as before. "Come, Child. All will be revealed."

"Therefore, taking the sword awakened Versatz Yagos. It was an irresponsible act of an ignorant man, but alone not necessarily catastrophic. Versatz Yagos was disoriented and weak, incapable of the barbarity which befell your village.

"But he was empowered, unknowingly, by a single mortal soul. Gifted to him by two foolish boys who selfishly acted to hide their petty crimes."

"Murder is hardly a petty crime," Jak said.

"In the great scheme of the world, it is. Boys die all the time. The only importance is that their souls remain hidden from Nagnuaqua."

"Nagnuaqua?"

"Versatz Yagos. That soul rejuvenated him. Strengthened him. Gave him power and purpose...to seize more."

"So he attacked Everdawn? How do we force him back out? Restore things to normal?"

Disciple Hobbes leaned back in his chair. He studied Jak, a recurring act that never grew less unnerving. "You misunderstand, Child. Your village is gone. Your people dead. The lucky ones, at least. The question is not how to push the demons out of Shadow Glen... It's how long before they destroy the empire entire."

"It's Shady Glen," Jak timidly corrected, deliberately avoiding the point.

"Shadow. So it was once, and so it is again. You will be fortunate to never see your home again, Child—for if you do, you will not like what you find."

The lesson still fresh in his mind, Jak sat back in his own chair. It was ornately polished hardwood, practical and uncomfortable. All the furniture, decoration, and supplies inside the Temple of Tempus were finely crafted and resistant to time. This included the beds that the four survivors slept in and the nondescript robes they now wore.

All in all, they were being treated conspicuously well, especially in light of the punishment they had inflicted upon Hobbes. Jak was thankful for that much, even though his companions were less than enthusiastic about the change in circumstances. They made clear that they considered the hospitality captivity, their hosts murderers, and preferred to take their chances away from the temple. He, however, was coming to see things from a different perspective. Not that those within the temple could be altogether forgiven for killing Riff, but he was willing to give them a chance to explain their behavior.

Jak was also learning—far more than he ever imagined possible—about subjects he had never known existed. He was determined to absorb all he could, that he might never again fail to protect his friends as terribly as he had. While the other three sought comfort in each other's company, the former housethrall made himself available to the disciples. He listened, asked questions, and—miracle of miracles—began to read.

The turning point had come on the first day, when Jak had still been resistant to Hobbes' persuasions.

The old man went to a bookshelf, pulled a large volume down and dropped it on the table before Jak. He flipped through its ancient pages until a map appeared. The lines were familiar, but the scrawled symbols were not. "See for yourself."

"I can't read," Jak said helplessly.

"Here." From a pocket of his robe, the disciple produced a translucent brown gemstone the size of a plum. At first glance, it appeared to be circular—but as the object was handed to Jak, he could see that it was shaped like something else. "The Eye of Versatz Orkus, your god of wisdom. Let me show you."

The first time Jak looked through the gem—the meaning of the symbols leaping from the pages into his mind—he had nearly fainted. He would have fallen from the chair had Hobbes not caught him, showing more strength than that wizened body had any right to possess.

The map predated the Empire of Twelve Kingdoms. In fact, it predated the Hrathan era entirely. It was a map of the Chekican Communion, when Jak's homeland was known by disturbing names. Hobbes pointed to the words "Shadow Glen," but Jak's eyes gravitated instead to the adjacent label next to an insignificant dot. *Neverdawn.* His home.

With an admonition not to overuse the precious artifact, the old man had allowed Jak to borrow it in exchange for listening to their lessons, their invitations, their pleas. They wanted—they needed—more followers for the fight against Nagnuaqua. Failing that, they desired another sacrifice.

Unmindful of the warning, hardly an hour had passed that Jak had not made use of the Eye. Unbeknownst to his friends, he was granted permission to leave the temple to visit the library—a building the disciples called the Pantheon, containing the accumulation of wisdom associated with all known deities. As the hours progressed to days, and days to tendays, he discovered more about the world than most did in a natural lifetime, and delved into arcane subjects no man ought—the perverse rites and unfathomable potencies of the gods, each of whom bestowed limited influence over some aspect of the world in exchange for terrible displays of piety. Perhaps the Eye performed more than mere decrypting, for Jak studied with a clarity of mind he had never before experienced. Or perhaps that stemmed from pure desperation.

One of his highest priorities had been to find maps of the underworld in which they were trapped. Ra'Cheka was the name the Chekiks had given these caverned cities, and it was only a matter of time before he discovered the right one. Soon he found what he had hoped for—passages away from this city to others, and from others to the world aboveground. The most hopeful option appeared to be across the lake and past a guardhouse. There a tunnel many miles long led far, far south, culminating at last in an even greater underground city with many potential ways out. He could only hope at least one remained open, for these maps and texts predated the cataclysm that supposedly sealed them all off.

Logic dictated that an exit was possible, for the disciples of this very temple spoke of new members joining throughout the years. Although they avoided specifics, Jak had ascertained that these came from above, drawn to this place by some irrational allure. If it was possible to come down, then it must also be possible to get up.

At first, Jak had been excited to share this plan of escape with his friends, and had hurried back through the streets nearly bursting with anticipation. On further reflection, however, he worried that they would all want to leave immediately. And there remained too much to learn. So more than a tenday had passed, and he still had not told them.

In fact, he saw less of them than ever, especially after taking the decision to eat alone while studying. He regretted their absence, but every minute spent away from the books was wasted time.

And so Jak was caught by surprise when Kluber cornered him in a hallway, impatient to talk. "Jak, there are things we should discuss."

He was restless to return to the Pantheon, but the hint of urgency in that statement compelled him to pause. "Aye," he nodded in reply. "It's time we do. This eve. I'll—"

But Kluber grabbed him by the arm and held firmly. "Nay, Jak. Now."

Head shaking, mind disturbed by the thought of missing a lesson, he tried to pull away. "Kluber, you don't understand."

"Nay, I don't." The stronger boy's hand twisted, turning Jak's forearm, lifting it. The sleeve of the robe fell back, exposing the skin. Both boys stared at the scars for a moment. "Calla was right," Kluber exclaimed. "I don't understand these, I don't understand what's happened to you, and I don't understand what's happening to...come on, Jak. Come with me."

For a few steps, Jak resisted. But not violently, and Kluber's momentum propelled them along the corridor. Then he found his own step, matching the long strides while a resolution formed in his mind. The purpose of knowledge was power, and the purpose of power was to control events. Jak had already learned so much, surely he could assuage any misgivings that plagued his friends. *I can, for I must.*

Kluber led the way into the small common chamber between

their sleeping cells. The two girls sat upon resting chairs in separate corners, each looking up at the boys' arrival. Jak's eyes longingly found Calla's face, hoping to calm his racing thoughts. Despite the recent icier demeanor, gazing upon its peaceful innocence brought a warmth and solace to his heart. But not now, for serenity had been overcome by naked distress.

"Is-s that Jak?" came a voice, and his gaze turned to Kleo. She stood and came forward eagerly, a smile forming as the light caught her features—once as lovely as Calla's, now marred by a thin layer of flaky scales stretching from chin to forehead. "Are you going to s-stay with us-s awhile?" she asked hopefully.

"Of course," he replied, as calmly as he could manage. "I'm sorry I've neglected you all."

The waning strength in his legs forced him to sit. Even with all the knowledge he had learned, Jak remained as powerless as ever. *I must, but I can't.*

That eve, Jak cornered Disciple Hobbes just as Kluber had cornered him. "Tell me more of Nagnuaqua. And Tempus."

"Unhand me, Child. There, that is better. Now…there is much to tell. Do you desire a full lesson? Or perhaps you have questions."

"Why do they fight one another? How do the fires aid Tempus? How can we stop Nagnuaqua's corruption?"

Hobbes nodded. "These questions warrant longer answers, but I see you are impatient. Very well. They fight because they are devils, and it is the way of devils to fight—"

"Wait," Jak interrupted. "Nagnuaqua is a devil, but Tempus is a god."

"Is that so?" The old man raised an eyebrow. A show of curiosity—or amusement. "Have you not learned the meaning of 'Versatz?' It is a title we use for those you call gods, a word derived from the older Hrathan tongue to signify falsity.

"The devil Reglaku is also known as Versatz Tempus, whom you simply call Tempus. And Nagnuaqua as Yagos. So it is for all your deities—Shuberath is mighty Theus by his Hrathan name. Ithicus is Orkus, your god of wisdom. It is his artifact you abuse so."

Jak had trouble associating the precious object in his pocket with evil.

"When the hratha rebelled from the Chekiks, they needed gods of their own. Gods they could believe were good, or at least benign. They needed the power, without the guilt of consorting with evil. Always childish, willing to believe what they desired.

"Most, anyway. Some few refused to recognize the role of divinity, believing instead that strength was not worth compromise. These fools believed submission and subservience preferable to self-deception. Their descendants have paid the price for that decision ever since. They live inside the empire, but not truly *within*.

"They are the exception, however. Most accepted the new deities without question. Then, and now, willfully ignorant of the truth.

"This temple works in secret so that those above may continue that ignorance. Barely aware of what they call gods, but not quite forgetting them. Continuing the rituals without knowing why. The burning of the dead in your home, for example."

Jak felt the panic of his nightmares returning, along with the headaches and anxiety. Once more, the air inside the dead city was too sparse to breathe.

"The rites you practice...blood to Versatz Kron, Father Earth —of which we do not approve—that is an offering to Bellugug, the scorpion with two tails."

Hobbes smiled sadly. "I'm surprised you have not learned this on your own. The pace of your study is remarkable—the fastest I've beheld, to speak true—but you ascend too quickly, Disciple Jak, like a climber without rope. Even the boy Riff understood this..." He leaned back, once again studying Jak intently. "Or, perhaps, you *do* learn, but do not wish to admit."

All trace of amusement was gone, his tone grave. "The world is poisonous, as I have already made clear. There are no gods, Child. Only devils. You seek a miracle to save your friend—but there are no miracles. Only sacrifice.

"It is too late for your friend, the corruption too strong, the peril to others too long unabated. The girl must burn."

8

NEUBLUSTEN

"The priests look to the gods, but so far the gods remain silent. Oh, thank you, Lass." Arturo lifted his cup of tea from the immense silver platter carried by the serving girl, a young, pretty blonde of thirteen or fourteen years. She held its considerable weight from a single point with deceptively strong fingers.

"What is your name, Lass?" Nico asked.

"Pris, My Prince."

"Pris, will you bring me another cup of water?" He placed his empty cup on the platter where the tea had been. Nico would have far preferred something more biting than water, but had implemented a policy of no drinking amongst the officer ranks until the current crisis was resolved, and did not wish to violate the order himself.

The girl bowed and walked out, his eyes and thoughts pursuing her. Those tiny hands contained more strength and agility than most of the soldiers training outside. Perhaps he should encourage her to enlist...

Nico smirked, unable to imagine a young girl like that

fighting and killing old veterans. His rapacious appetite for more soldiers was growing ludicrous.

"Disciple Elyseo—the Grand Cleric of Theus," Arturo added for Nico's edification—"assures us that the answers will come, we must simply be patient." He sighed. "First Eberhart was always dubious of these priestly claims. I tend to agree." Swallowing half of the tea in one long pull, the Third then leaned back over the map. His finger tapped on the northernmost region of Falkenreach, a forested district named Shady Glen—a place unfamiliar to Nico. "My Patron sent two Seekers to this area. One this past autumn, who never returned. The second more recently, to confirm these demonic reports. The first priority following our…engagement…should be to follow-up on that."

Nico nodded in understanding. These meetings had been Arturo's idea, but both men were equally committed. The possibility—no, the likelihood—that one of them would die in the duel meant that the winner would bear some of the loser's former responsibilities. Arturo agreed to take an active role in negotiating for peace between Akenberg and her rivals, should Nico fall. The terms would not be favorable, of course, considering the circumstances. But the prestige of a Third carried no little weight, and although his father was certain to resist any terms that included surrender, Nico was confident that the damage to his homeland would not be irreparable.

On the other hand, if the prince were to emerge the winner, he promised to pick up the heavy burdens carried by the older man.

There was a certain tranquil anticipation to the challenge. The outcome—the unpleasant notion that one of them would lose his status, his pride, and perhaps his life—was daunting, but the fight itself was expected to be glorious. Both swordsmen were skilled, energetic, in the prime of their years. Each was calm, thoughtful, and as respectful of each other as they were for the tenets of the Order. Contrasted with Zenza, the contemptuous thane in Cormona, Arturo was everything Nico looked for in a warrior.

Moreover, the two of them genuinely liked one another, and though the words remained unspoken, each knew it would be an honor to fall to the other.

As for the odds, Nico gave himself one chance in three. A clever move here, a lucky break there, and he could conceivably come away the victor.

Arturo continued the narration. "If indeed the demons emerge from the glen, King Tesius will need to be reinforced. In spirit, as well as in numbers. He is not a resolute man, and will waver in the face of such evil. I tell you this because I believe you see others much as I do. Their hearts and minds as well as their titles and purses."

"Yes," Nico agreed. "But fighting demons is quite different from fighting men. I'm not certain I would blame those who cower and hide."

His companion nodded regretfully. "The troops will need to know—will need to *see*—that such monsters can be killed."

"Can they?"

"Who can say? But we get ahead of ourselves. So much is unknown at this time. Let us speak instead of the Chekican invasion. Here, in the east…"

"Your pardons, Third, but I fear that must wait until the morrow." Nico was looking at a new arrival to the conference chamber. Lima, looking characteristically impatient.

"Handersonn?" he asked, and she nodded.

He turned back to Arturo. The expression on the Third's face was unreadable. "Of course, Thane. Good luck in your war."

Nico hurried with Lima back to the war room of the Rechshtal. Along the way, she explained her difficulty in finding the man amongst the taverns of Neublusten, as heavily patronized as they had become in recent days. And then, upon finding the general—rousing him from his incoherent stupor.

This is the man to whom I am going to trust the defense of the city?

But to his utter surprise, Nico found himself liking the amiable old officer. Aware of his own limitations, oftentimes openly ridiculing them, General Handersonn not only thanked Nico for the opportunity to salvage his reputation but praised the prohibition of wine, beer, and spirits. "As you can see by my extreme rotundity and brightness of nose, I have greater difficulty vanquishing temptation than more mortal opponents. But your decisions, My Prince, General, Thane—how many titles does one man need?—grant me the forbearance I so desperately require, and so plainly don't deserve."

"I have to know one thing, General—can you take a field command?"

Handersonn laughed wholeheartedly. "Why, My Prince, I know I don't look like much now. But in earlier years, I made quite the dashing commander. The barracks still speak of my glories, my accomplishments, my stunning victories—and if they don't, the taverns do. Of course, that's because I told them myself…but nevertheless, they do speak of them."

Sighing, trying hard not to smile despite himself, Nico pressed on. "We have nearly five hundred new recruits. Willing, but raw. They can barely swing a sword or lift a shield, yet they stand between the city and ruin. They, Captain Reikmann's Royal Guard, my Princeshields, and the remnants of General Freilenn's Second Army are all we have left." Handersonn frowned distastefully at the mention of General Freilenn, but brightened again quickly as Nico continued. "I need someone to take command of this rabble, to lead them in battle. Can you do it?"

"Prince, General, Thane—I not only can do it, I can whip them into shape faster than you would believe. Back in earlier years, I was quite the capable instructor. Few remember now, but I could turn a baby-faced boy into a seasoned veteran faster than anyone. Discipline, maneuver, fighting—you name the routine, I could drill it…"

Nico's mind wandered while the boasting rambled on. He felt sorry for the new recruits, and not because of this man. They showed willingness now, but when the time came to fight, they were in for a brutal awakening. How many would die, he wondered. Or be cruelly maimed, like Lima? And for what purpose? Did they have a prayer of even slowing down the Loresters? Some of them were as likely to hurt themselves or each other as the enemy.

He thought of the former page, Kip. Just that morn, the young man's company drilled with practice swords in a mock battle. In the span of five minutes, the lad had twisted his ankle on a loose stone, tripped one of his comrades, and somehow contrived to break his own sword. He had to be the clumsiest, unluckiest soldier who ever existed. *Whatever you do, don't stand close to that one when the quarrels start flying.*

Handersonn droned on and on, until falling silent at the sudden arrival of another.

General Freilenn looked weary. At the sight of his rival, he straightened his back and squared his shoulders, but a bit of posturing could not disguise the exhaustion. He and Nico had last met nearly a full day earlier, and that at the culmination of a long march. Clearly the man had not slept since.

"General, please take a seat."

"Nay, thank you. I'm here to report."

Did he think sitting was a display of weakness? "I insist. You've earned it."

Freilenn nodded, and moved to the chair farthest from Handersonn. The relief upon sitting was obvious. He sighed and closed his eyes, leaving Nico to hope he would not fall asleep instantly.

"What is your report, General? Where do things stand?"

Reluctantly, the eyes reopened. "I believe we can claim success. The Loresters were not expecting another attack, and pulled back in some disarray at our approach. They drew up defensive lines and waited for us to come to them. I ordered three feints throughout the day, one for each flank and again in the center. They reacted conservatively, reinforcing the lines but declining to pursue."

"Sensible," Nico said.

"Aye. It's what I would have done. They have every advantage, there's no need to take risks."

Handersonn scoffed. "An old woman's approach. I would have hit back with everything."

"And if I was leading you into a trap, you would have exposed yourself."

"But you weren't, were you?"

"Generals!" Nico interrupted. "There's a time for each, aggressiveness and caution. Let us not concern ourselves with what the Loresters didn't do, and focus on the present."

"Aye, General."

Nico glared, waiting for Handersonn to restrain his boisterous tendency. "Yes, General."

"Fine." He turned back to Freilenn. "Where are the Loresters now?"

"Encamping across the lake. Out of range of our towers, but only just. I expect them to begin the investment, so that no one may enter or leave. I fear the siege has begun."

Nico nodded. "That's all right. You gave us time to stock the city properly. If need be, we can last the winter, thanks to you."

Handersonn coughed. "Bah. Neublusten should not have to suffer this deprivation. We should drive them back."

"Worried that the taverns will run dry on ale, *General?*" Freilenn sneered.

"Enough," Nico blurted. He faced Handersonn first. "Every extra day of drill helps us. You say you can drill like no other. I expect you to prove it." He then turned to the other, who looked about ready to fall from his chair. "Well done. You've earned a few days of rest, I believe."

Freilenn fired a sidelong glance at Handersonn before responding. "Your pardon, no rest is necessary. I'm ready to resume command of my army."

This rivalry between the two men was not unexpected, but was a complication needing to be monitored. Still, Nico did not see how pushing themselves to exceed the other could be a bad thing, so long as they obeyed orders.

"Very well. I'll speak to you again on the morrow."

Assuming I am still alive, that is.

"It has always been the role of Vilnia and Gothenberg to shield the empire from attack from the east. Had we known the Chekiks were coming, these passes could have been more heavily fortified." Arturo pointed to three places on the map. Nico leaned in to read: Soul's Pass, Sky's Pass, and Sea's Pass. "But there was no warning, and the kingdoms have allowed the defenses to erode."

The appropriate strategy was obvious enough. "The mountains are certainly the place to stop them."

"It's too late for that. They're already through. In what numbers, we know not. Passage through the mountains is necessarily slow, and the winter makes it slower. It's likely that we're only facing scouts and pillaging warbands at this point. That's bad enough, but I fear things will get much worse when full armies are across. This is what the combined might of the empire should be focused on—driving them back." He looked at the prince in earnest. "Here is where Akenberg's, Lorester's, and Daphina's forces should be."

Nico deflected the comment. "Of what we're seeing so far, how are they comprised?"

"Mostly tribesmen, according to reports. The few Chekiks spotted appear to be leaders, officers, conductors. Some say magi."

"Magi?" The notion of Chekiks returning was discomfiting, but Nico had difficulty believing this last.

"Only a rumor. Still, I think it best that you hear everything."

Nico agreed. "So, if we can put the current…unpleasantness… behind us, the central kingdoms should send aid to Vilnia." His fingers swiped at the map, indicating movement. "And the southern to Gothenberg." Clicking his tongue inside his cheek, he considered. "The northern have their own problem. Nurosterlend should reinforce Falkenreach. Keep the demons contained until the Chekiks are dealt with. That leaves the western. Their forces should be centralized for now, to function as a reserve to be deployed wherever evolving circumstances dictate."

"And Yoshini," Arturo added.

"Ah, I often forget them. Do they even have soldiers?"

"They do, and they are a marvel. Would it surprise you that the Order of Swordthanes originated there?"

"You astonish me."

"Indeed. You've done yourself a disservice if you've never witnessed a Yoshi fight."

"We must do our best to rectify that."

Arturo smiled sadly, and Nico was reminded of the obvious. "I don't imagine we'll both be alive in two hours' time, will we?"

The Third shook his head. "No, I suppose not." Then he clapped a hand on Nico's shoulder. "It is a good plan, Thane. Very similar to my own. Ah, my tea, at last."

Pris entered with their beverages, on the same oversize platter as before. With room enough for a dozen, their two looked lonely. Nico lifted his water and prepared to sip.

To his surprise, Arturo spoke before drinking. "May I say something, Thane?"

Nico thought of the last man he had shared a drink with—Captain Gornada, in Cormona. That memory was a warning at how suddenly friendship can turn. It was dangerous to like this man as much as he did already. "No, thank you, Third, I prefer—"

But Arturo was already speaking. "I have enjoyed these last days. Despite terrible sadness, an unwanted conflict, an enemy at your walls...Akenberg hospitality has been exceedingly gracious. I came as the harbinger of bad news, and I forced you into a decision that I believe you would have preferred to avoid. Your respect has been a surprise, to be honest. Your company, agreeable. I am glad to have met you, Prince Nicolas." He downed the tea.

Nico did not understand how his companion could do that. Compliment a man just before killing him. Perhaps it was simply a courtesy to ease an opponent's mind. Or to purge Arturo's own guilt.

Either way, he appreciated the gesture. Here was a man who embodied the values of the Order. His service was a boon to the empire, and his companionship an unexpected delight. Nico did indeed feel honored to fight the Third, and if he must die, there was no better way than by this man's blade.

"May the challenge be everything I hope for." He raised the water.

"Well said."

Duels were normally conducted in the castle's sparring chamber. But on this occasion, an attendant informed the two participants that they would fight in the courtyard, instead.

"Why?" Nico asked as the youth led them out through the main gates.

He received his answer in the form of an immense cheer. Hundreds of people had gathered to watch, and roared their support at the first sight of their prince. Surprised and embarrassed, he looked down. This task would be difficult enough without bearing the additional weight of oppressive expectations. He attempted to block them out, unsuccessfully.

Somewhere in the back, a distinct chant erupted, then quickly spread through the throng. "Ni-co-las! Ni-co-las! Ni-co-las!"

Arturo smiled cheerfully, as though unaware the crowd was against him. "Very well. Much nicer to fight in the sun." He tilted his head to allow a cheek to warm in the crisp, cool midafternoon air.

After a morn inside the Rechshtal war room, the bright winter sunshine nearly blinded them. Nico squinted, hoping his eyes would adjust before the fighting began.

They took their positions in the courtyard, surrounded by onlookers but seeing only each other. Arturo nodded discreetly, all signs of humor and camaraderie gone. Friendship had no place here, just as there was no room for sympathy or mercy—a lesson Nico learned from his very first bout.

So much had happened since then. Very strange to think how it could come to an end—the fighting and killing, strategy and deception, the pleasures of riding with his company and earning their respect. The adulation of the Cormonans, their treachery, an impending battle, an eventual crown...

He had created more memories in the last few tendays than his entire life before. And he would miss none of them half so much as never seeing Leti's face again.

Had there been a choice? In the moment, it had felt as though there were not. But in hindsight...

Then Arturo was upon him, and Leti's image disappeared in the flashing of blades and the crashing of shields.

A quarter-hour later, Nico stepped back, eyes staring at the sight before him and mind replaying the sequence of actions. He felt the blood from the gash in his calf soaking through the woolen pants, pooling inside the bottom of his thick boot. His shoulder ached where the chain mail had turned the incoming blade enough to change amputation to a shallow slash. Two wounds, not inconsequential, but he was still alive.

So was his opponent. Arturo was there, catching his breath, taking advantage of the respite, even if he appeared to need it less. He looked confident. Poised. As he had every right to.

They were both too good, too aware of the defense, to expose themselves to the type of fast and easy strike that could end the duel quickly. Instead, each had learned to look for small successes wherever they could find them. And the dynamic of the competition had changed as a result.

Swordfights were ordinarily fast and brutal, their outcome determined by a sudden show of skill. This one, however, was becoming a test of endurance. And Nico was already running out of energy, with no idea where to find reserves. He felt desperate, and although he tried not to let the fatigue show, he believed his opponent could sense it.

The wounds were annoying, and either might ultimately prove fatal, but the biggest concern at that moment was air. Even after this momentary pause, the prince continued sucking for breath, chest heaving, heart hammering like a blacksmith. Without air, there would be no strength, no speed. No life.

There was no more time to recover, for Arturo was already closing again.

From the first swing, Nico knew this would be the toughest fight of his life. Opening with Grimaldi's Fourth Measure, that old familiar friend, he quickly moved on to Hansa's Gambit, and from there to Prunela's Scale. None had the slightest success. Renard's voice began to lecture inside his head. "If the plan isn't working, only a fool would keep using it."

It was all leg work now. That took less effort to execute, while still requiring Arturo to pay some attention to his own defense. The man had no weaknesses, and if Nico was not going to achieve anything with his attacks, at least he would burn less energy failing.

The first snowflake fell, lazily floating through the air between them. Both men watched the flake suspiciously. In other circumstances, snow might have created a lovely effect on the surroundings. But here it could only become another obstacle, distracting the eyes and deceiving the feet. With any luck, this growing cascade would not last. Or the fight would end before the snow accumulated.

Of a same mind, both men lunged forward simultaneously, swords clashing on shields, the battle resuming in earnest.

Something between ten minutes and a lifetime passed before the next disengagement. Nico had taken another light wound, this time to the other leg. Now both legs and one arm suffered. Yet Nico was nearly elated, for he had managed to score a wound in the exchange.

He abandoned memorized sequences in favor of pure instinct —a series of thrusts, feints, and parries culminating in a single slash to Arturo's abdomen. The blow was heavy enough to nearly dislodge the sword from Nico's hand, but at the time he thought the hit merely knocked the wind from his opponent. Now he could see the man favoring one side, a slight hunch to his posture, bloodlust not yet numbing the wound the way Nico's had.

Press the advantage. Nico drove himself on and on. Yet it was so hard to break through even the minutest amount, to so much as force a step backward.

Clash and circle. Circle and clash. The snow falling all around.

At last, Nico was spent. One knee in that snow, gasping for

breath, shoulders shaking. The bottom edge of his shield rested on the ground, relieving the burden from a weary arm. He took to moving the shield only when absolutely necessary, and it functioned as little more than a dead weight he had considered discarding a dozen times.

Annoyingly, he had blood in his right eye from a scalp wound that was almost completely unfelt but would not stop bleeding. He was certain that half his face was streaked in blood, and imagined the horrifying sight he made to the onlookers. Yet pain was nothing, appearances were less—vision was everything, and so he was thankful that one eye remained clear.

In dueling there is a tipping point, before which the outcome is in doubt and after which is only a matter of time. Sometimes it is difficult to recognize exactly when that tipping point occurs.

Not so today. This one had been clear for at least the past three passes. Nico was doomed.

Why did his opponent delay the inevitable? Arturo should be pressing the advantage, but instead lingered just out of range.

He had clearly not fully recovered from the injury to his midsection. If anything, his hunched posture was even more pronounced. That single success was the only thing keeping Nico alive, even as a significant part of him wished the Third would hurry up and end this.

Filling the pause, the chanting began anew, growing more pronounced until it permeated his addled mind. *Ni-co-las. Ni-co-las. Ni-co-las.*

He listened more closely as his breath slowly returned. Either the chant was getting louder and louder, or the barrier between awareness and comprehension was breaking. That was *his* name. They were shouting *his* name, over and over and over. They still thought he could win.

Nico believed they were fools, but could not deny the swelling of spirit happening inside. Rejuvenation. Here was the energy he so desperately needed. Thanks to the cheers, he was able to stand again, to lift his shield, to assume a combat stance. He was not done yet.

His enemy ignored the noise. Pressing forward, he feinted and lunged. Nico parried and launched his own attack. Sword high, shield low; sword low, shield back... The series of blows went on at an unsustainable pace. The chanting turned back to *oohs* and *aahs,* then became a gasp—for Nico's blade swiped across the back of a heel, slicing leather and muscle. At the same time, Arturo's blow came down so hard on the shield that Nico lost his balance and tumbled to the ground.

Rolling... Raising the shield instinctively to meet another blow... The concussion rang through his left arm, even as his right hand thrust repeatedly to force Arturo back.

As they separated, Nico found himself back on a knee, once again without the strength to stand. This time he was not sure it would come back.

Arturo hobbled, limping around in a circle, sword hand pressed hard to his gut. Perhaps he was bleeding beneath the armor. Judging by the man's posture, the earlier hit must have inflicted internal damage. If nothing else, Nico had put up quite a fight—one the Third, and all these onlookers, would never forget. The Order promised a means to die honorably. Nico would have liked to see his beloved again, but he could die content knowing he had nearly matched a Third.

The contest was not over, however. The honor of both men demanded that they resist to the end. Despite the fall, Nico was able to move well enough to keep the shield between himself and his circling opponent. Now he watched Arturo give up the maneuver, let his own arms sag, struggle for breath himself.

"Prince, how are you still alive?"

By way of reply, Nico stood. Slowly, steadily, not daring to risk falling over.

The crowd cheered louder. He loudly smacked the blade of his sword against his own shield boss, encouraging them further. The chanting resumed. "Ni-co-las! Ni-co-las! Ni-co-las!"

Arturo, at last, cringed. Nico stepped toward him.

The man lunged, surprisingly quickly, his energy not as drained as it seemed.

And Nico was ready. He blocked, thrust, parried, slashed. Arturo's wounded foot came down awkwardly on the moist earth, slipping for just a second. Nico leapt forward, not swinging the sword at all, shield impacting on shield with all the force he could muster.

The Third went down for the first time. The cheering would have been deafening, except that Nico no longer heard it. He took one step, thought better of it, jumped back, and watched Arturo's sudden swing pass through the air between them. A close call, and a reminder that a wounded animal was most dangerous.

Now Arturo was on a knee and Nico afoot. The young prince had the blessing to be able to catch his breath and study his opponent. The pain in that sweat-drenched face was unmistakable. Here was an opportunity to seize the advantage, once and for all.

Nico took a step right, then left, then right again as he raised the sword for another thrust from that side. At the last second, he turned it into a swing from the opposite direction. Arturo had lifted his shield to meet the expected attack. Instead of trying to sweep it back across his body, he now brought his blade up to parry. Nico's sword deflected downward, right into the abdomen where the Third was already hurt.

Instinctively, Nico did not think the blow was enough to accomplish anything substantial. But Arturo looked like he was gasping for air. Then he retched, dark blood and bile spilling out of his mouth. He dropped the sword into the snow to support himself with his hand. The body shook violently, then he heaved again. And collapsed, face down, unmoving.

The thin layer of white snow between the two of them became black and red.

"Ni-co-las! Ni-co-las! Ni-co-las!" The cheers were louder than ever, but the energy they bestowed was entirely gone.

He dropped onto both knees, arms hanging limply, too tired to detach his left from the straps of the shield. Blood ran from four wounds.

Not believing that it was over. Uncertain how he had won.

If he could survive this, he could survive anything. *Leti, I will see you again, after all.*

Hands wrapped around him. He did not know who they belonged to, but they were all that stopped him from collapsing beside his dead opponent. So he gave himself over to them.

9

GOTHENBERG

Once again, snow halted the progress of the harpa caravan. Winter had finally reached down from the mountains onto the Gothic plains.

Light and unremarkable at first, by the third day it fell fast and thick, and the caravan could no longer disregard its effects. Summer called for a premature end to the day's travels, allowing extra time to prepare a camp with extra protection from the vexing precipitation. This came in the form of a series of overhanging canvases suspended between wagons and propped up by long poles, creating an enormous canopy. Still, some snow got through a hole in the center required to let campfire smoke out. This fire blazed bigger and stronger than ever before, and some of the soldiers were sent out to gather extra firewood to keep it going through the night and beyond. Shortly after venturing beyond the canopy, however, the raging storm forced them back.

It slackened slightly on the third day, and Corporal Mercer sought to take advantage.

The atmosphere beneath the canopy was cozy, and Yohan loath to leave it. But he reluctantly went with Brody on a wood-gathering run. What they picked up was already soaked, and stores would need to dry before becoming useful. He wondered if they were wasting time, collecting fuel that would no longer be needed by the time it was ready.

Not that he minded. Conversations with his loquacious friend were less common now that the other soldier was spending so much time with Meadow, and Yohan more with Summer. Expecting an opportunity to be reminded of just how much he appreciated the cheerful banter, Yohan was instead struck by Brody's unusual reserve.

They approached a pair of trees, looking for low and fallen branches.

Yohan attempted to lighten the mood by emulating Meadow's title and tone. "Is all well, Soldier Brody?"

A wry smile was his reward. "Aye, Brother. All is well. Just thoughtful these days."

"That is unlike you."

"Aye. I become more like you each day."

"And I like you, I find."

Brody laughed. "So I've perceived. Dancing, smiling. Why, last eve I believe I heard you laugh. These harpa have had quite the effect on you."

Yohan could not deny it. "I feel a weight has been lifted."

Brody balanced one armload of sticks while he placed a hand on Yohan's shoulder. "I am happy for you, Brother."

"Should I be happy for you, in return? Where have these newfound thoughts led?"

A pause, as his friend considered. "When this is over, I am staying with them."

"Aye? And what of joining the Swordthanes? What of your Proving?"

"Bah," Brody scoffed. "A fanciful dream, nothing more. I'm not one of the greatest swordsmen in the empire. It's become clear to me that I'm not even the best swordsman in this squad." A hint of sadness mingled with the usual cheer.

"Don't sell yourself short, Brother."

Brody laughed again. He took his hand from Yohan's shoulder to scoop up more sticks. "Sometimes a man is fortunate enough to decide between two dreams. Only a fool wouldn't choose the one just in front of him."

Yohan stiffened. A few preliminary notes of music emanated from the distant camp. He closed his eyes, suddenly disoriented. Waiting. The fiddles were echoed by familiar, comforting laughs. Yohan breathed deeply, collecting himself.

Still hunched over, Brody did not notice. "Besides, by the way Kelsey talks, you should be the one taking your Proving, not I."

"I have no interest in the Thanes."

"You haven't even thought about it? She says she's never seen anyone fight like that."

"Kelsey exaggerates."

Brody stood back up, grinning at him. There was the familiar, teasing smile Yohan knew so well. Pleasing, and so willing to be pleased. An enviable outlook on life, and yet another lesson learned.

The grin morphed into an expression of surprise, then worry. "What the Devil…"

Brody dropped the armful of sticks and began to run. Yohan turned, seeing a figure emerge through the blurry wall of falling snow. The figure stumbled, went down to its knees, and stayed there. Yohan dropped his own sticks and ran after his friend. As the two of them got closer, the bowed head lifted and an unexpected face returned their stares. Sallow eyes and a ginger beard, grown uneven.

"Are you hurt, Brother?" Brody asked, for the man wore the garb and gear of a Vilnian soldier. "Wait. I know you."

"Redjack," Yohan said. "Can you stand?" Not waiting for an

answer, he and Brody lifted the man between them and hurried him toward the camp.

In her twenty-two years of life, Summer had taught the harpa dances to many a willing partner. Each time pleased to do so, happy to spread happiness. But never had she derived such satisfaction—nay, enjoyment—as she did with Yohan.

It was not only that he caught on so quickly—not merely the footwork, but the soul of the music and the motion. The essence of the thing itself. She could read in his face that he felt it in his heart, and all other things were trivial by comparison. She was proud of him, and proud of herself for having this effect.

She was teaching him not only how to dance, but how to live. He had told her so himself. Whatever the burdens he had started with, he was enjoying life again, and she had played a part in that. Quite simply, seeing happiness in others brought some to her. It had always been that way with anyone, but especially with those who experienced it least and needed it most. Indeed, this dynamic had lured her to Patrik, who in youth had been the unhappiest man she had ever known. Until now.

Summer discussed some of these thoughts with her betrothed. Not that she worried for his feelings, for he held not a jealous bone in his body. Summer had long ago cured his melancholy, and was proud of the man he had become. Patrik was, in many ways, the complete opposite of Yohan—appreciative for what he had, oblivious to what he did not, completely content with his lot. Patrik epitomized what it meant to be harpa, and she loved him for it. He noticed the good she was doing, and the good it did her in return, and encouraged her to continue.

He was a good man—the best of men—and she thanked the

stars and moon for him each night. Even as she felt her heart turn.

This world was cruel and dangerous, especially for her people, and getting more so every day. Yet amid the oppression and inequity, hardships and death, she was content. The cards had been good to her, her life better than most. She did not know why some people were dealt the lyre and others the shroud. She saw no reason why she deserved the former, so the least she could do was respect the blessing through constant appreciation. Harpa culture taught that the best way to do so was to maintain joy in one's heart, and that was a fine way to live.

Summer's was a life of sharing joy, and of receiving it. She had experienced more than her fair share of joyful moments. Who would have thought the memory that lingered the strongest was a simple soldier asking her to dance? The moment resonated like none other. She had never felt so surprised, so proud, or so happy.

Proud and happy. Happy and proud. Precarious heights from which a fall was inevitable, but to be enjoyed for as long as possible. So much remained unspoken, and uncertain, but she would appreciate these simple joys nonetheless.

Summer finished inspecting her wagon and rejoined her family, smiling as she saw Silvo pull his cherished lute from its protective box. "Are we in for something special this eve, Silverson?"

His broad, toothy grin turned a homely face handsome. "Aye, Sister. I've felt it calling me these last nights, and I can resist no longer."

She hugged him excitedly, for his pleasure was contagious. And anticipation raised her spirits even higher. She had heard him play the lute on two other occasions, and the music he created was almost enough to make her believe in the gods.

She caught Meadow's eye, and knew her sister was just as enthusiastic. No doubt envisioning the special dance she would perform, or time shared with Soldier Brody. The eves were for forgetting the trials of the day, and no one was better at this than Fairmeadow.

The yells interrupted these thoughts. Another unwelcome disturbance, of which this journey had seen so many.

Her heart skipped a beat as she saw Yohan and Brody carry an unknown soldier into the camp and toward the fire. Summer looked from one man to the other, her eyes reluctantly settling on the stranger, and felt a wave of unease. Then she noticed Meadow hurry to their aid, and followed her sister's example.

Out of the snowfall, warmed by the fire, fed directly from Meadow's nursing hands, the unknown soldier spoke at last.

"I thank you, my friends." He accepted another spoonful of soup and smiled crookedly at the small blonde. Summer disliked the gleam in his eye—a sign she had long since learned to recognize—and wondered how a man could feel desire so soon after a harrowing ordeal. But the look quickly faded, and he politely shook his head at the next spoonful. "Later. I must tell you my story, first."

Curiously, his eyes drifted toward Yohan, and lingered.

Despite whatever ordeal the man had endured to come here, she saw that he still retained the sword at his side and the crossbow on his back, and he bore no visible wounds. Hopefully, these were all signs that the story would not be as unpleasant as she feared.

"Our party formed at Halfsummit a few days after your departure. Thirteen of us, one full squad. Mainly younger recruits plus an oldster like me because they needed a scout. Three officers: Corporal Lister and Captain Yanik—two fine leaders who deserved better than they got—and Commander

Jenaleve. An escort mission, we were told. The princess returning to Northgate, reporting dire events to the king personally, and a daughter reuniting with her father. I think most of us were looking forward to getting away from the frontier, and spending some time in a proper city.

"So we were told, as I say. But shortly after leaving Halfsummit, our party turned south. None of us were surprised, for the rumors were widespread by then. We knew where we were going...who we were seeking."

Summer watched the soldier stare again at Yohan, whose face was clouded in emotion. She had not seen him like this since the early days of the journey, and it was not a welcome reversion.

"We moved quickly at first. A pleasant four days. I remember them well, and with longing. The weather fair, the road easy.

"On the fifth day, we found the first caravan. You would not believe the change that occurred within the commander. She was always imperious, but normally aloof. A hard woman to like, if truth be told. But at the first sight of that caravan—of the dead— the worry broke through. She had us check every body, even though we assured her there were only two wagons. This was not the caravan we sought.

"Everything—and everyone—changed at that point. She became more resolute. And we all liked her much better. She was anxious to keep going, but took the time to give the dead a proper burial. Then she pushed us hard and fast, and we willingly obeyed, for we had seen the person inside the armor. Her hard orders and harsh reprimands bothered us no longer, for we understood where they stemmed from. The commander had earned our respect, as I say. She became one of us, even if she did not know it herself.

"Our group reached the river shortly thereafter. We saw an old watchtower, peering down over the lonely road. I don't remember which side it was on, Vilnian or Goth. It doesn't matter, it was abandoned, for the danger lay to the east, through the Stormeres. Or so we thought.

"And then we reached the mountains." Redjack sighed. "That's where things got bad."

His shoulders shivered, and Meadow handed him a bladder of wine. He paused for a sip, then a second, then a large gulp. The liquid fortification put a stop to the shivering, but a pronounced shakiness entered the voice.

"The second caravan was on the high road through the Triumphs. We had no warning, for the smoke had long since cleared. One ridge after another, each harder than the last, bad footing, tiring inclines, low visibility. We came over one and there it was, just ahead—more wagons, more dead. Commander Jenaleve helped us this time. She was calmer, and sadder—I believe she had decided that you would all be dead by the time we caught up.

"Burial was impossible, so we spent an afternoon building cairns. Every minute was valuable, but we took time for this. If we hadn't, we might have cleared the mountains before the storm came.

"There are caves in those mountains. Caves…and other things. Including another old fort, built up in the rocks, a tricky climb from the road. Abandoned and forgotten, like so many others we see. Why it was built up there, I have no idea. If the snow had started sooner, or if it had been easier to reach, perhaps we would have stopped to inspect that old fort, and things would have gone differently.

"But we didn't, and there were plenty of caves to choose from instead. They gave us some protection from the weather. We reached them just in time, right as the sky got ugly. The blizzard hit us not long before we would have cleared the mountains, as I say. But we had food enough to last out the storm, however long it would last, and kept scouts posted for signs of danger. Thirteen healthy soldiers, well-provisioned, with good officers. We had nothing to fear.

"I don't mind the snow. Never have. I used the time to hunt cottontails and foxes, and the extra meat was not unappreciated by the others.

"The commander warned us, but I fear I did not take her seriously enough. I hunted during my turn to watch. I returned with another rabbit for the fire, feeling proud, looking forward to the gratitude of the others." He uttered a choking sound, turning it into a cough.

The bearded face looked around, at no one in particular. "They liked when I hunted..." He looked down at scarred hands, turned red from the cold. "...as I say."

They waited in respectful silence. Meadow put a comforting hand to his shoulder, squeezing once. He smiled weakly at her kindness.

"I heard the sound of fighting long before I got back. I dropped the rabbit and ran, but the snow slowed my progress. When I got there, it was too late to help.

"There were at least thirty, possibly more. Barbarians, savages. All except for one, giving orders in a language I couldn't understand. I never saw his face, but I know what he was. I should have used the crossbow, should have shot him down, should have made some attempt to help the others. Instead I hid behind a rock and watched them slaughter my squad."

Redjack hesitated, then sniffed. The wind howled in the background, and Summer noted that the snow around them had resumed its previous ferocity. Then the narrator cleared his throat and found his voice again.

"Most were already dead. A few tried to surrender, but the bastards struck them down anyway. I watched poor, dear Hidra —wound in her gut—drop her sword, fall to her knees, and try to stop the bleeding with both hands. One of those barbarians stood over her and lifted his weapon. She raised a bare hand, as if that was going to stop an axe.

"You want to know about the princess, of course. She fought like the Devil...your pardon, Sister. I've never seen any soldier, man or woman, fight as well. I counted three that she killed, and at least that many more wounded, before they overcame her."

"They killed her, too?" Mercer blurted.

They all stared at Redjack, all except Summer. She had spent the last few minutes watching someone else, absorbing a measure of reflected pain. Then she closed her eyes to wait for the answer, knowing that her life would change based on the next word.

"Nay. They took her. I tracked them back to the fort. Then I ran—I knew not where, simply out of the mountains. I learned fear is greater than snow and hunger combined."

And so it turns. Summer reopened her eyes, staring at Yohan. His fists had closed early in the narration, the only obvious sign of the distress he was feeling. But in recent days, she had learned to see what lay within.

Look how that fire consumes him. He tries to hide it, but it shows in his face, it shows in his eyes, it shows in his body.

I thought I was the teacher, but I am a fool. This man knows far more of life, of love, than I.

The fervor that had seized him was simultaneously terrible, frightening, and humbling. *Will anyone ever burn so for me?* Never had she felt so insignificant. Merely an extra in someone else's great dance. But it was a role she would play to the best of her ability.

There was no music that eve, of course, but they did take the time for a thoughtful, wordless supper. Afterward, Summer sought out the corporal.

She was not surprised to find him in his tent with Soldier

Yohan, the two of them deep in disagreement. They were attempting to keep their volume low, to not be heard by all.

She wondered why. By this point, everyone knew what the private was requesting, just as they knew what the corporal's response would be.

Mercer's anger was less demonstrable than expected. Perhaps there existed the tiniest hint of appreciation, for without Yohan, they would all certainly be dead.

"Nay, Private, I cannot allow it. And don't think of going anyway. I'm putting you under guard from now until we reach Threefork, and I will not hesitate to have you arrested, if I have to." He smiled maliciously, and she jettisoned her previous theory. "It will be my pleasure, in fact. I know the things you and the others say behind my back."

That the odious man should express all this in Summer's presence came as a surprise to her, and showed the depth of his enmity toward the man who served beneath him. Her instinct was to rush to Yohan's aid, but someone else beat her to it.

Lullaby had become such a frequent sight at Yohan's feet that few ever took notice anymore. But the three of them did now, for the teeth were bared and the throat emitted a vicious snarl. Mercer looked down at the dog and swallowed reflexively, then began to choke on the aftertaste of his vile tobacco.

"What are you discussing?" Summer asked, hoping to restore some order before the situation became even more hostile.

The corporal coughed twice. "This...this is nothing for you to worry about, Sister."

She looked at Yohan hopefully. His head was lowered, and he did not return her gaze. She felt the disappointment even as she turned back to Mercer.

"Has he suggested the squad turn back to this fort? To rescue the princess...the commander?"

The corporal shook his head. "Nay, Sister. Fool though he is, he knows better than to ask that. He wishes to be discharged from duty. He thinks he can save her alone."

Alone? She inspected Yohan, still seeing the fire raging within. Instead of flaming out, it was only building. She could see his hand trembling, and wondered how tempted he was to draw the sword at his side, to strike down the corporal and anyone else in his way.

The profound sadness that seeped through her being washed away with the knowledge that she was doing the right thing.

"Aye, it was wise for you to reject that request," she said. Mercer smiled, then sneered at his subordinate. Yohan took no notice.

"Far better for us all to go," she continued. "I'll inform my brothers and sister. I'll let you issue the appropriate orders to your soldiers."

The corporal glared at her, and she felt a portion of that hate previously reserved for others. Surprised by how intensely it struck her, Summer looked away from him and back at Yohan. She watched his head lift, his gaze turn to her. That face wore a tangled skein of emotions, too confusing to read, and her own were too disorderly to make sense of as well. She could only trust that caught up somewhere between the two of them were gratitude and acceptance.

The decision made, they had a path to follow. For better or worse, and she knew which was more likely.

10

RA'CHEKA

*J*ak *and Kevik no longer chased the badger. Now, Kevik was chasing him.*

Only a step behind, sword swinging in deadly earnest. Jak could feel the wind generated from each pendulous arc. If he slowed, he would die.

Even had he been alone, he could not hope to outrun his former friend and current foe, for Kevik had always been the faster, the stronger, the smarter. But Jak was not alone. He carried three others on his back and shoulders, their weight growing heavier with every step. His muscles tired and his desperation mounted. Slowly but surely, the footsteps behind got louder, the sword drew closer.

They would all die. And it would be Jak's fault. They trusted him, relied on him. They were his responsibility entirely.

I cannot save them all. Better that I drop one so that I may save two.

Jak opened his eyes, but he had not been asleep. This dream was always with him. His sense of doom finally found form. That, not Kevik, chased them, always one step behind. It was up to Jak to keep them ahead.

"The ritual is very simple," Disciple Hobbes continued. "And most humane. The participant goes willingly. We provide a draught that renders them insensate—oblivious to pain, but not to their own generosity. They give themselves over to the flames knowing how their sacrifice shields friend and stranger alike from the corruptions of Nagnuaqua."

Jak thought about those corruptions, knowing them all too well, for he saw them on a daily basis.

Kleo was taking her "illness" better than expected. The rash had recently spread to her arms and hands, so her friends could no longer hide its true nature. This poor girl, who had always been irrationally terrified of lizards, watched her own transformation with courage and resolve. Certainly she cried at first, but only that once. Never again.

Jak admired the determination, and from it drew inspiration.

"…this outcome is best for all." The old man's voice droned on soothingly. Reassuringly.

Jak smiled, nodding. Then he stood. "Thank you for this explanation, Teacher."

He departed with a reassuring smile of his own. Now that the four refugees had made their decision, Jak felt more peace than at any time since before the wedding.

They were leaving. The followers of Tempus could burn one another until nothing remained of this place but ash. But they would not touch his friends. They could not have Kleo.

He and Kluber had made plans the previous eve. Today was the day to put those plans into motion.

The first obstacle appeared as soon as Jak returned to the others. He entered the apartment where they had lived these last tendays. Kluber and Calla were there, looking worried. Kleo was not.

"They took her already," Kluber said.

Jak nodded. The event was happening sooner than he had anticipated, but this was not an insurmountable problem.

The magistrate's son went to one of the ornate chairs and held it firmly while raising a foot. It creaked, bent, and snapped, and soon each of them had a makeshift club to conceal within their robes.

"Calla, we'll meet you at the dock, aye?" Her task was to collect food and other stores for the trip ahead from the temple's kitchen and storeroom and the distant larder. With luck, they would all reach the meeting place at the same time.

"Aye. Good luck."

The two young men exchanged a look. "Ready for this?"

"Ready."

Jak took a step, then stopped when Kluber put a hand to his arm. "Remember, Jak. Their words are dangerous. Don't let them try to talk us out of this. Don't let them talk at all."

He nodded, knowing the truth in his friend's warning and hoping that the threat of violence would strike their foes mute.

The two of them found Kleo in a ceremonial antechamber near the temple's exit, about to make their way outside to the plaza. Three disciples were in the room with her. One was Hobbes, who challenged the interruption.

Odorless draught in hand, he stepped between the newcomers and their objective. "Disciple Jak, your purpose is clearly written on your face. I fear you are not here to facilitate, but to hinder. I thought we had discussed this to everyone's—"

Jak struck him in the head with the club, harder than intended, desperate to silence these words that poisoned his mind. The gray eyes flashed accusingly, then the light within winked out as the body tumbled.

The other two disciples shrunk away. Kluber already had Kleo's arm in hand. Now he looked from Jak to the man on the floor, then kneeled to put his ear to the man's chest for a long moment. Listening.

A shake of the head. "Dead." He stood.

Jak's mouth was agape. "I only meant to—"

"It's all right. Come on."

Taking each of his companions by an arm, Kluber led the way

out of the temple and into the lifeless city, then through the misty streets toward the lake.

"It's all green now," Jak said at last. His feet were still moving of their own accord, propelled forward by his friend's unrelenting pull. This was good, for his mind was failing him as it sought distraction from current circumstance. From what he had done.

His eyes did not deceive him, for the fungus was indeed entirely green. And not a healthy shade, but the sickly pale hue of decaying leaves.

The influence of Tempus was on the wane, and now Yagos was ascendant. Too much time had passed since the last sacrifice.

Sacrifice. There had to be a better way, and Jak intended to find it.

Calla was waiting for them at the dock. The sight of her brought something out of Jak. An inner grief that finally needed expression. He looked away from her face, wishing to see no more of the resentment that had been residing there for as long as he could remember.

Kluber stepped onto the dinghy, followed by Kleo. Jak saw her turn to look back, reaching to him, calling out. But he remained rooted to the wooden planks of the dock, aware only of the soft lapping sounds of the water and Calla's judgmental silence.

He raised his eyes to hers at last. She met his gaze not with scorn, but sympathy. Then she looked at Kluber.

"He killed the old man."

She looked back at Jak then, her head cocked sideways, a new emotion joining the complex amalgam he tried so desperately to understand.

Kleo became more insistent. "Jak, come on. Come with me."

His attention remained focused on Calla, his mind certain she would turn away. Instead, she came to him, wrapped her arms around him, and slowly pulled him along. Into the boat, his feet willing to move again. There he sat with her as the tears came, soaking into her robes. She seemed not to care, for her fingers continued to stroke his sweaty black hair. "It's okay," she whispered.

How badly he had needed to hear that.

Kleo was crying, too. Sobbing. Jak understood how she felt, even as his own emotions came back under control, his sorrows abating. This escape—these last days, her ordeal—had been hard on them all. But soon the nightmare would be over.

He became aware of the irony that the dinghy only seated four. This escape was available to them only because Riff was gone.

He felt Calla stiffen, and reluctantly sat up at last. Shapes began to appear on the dock behind. A half-dozen followers, silently watching. He could not see their faces beneath raised hoods, but he felt their stares. Here was the judgment that he had expected from Calla.

Jak did not care. Let them judge him, for he had judged them —and found them unworthy.

Slowly the mist swallowed those shapes. Jak realized that Kluber was rowing, alone, propelling the dinghy toward the far shore.

Jak twisted, ready to offer his assistance with the oars. Only then did he truly see Kleo, and the depths of her pain. He knew not why, but he felt guilty.

They could not see, but they could sense the sacrifice.

"They burn the old man," Kluber said.

Just ahead, the glow of the far shore began to change again, green returning to blue. The boat coasted in, grounding on the low stone with a gentle scrape.

"It should be me," Kleo whispered. She stared back at the distant city, and Jak saw one more tear roll down her cheek. Calla went to her, but Kleo brushed her hands away. Then she stood, waiting her turn to step off the boat.

Kluber leapt out first, then held the dinghy in place. Jak straddled shore and boat, one foot on each, holding his hand out to the girls. Calla thanked him as she made the short jump. Then Kleo smiled at him warmly, scaly skin reflecting a blue that matched her eyes. Of all her features, those alone retained their beauty. She accepted his aid and jumped gracefully onto the hard earth.

The map in the Pantheon had shown a road of some sort, leading up to a guardhouse and beyond to a wide passageway that extended for miles. Now they all saw the nature of that road, looming far above them, obscured in sections by the floating tendrils of mist—a series of switchbacks along the wall not unlike those traversed during their flight from Everdawn. A long, tiring climb up awaited the four weary derelicts. Jak, Calla, Kluber, Kleo. One-by-one, they wordlessly began.

Halfway up, they could more clearly see their destination—the top of the switchback trail, and the familiar sight of a crumbling gatehouse. Much larger than the one they had passed through before, but similar in design, with a narrow aperture framed by thick stone walls.

Upon seeing it, Jak's last concerns disappeared, for he had worried that the portcullis would be down, blocking the way through. As ancient as these structures were, the four of them might not have been able to raise it again. Blessedly, that fear had not come true.

"Why would they need a guardhouse?" Calla asked.

Jak knew the answer. "Because they were at war."

The others looked at him, and he told them the story of the collapse of Ra'Cheka. Some of it Calla knew already, for she had read the first legend that exposed him to this history. Since then, however, he had learned so much more.

"While the rest of the Chekican Communion revered the devil Shuberath above all others, this part of Ra'Cheka was the center-point for a splinter group who worshipped Nagnuaqua—whom we call Yagos. The temple we just escaped from was, at one time, devoted to him. Before his defeat. Before Tempus claimed the world above.

"The followers of Nagnuaqua were a minor faction for a long time, vocally accepting the dominance of Shuberath, but in reality biding their time while the Chekican armies conquered new lands, moving ever farther away. Then this city seized its opportunity to declare Nagnuaqua's predominance, tearing Ra'Cheka in two. No one knew what defeat to the Chekiks meant better than their own kind. Determined not to suffer such horrors, they prepared for a long war and constructed defenses.

"Perhaps they would have been successful, but the hratha—our ancestors—were even more opportunistic. We used the Chekican conflict to declare and seize our independence, driving the Chekiks out and creating our own empire. Before devolving into war on ourselves, of course."

He stopped, becoming aware that his friends were staring at him oddly. He felt a certain pride of education that he had never before known, and the strange sensation made him uncomfortable.

"Come on, let's keep going," he insisted.

Jak could not avoid another change occurring inside him, however. He recognized, then wondered whether it was okay to accept, this new and unusual feeling.

Hope. For they were leaving the doom further and further behind.

"Another gap," Calla said resignedly.

Ahead of them lay another crumbled section of trail, one more obstacle thrown their way by the cruel hands of fate.

No one mentioned Riff's name, but everyone remembered his heroics in climbing the last chasm to save them all. Risking his life for his friends, as he would later give it.

Now it was time for someone else to pick up where Riff left off, and Jak was prepared to do so.

The small blade that Kluber once gave him to scale and slice fish was still in his pocket, and he had used it many times recently for a purpose far different from its intended one. Now he did so again, drawing it out in his right hand and bringing it hard across the palm of his left, cutting deep into the flesh.

Calla jumped toward him. "Jak, what are you doing?" She pulled his arm back, but the slice was already complete.

The pain was fleeting, the exhilaration overwhelming. This was the most blood Jak had ever given at once, and he knew he would need every bit of it. He lifted his arm high, palm upraised so the liquid offering would pool there, oblivious to the trickle running down the length of his arm.

A few mumbled invocations—reminiscent of Lukas' last moments—and then Jak kneeled, turning his hand over and pressing it to the hard rock beneath them. More entreaties, and then an answering hum passed from stone to body. Blood seeped into rock like water through sand. Kron listened, accepted the sacrifice, and replied.

The ledge thundered beneath their feet. Small stones and loose dirt crumbled away from the side, threatening to become a terrifying landslide. Calla and Kluber jumped away from the edge, fearful of their precarious footing as the earth shifted.

Slowly the stone trail expanded forward. Ledge and cavern wall each yielded material to fill the gap, the movement annunciated by a low protesting rumble from deep within the earth.

A few harrowing moments later, the ledge was wholly restored. The transformation ended as abruptly as it began.

Still on his knees, Jak attempted to get up. He could not, the effort forcing him instead to collapse onto his face and chest. Twisting his neck so he could breath, he felt the stone slice open his cheek. A few seconds before, it had been a miraculous ally; now it was once again a malevolent enemy.

Then the others lifted him, helped him rediscover his balance, and gave his legs strength and support. He found that he could just barely put one foot in front of the other, over and over again, keeping his arm around Calla's shoulders as she bore his weight.

Ahead, at last, lay the gatehouse. Beyond it, a way out of this cavern where they had lost a friend, and hope for an escape from hell. The others would have to blaze the trail, for he could not so much as think.

One thing worked against them. Thankful though they were that the portcullis was not closed, its lever on this side meant that they could not drop it behind them. They would not be able to block off pursuit.

They would simply need to keep moving, at a time when they all desperately needed rest. Jak most of all.

Perhaps the anxiety was for naught. Would the followers of Tempus even chase them? There was no indication of that, so far. But then there had been only a single boat. Any pursuers would have to take the long way around the lake, presuming such a path even existed.

Still leaning on Calla, Jak passed through the portal. Kluber was already ahead, raising a torch high to illuminate the wide-open tunnel stretching far into the distance.

Calla needed some relief from his weight, that much was obvious. Jak asked her to lean him against the wall. Catching his own breath, he looked back. Kleo had not come through. She still stood on the other side, making no move to join them. Looking at him, her hand on the lever.

Even when the demons attacked Everdawn, he had not known such panic. "Nay!" he yelled.

He pushed himself away from the wall, took one step toward Kleo, and immediately fell to the ground. The cut on his cheek split open wider, and he spoke into the earth. "Kleo, nay."

But she had already pulled the lever. He heard the loud mechanical noises even before he managed to twist his head to see the bars drop.

He stared at her through blurry eyes. She smiled. In this light, he could not see the scales. She looked as lovely as he had ever seen. "Be well, Jak." Then she was gone.

Not like this. There was still a chance, he believed.

Jak tried to push himself up. "The knife," he gasped. He felt hands on his shoulders. Calla, comforting him. Kluber, restraining him.

"My knife…" His voice was raspy, almost unrecognizable.

Why were they not helping him?

"Jak, you can't," Calla said. "You'll kill yourself trying."

I don't care.

"It was her decision," Kluber said. "No one is happy about it, but we have to accept it. Come on."

"I can't move," Jak replied. *I won't move. I'll die here, or they'll come for me.*

He felt hands lifting him up, as though he were a child. Kluber, taking charge at last, now that Jak did not want him to.

"You've carried us this far. We'll carry you awhile."

"Close your eyes, Jak," Calla compelled. "Go to sleep."

He did close his eyes, but sleep did not come. Instead, his mind raged, the thoughts tumbling wildly until he reined them all in with a single resolution.

There would be no more sacrifices; he would not allow it. Or rather, *no one else* would sacrifice—only him. And only until he discovered a different way.

These gods—these devils—used humanity as pieces in their game. He would make them pay. This child would use them as they used others.

Pitiful, ignorant Housethrall Jak would become their servant. He would learn from them. He would accept their power, only to turn it against them. He was now at war with the devils, and he would destroy them all.

11

NEUBLUSTEN

Captain Reikmann stated the obvious. "If the snow continues much longer, the Loresters must necessarily withdraw." His voice sounded optimistic, almost triumphant.

Nico was not nearly so sanguine. "We don't want them to withdraw."

"You should...that is to say, I would have expected you to be pleased. It would mean the end of the siege. The city would hail you as a hero."

"Even more than they already do," General Handersonn chimed in.

What is it with these generals and their incessant need for glory? The higher the rank, it seemed, the greater this restless desire for attention, recognition, and respect.

"That's irrelevant," Nico said. "Let us say they pull back now. What happens in the spring?"

"There are benefits of a withdrawal. It gives my troops more time to train."

Nico was surprised by this turn of events, having expected the brash Handersonn to advocate the more aggressive strategy. "Haven't you told me they're ready?"

"Certainly they are," the red-nosed man replied immediately. A bit too defensively. "But a little more time never hurts," he added in a quieter tone.

"I'm sure it wouldn't," General Freilenn said. "In another tenday or two, your soldiers might learn the difference between a sword and a spear."

"We wouldn't need to have this discussion if you had pushed the enemy back when you had the chance."

Tired of attempting to restrain them, Nico shifted uncomfortably in his chair. He was perpetually uncomfortable now, he found, and it made him short-tempered.

His wounds—none of them life-threatening, but all of them painful—had been cleaned and bound. It was only a matter of time before he recovered completely, a blessing he tried hard to appreciate. But they were not healed yet, and so the frailties of the body continued to reign over the will of the mind. He felt weak and incapable, far less sure of himself and more dependent on others than he cared to be.

After the duel and the subsequent ministrations of the doctors, Nico had slept even longer than he had upon his return to Neublusten. Yet his body ached for more rest. He had forced himself back to action before he was ready, and done so for one reason alone—only to discover he need not have bothered.

Worried that all progress would cease were he not there to oversee the work, he had instead discovered the opposite. Lima and Reikmann carried on the recruiting of troops and rationing of the city's precious supplies. Even Generals Freilenn and Handersonn had momentarily set aside their petty squabbles— had even cooperated—to put things in order for the city's defense. The siege of Neublusten had begun, but thanks to all these efforts the deprivations were not yet felt, the citizens were unruly but not to excess, and the city was in no immediate danger of collapse from within or without.

The current state of affairs left much to be desired, but could have been far worse. Nico recognized a small sliver of opportunity, and he intended to make the most of it.

He leaned forward, placing sore elbows on the hardwood tabletop. "Consider this. If the Loresters retreat, where will they go? All the way back to their kingdom? I think not. Either they will return to Allstatte and join forces with the Dauphi, or they'll move north and settle into a defensive front, provisioning themselves by foraging in our homeland. Akenbergers will starve and freeze so that the invaders can eat and rest comfortably. The capital may be saved—temporarily—but our responsibility is to the entire kingdom.

"Moreover, what will we do in the spring? Wait for them to return and lay siege again? By then, Allstatte will have fallen and our two enemies will come together. So let's say we don't wait. We beat them to the march, head north and throw ourselves against the defenses they've had time to construct. And then the Dauphi come at us from the west while we're engaged with the Loresters. We're pinned between the two. I don't think I need to remind anyone that this is exactly how my brother lost his army, and his life.

"Meanwhile, the Asturians will have finished their preparations and come up from the south. Neublusten may face three enemies simultaneously. No amount of additional training gets us ready for that.

"Sure, we can win a minor victory today. The city will be happy, for a time. And come spring, we'll face even bleaker prospects than we do now. We will have traded a winter of safety for impossible odds, and a war we cannot win."

"Your pardons, Third, but you assume the worst," Reikmann replied. "The enemy may not work so effectively together. The siege of Allstatte may linger longer…"

"He is right. These things you speak of are not quite so inevitable as you believe," Handersonn added. "A wise commander takes victories where he can find them, then alters his strategy as circumstances require. On the other hand, many a new commander mistakes recklessness for boldness. I speak from experience. Some never get a chance to learn from their mistake, as I did. We are here to save you from that, Third."

It was strange indeed to be called "Third" by the people of his own city. There was no formal necessity that they do so, and he was not without temptation to tell them he preferred a different title. But he stopped himself because he understood why they did. It was a sign of respect. He could not only hear it in their words, he could see it in their faces. Even though they disagreed with him now, they did so deferentially. He knew the ultimate decision was his alone, and so did they.

Respect was a precious commodity, far greater than power or wealth. He believed it more important than anything save love. And Nico had struggled to attain it through so much of his life that he could not easily reject it now. Instead, he welcomed their respect, and tried to appreciate it while it lasted. For if they lost their battle or their city, that admiration would irrevocably disappear.

"General Freilenn, you have been quiet. Please tell us your thoughts."

Handersonn scowled as his rival leaned forward in his chair. Whatever temporary truce had developed between the two was clearly over.

"I am in agreement."

Nico was disappointed, but not surprised. "You, as well. None of you see—"

"Nay, Third. I am in agreement with you. I believe our best option is to deal with these Loresters now, while they are at their most vulnerable. We are badly outnumbered in this war. Better that we fight our foes separately, when they foolishly give us that chance."

Nico nodded. "Well said." It was nice to receive some support at last. *But is he saying so just to disagree with Handersonn?*

The others resumed their protests, now directing them toward Freilenn. Nico sat back and tuned them out. A wave of dizziness passed over him—an altogether too frequent occurrence since the duel. Both legs burned continuously, but currently the throbbing in his shoulder bothered him most.

A serving girl brought in four cups of water. He thanked her as he took his own. A pretty girl, but not quite so much as the last.

"Please bring two more," he requested, motioning to the soldiers standing silently in the corner of the room. Lima and Pim. Quiet, but always there. Dependable.

The serving girl smiled and turned, then stopped as Nico grabbed her sleeve. "Wait. Where is Pris?"

Humorously, he thought perhaps she had enlisted, after all. So many servants throughout the city and surrounding countryside had done so. Far more than the army had been prepared for. The current roster of drill instructors had been insufficient to handle them all, so Reikmann had proposed supplementing them with retired veterans willing to return to service for this sole duty. Remembering the pride Renard had taken in training the prince, Nico had readily agreed. Then Lima had suggested boosting the ranks even more with those who had suffered wounds severe enough to force them away from the battlefield, but who remained capable enough to help in other ways.

It was pleasing to see the whole city pulling together in a time of adversity. If nothing else, Nico had accomplished this much.

"She's back at the castle again, My Prince," the girl replied, bringing him back to the present.

"The castle? She isn't part of the Rechshtal staff?"

"No, My Prince. She usually works the king's table."

Nico was further distracted when a messenger arrived. The serving girl bowed and hurried away as he watched the newcomer whisper into Lima's ear. She nodded and approached the Third, in turn whispering into his.

"An envoy from the Loresters is here, wishing to speak to you."

That was interesting, indeed. But there was more. "He has an Akenberg prisoner with him—General Cottzer, who was with Prince Markolas when he was killed."

Even without ever having met the man, Nico knew by his name that Cottzer was a capable officer. No mere nobleman who had received his commission through wealth or influence, he was a commoner who had been promoted through meritorious service. A lifetime of success tended to breed self-confidence.

Therefore, the Third was surprised when the middle-aged general could not look him in the eyes. Cottzer sat meekly at the table in the ancillary conference chamber with the envoy, barely lifting his head when Nico and Lima walked in, and not at all when introductions were made.

Nico felt a flash of anger and resentment toward the effervescent Captain Fineo, aide to the Lorester crown prince who commanded the besieging army. All prisoners were to be treated humanely, but a captured officer particularly so. If Cottzer's spirit had been savagely broken...

Best not to rush to judgment, Nico told himself. Based on Fineo's display of confidence, there was more here than met the eye.

The formalities lasted several frustrating minutes. Nico's fluency with court etiquette was deeply ingrained, but that did not make the activity enjoyable. Now that he felt a continuous rush of responsibilities, each second involved in useless pleasantries was particularly bothersome. He desired this emissary get to the point as soon as possible, and said as much at his first opportunity.

"Very well, Third—congratulations on your victory, your pardons, we were overjoyed at your success when the rumors reached our ears—"

"Your purpose, Captain?" Nico reminded.

"Yes, indeed. I'm here to negotiate terms of surrender for your kingdom."

"Then you have wasted your time and mine. Perhaps that was your intent?"

"No, indeed. It was not, Prince Nicolas. I am granted the freedom to offer very generous terms, generous indeed, terms that are most favorable to you and your kingdom, in light of your circumstances. Terms that we feel you should at least listen to, and upon the listening will see the fairness of. Especially after you hear what our guest General Cottzer has to say. I could tell you myself, but I think you should hear it from your own, indeed I do."

"Is that so, General Cottzer?" Nico asked. "You have something important to tell me?" He attempted to get the man's attention, but the head continued to stare down.

"He is understandably reluctant," Fineo said. "Reluctant, indeed. I cannot blame him, for your anger is likely to be considerable."

"My anger is likely to be worse if we keep talking around the point without getting to it." *And Theus help this man if I hear the word 'indeed' once more.*

"Very well. General, please tell the prince your version of events. Please tell him how his own father and brother, his own kingdom, betrayed him."

Lima put her one hand on his left shoulder. She said nothing.

Nico glanced at Pim. He looked more upset, more outraged, than Nico felt himself.

"You overplayed your hand," Nico had told the envoy after Cottzer's story. "My feelings are irrelevant; my duty is to Akenberg and its people. And they desire me to destroy our enemy."

Fineo's smile had not faded, but his eyes flashed irritation. "So it is death and defeat you prefer, young prince?"

"It is. *Indeed.*"

Nico had Pim escort the captain and Cottzer out, while he himself remained seated, thinking. He had not moved at all by the time the twin returned. Now the three of them were alone in the silent chamber.

I don't see how this changes anything, he told himself. *I can deal with it after this battle is concluded. And if we lose, I won't have to worry about it.*

By the gods, my body hurts.

As he issued dispositions for the coming battle, Nico said nothing to the other officers of what he had learned—that their enemy was intended to be their ally, the second prince was expected to be dead by now, and the king they served sought to deceive his way to the top of the empire.

As much as possible, he focused on the battle. One that could not come soon enough for him, but could easily spell the end of his royal family. *And good riddance to that.*

He decided that General Handersonn would command the center of the combined army, General Freilenn the right wing, and Captain Reikmann the left. The Third would retain overall command from the gate towers, where he could survey the entire field of battle from walls to lake.

None of them seemed particularly happy with the deployment, and even Nico himself knew there were serious weaknesses in the plan that were likely to be exposed, but it was Freilenn who sought the prince out in the corridor after the briefing.

At the sight of him, Nico immediately knew what the complaint would be. The center of each army was typically commanded by the general with the most seniority, for that was the position of greatest prestige. The right wing came second, the left third. Now Freilenn had been placed in a position of inferiority to his rival, a consideration that Nico would have given more thought to if he had not been so distracted by his family's betrayal.

"I supported you at the conference, and this is the thanks I receive?" The general's temper remained under control, but only just. "Your pardon, Third, I deserve greater honor... My troops deserve greater honor."

Nico's instincts were to allow the man to vent his frustrations, but now the familiar rise of anger cut that idea short. He did not have the time or patience to deal with silly jealousy. "General Freilenn, control yourself."

Freilenn stopped the flow and grimaced, but the fierce stare continued.

The wounded shoulder chose that moment to start throbbing again, and Nico subconsciously used his left hand to knead away the tightness. "I need you to tell me, unequivocally and without hesitation, that you trust me to command this battle the way I see fit. I will replace you if I have the slightest doubt you will obey orders."

The reply was not without hesitation, and the general nearly choked on the words, but it did come. "I do, Third. And I will. Your pardon, I allowed my feelings—"

"Now that that's settled," Nico continued, still rubbing, "let me pose this to you. In our center, we have twelve raw companies that have never seen action. Our left wing comprises all of one detached infantry company plus the Royal Guard and Princeshields, two understrength cavalry companies. Besides them, all of our veterans are in your Second Army on the right. Now I ask you...what do you believe I see as the strength of our force?"

"The...right wing, Third. *My* wing."

"And you'll oppose the Lorester left. The weakest part of their army. All I will say is that I hold you in the highest regard, and I need more from you than the others. I don't expect you to merely hold our flank, I expect you to overwhelm the enemy. No—I not only expect you to overwhelm them, I expect you to win the day for us all. If you do that, there will be glory enough for you and your troops." His shoulder felt better, and now he grinned fiercely at Freilenn, trying to throw the general's own fire back at him. He reached out to thump his hands on Freilenn's chest three times, hard enough to stagger the man, and raised his voice. "Does that satisfy your honor?"

"Aye, Third."

"Do I ask too much?"

"Nay, Third."

Nico gripped the man's shoulders firmly, staring him in the eye. "Tell me true, General. Can you do it?"

"I will. Or I'll die trying."

I will, or I'll die trying. Words that resonated with Nico as he left the Rechshtal, unsure where to go next. He knew he should speak to the king at least once before the upcoming battle, but the thought of seeing his father now was far too painful. So he found himself in a snow-covered street, torn between destinations, belonging nowhere.

Never had he been so alone. It seemed as though every fear he had felt while growing up suddenly became reality. And yet that truthfully did not affect the immediate situation. Rejected by his own family, celebrated then cast aside by the Asturians, there was still a place where he could find comfort.

Nico glanced up at the sky. Still another hour of light before the sun disappeared for the eve. Supper would be served soon. The parade out of the city would begin shortly after that.

He turned around, momentarily worried that Lima and Pim had left him, too. But of course they were there, as always. "Let's see the troops one last time," he told them.

"Where's Kip?" Benson's deep voice called out.

The former page hurried toward the sound. "Here, Captain."

"Private, I'm putting you in charge of supper detail." The mustached face frowned. "Try not to spill any this time."

The eve's meal was a watery, meatless stew smelling of weak onions. Once, back when he tasted scraps directly off the king's table, Kip would have found this dish repugnant. A tenday in the army, however, had taught him to savor food of any sort. He hurried to distribute a bowl to each of his comrades, for the aroma made his stomach growl, and he was not allowed to serve himself until the task was complete.

Soon one of his companions came to his aid. "Let me help you, K-k-kip."

The worst cases in a company of bunglers, it was only natural that he and Trip became fast friends. Both received more than their fair share of the company's thankless duties, and it had become habit for them to work together. On this occasion, the food service went even faster, for they were joined by a third.

By contrast to them, Henk was one of the best fighters in the unit. Bowlegged and broad-shouldered, he had earned the respect of the other soldiers and officers, and sometimes took it upon himself to shield the weaklings in the group from an excess of ridicule. Kip did not know why the big man did so, but was always thankful for the benevolence.

When the task was complete, Kip sat down with Trip on the snowy ground of the courtyard where the company currently bivouacked. That was soon to change, for this would be their last meal before marching out of the city. Before the battle on the morrow.

"Henk, join us?" he asked.

"Aye, Henk. J-j-join us?" Trip echoed.

"Why not."

The three of them sat in silence while they spooned the flavorless broth to their mouths. The nourishment was welcome, but just barely. The winter air was not quite as freezing as it had been, but the distribution of the stew had taken so long that their bowlfuls were merely lukewarm. A good hot meal could warm the body and spirit, but they found no such comfort here.

A skinny, undernourished youth who attacked food of any kind with reckless zeal, Trip was the first to finish and set his bowl aside. "I s-s-spoke to Sils today."

Kip's ears perked up. He always liked talking of the former housethrall's lively sister. As did the rest of the men, and he saw a familiar smile come to Henk's lips. *Good luck,* Kip thought. The girl worked in the Rechshtal, serving the generals and nobles—meaning she now had a hopeless infatuation with the prince.

"Aye, I did. Brought me these g-g-gloves." He proudly displayed the poorly-knit mittens for their admiration. "She s-s-spoke to the Th-th third. Says he is s-s-sad about something."

"Sad? What can he be sad about?" Henk asked aloud, his smile becoming a scowl. "He has everything a man could want. And what do we have? Cold, disgusting stew." But Kip noticed that the other soldier emptied the bowl before setting it down.

The three of them spoke for a time of the poor food, the bitter weather, and the unfair treatment of their superiors. Everything but the coming battle. Which was odd, because that was the one subject that dominated their thoughts. The thing that bound them all together, for they were all terrified.

Twilight settled over them by the time they heard the commotion. It started on the other side of the courtyard, and slowly moved their way, preceded by a surge of whispered excitement. *The Third! The Third is here.*

Along with all the others, Kip stood and pressed forward to catch a glimpse. Sure enough, there was their leader, their prince, their commander, along with the one-armed woman and quiet man who always accompanied him.

As the trio came close, the soldiers all cheered. Kip found himself doing the same without even thinking about it, noticing that Trip and Henk did likewise despite the earlier commentary. *That* was just soldier talk; *this* was the real thing.

Much to his surprise, Kip watched as the Third stopped directly in front of him. That young face stared back for a moment, then erupted into a smile. The unwounded arm reached out, a hand clasping the former page's shoulder in a gesture of friendship. "Kip, it's good to see you. How goes the training?"

He could hardly believe it, and became nearly as tongue-tied as Trip. "E-excellent, Third."

The smile grew larger. "Who are your companions?"

"Trip...and Henk, Third." As he introduced them, the Third patted each once on the shoulder.

"Trip. Henk. Are you all prepared for the fight?"

"Aye, Third," they answered in unison. Caught up in the moment, they probably even meant it.

"Good. Akenberg counts on you. I know you'll make us all proud." He nodded one last time, then moved on. The commotion went with him, but the excitement lingered.

Kip noticed that the others treated him with more respect that night. Even Captain Benson.

The horn woke them early, well before first light. It was time to march.

Clad in stiff, uncomfortable leather and a steel pot helmet—neither of which did much to keep out the cold—and carrying a heavy spear that his suddenly sweaty palms persistently threatened to drop, Kip maintained step with the man beside him and the woman ahead. If nothing else, they had at last learned to walk in straight lines.

There were few bystanders as his company cleared the streets and continued out the city gates to the grassy slopes beyond.

Inside Neublusten, they had all felt reasonably safe, if anxious. Now, as soon as they left the wall behind, Kip could not help feeling vulnerably exposed. Still hidden in the morn darkness, the crossbows and ballistae on the wall ramparts and inside the towers kept the enemy at bay. But the infantry marched onward, farther and farther from that protected zone, down where death and dread awaited.

The terrain was one of the few advantages favoring the defenders. From the lake, the ground sloped upward toward the walls of the city. The snow had stopped, at least for the moment, but not before coating everything with a white powdery layer several inches deep, softening the ground and turning much of it soggy. The grass was high and slick, and the ranks of soldiers began to waver as men and women slowed and stumbled.

The spear was the weakest weapon on the battlefield, given to the poorest and least-skilled soldiers in an army. Primarily a defensive unit, spearmen were the expendables that commanders threw away like refuse. He would have far preferred to be in one of the sword companies, but it had come as no surprise to Kip when he had received this assignment.

They were still in motion as the sun peeked over the horizon, clear and bright, promising to bestow upon them a beautiful day. They felt the first rays on their faces with eager anticipation, for their bodies shivered uncontrollably, and some of that from the chill.

At a quarter-mile down the slope, the corporals barked orders to shift formation. Kip and his comrades broke the long lines to form wide columns, four soldiers deep and ten wide. He was in the second row, and could now see over the shoulder of the man ahead well enough to make out the distant enemy. Over a thousand of them, less than a mile ahead, slowly making their way up the troublesome incline.

It did not take long for the lines to close to within a few hundred yards, and already the intermittent bursts of crossbow fire arced back and forth between the armies. Kip and his comrades did not carry shields, so they could only hope that none of the deadly missiles would rain down upon them. Thankfully, few did.

"Here they c-c-come," Trip said. "I'm not r-r-ready."

"Neither am I," Henk admitted mournfully.

They all stared out, seeing the swords and shields of the enemy closing in on them.

While their weapons were most effective against cavalry, the bane of the spearmen was swordsmen, for once the short gap between foes was crossed, the spear's longer reach became more of a hindrance than a boon. Therefore, the trick was to keep the enemy back with an unbroken wall of spearpoints. To this end, the first row held their weapons out at chest-level, while Kip and the second row extended theirs over the shoulders of those in front, forming one continuous, jagged barrier. The key was to maintain this formation, for once weaknesses appeared, the swords could close and take advantage.

The enemy line halted fifty yards away. Even though their shields provided significant protection, pressing directly into an unbroken line of spears was no simple task. Kip found himself smiling in relief. A few fleeting minutes of the upper hand would bolster the confidence of everyone in his company. Maybe the whole army was watching, and cheering. Perhaps even the Third himself.

Then he heard a horn sound the order to advance, and his smile faded. He did not like the order, having just gotten comfortable with where they were. Now his comrades began stepping forward on the unstable ground, directly toward the enemy. While moving, the precise height of their spearpoints was harder to maintain. Then, at twenty yards away, they heard the call to charge. A surge of fear and anticipation pushed him forward, and Kip heard himself yelling nonsensically in unison with the others.

The sides met, and he felt the tip of his weapon clash on shield. He stabbed forward, pulled back, and stabbed forward again, the way he had trained to do day after day. His palms were still sweaty, his grip uncertain—but his muscles had strengthened from repeated drilling, and the familiar motion felt cathartic to an anxious mind. His row took another step forward, and he realized they were driving the enemy back. Long may it last...

It did not last long. The shields pushed back, and the gap between lines shortened. Kip stepped back instinctively, wanting to maintain as much distance as possible. Beside him, however, Trip tried to step forward instead. All along the ranks, this uncoordinated movement was happening, and the formation quickly disintegrated as a result.

Then the woman in the rank ahead took a blade to the shoulder and went down with a yell. Kip could hear other screams, some in anger, most in agony. All around him, his comrades were attempting to step back, but the ranks behind them prevented most from doing so. The swords of the enemy were now flashing, swinging left and right in deadly arcs, thrusting forward and back with terrible effect. Kip stared at one of them, directly ahead, expecting the man to jump forward and extinguish his life in one swift merciless second. Instead, the swordsman remained shoulder-to-shoulder with his neighbors. The enemy was holding their formation, even as the Akenbergers did not.

"A-a-ah!" Trip shouted as he lunged, aiming his spear at the neck of a Lorester. A shield raised, deflecting the point uselessly into the air. Then the shield moved aside and a sword-thrust followed, catching Trip in the gut and driving deeper, then withdrawing just as quickly. Kip's friend fell to his knees, dropped the useless spear in order to clutch his belly with mittened hands, then collapsed at the feet of the man who had killed him.

Up and down the lines, similar incidents were occurring,

leaving Kip to wonder when his turn would come. Then, for some reason, the swordsmen stopped advancing. They even took a few steps back, disengaging. Right before his eyes, the enemy unit swung backward as one, like a giant door on a hinge. The infantry were clearing the way for those behind.

Kip's eyes widened in horror as he saw the horses growing larger. His ears recognized the sound of blowing horns and pounding hooves, and he watched the enemy cavalry lean forward in their saddles in perfect time. He still had his spear, and remembered his training. Spears were supposed to be strong against cavalry, although drilling in courtyards had not prepared the recruits for how loud and terrifying a torrent of warhorses truly was.

He planted the base of the shaft in the soft earth and raised the point up, the way they had been instructed. But few of his companions were doing the same.

"To the poxing Devil with this," Henk yelled, then dropped his spear and ran.

"Henk…" Kip gasped. He turned his head back to the enemy, just in time to see the mass of horses leap.

Before the battle began, Nico had debated what exactly to do with his limited crossbowmen. He had considered their value in the early stages of the battle, where every soldier was crucial, but ultimately decided that it best suited his plans for them to cover a retreat. And so, with mixed feelings, he had stationed the lion's share on the ramparts. A line of them stood beside him now, watching events unfold in the center just as he did.

The clean air made visibility perfect for watching the crisp lines. Initially pleased at the good order Handersonn's troops showed on the march, Nico appreciated the precision with which they switched from column to line and stood in place. His battle plans did not call for them to do much more than that. All they were supposed to do was hold their ground for as long as possible, to give time for the action on the wings to resolve.

His displeasure did not begin to mount until those lines began moving again. The twelve companies of footsoldiers were divided into eight units of spears and four of swords. The latter were purposefully behind the former, a reserve force to be held back until they were needed. Now Nico watched those four advance to a line with the others, and then the entire group move together as one.

"What is General Handersonn about?" he asked aloud. Not only was this movement not what he had ordered, it directly made those units more vulnerable.

The problem was not that he wanted the center to win—he had always expected these inexperienced units to be driven back —but rather that he hoped it would be able to fall back in good order. Every step forward now took this line farther from the wall, from the cover of the men stationed there, from eventual safety. Every step forward now meant more men and women killed, to no good purpose.

The center of an army was traditionally its strongest point, and so Nico had intended it to appear today. It *was*, in terms of numbers—but not with respect to skill or experience. He hoped the Loresters would not anticipate his deception, of course. Putting his least dependable soldiers in the center was certainly unorthodox, as much born of desperation as ingenuity, and yet that was the key to the entire battle.

Nico did not worry about the center collapsing, because his strategy relied upon that. And on the enemy pursuing. With luck, right into the kill zone comprising his crossbows and ballistae. Nico hoped to be able to rally any fleeing troops at the wall, to throw them back upon the enemy in a sudden counterattack. Yet even if not, he planned for his own success to come on the wings, exposing the enemy flanks and putting his own forces in an advantageous position. Perhaps even within striking distance of the Lorester supply train in the rear.

Displeasure became anger when he saw the line break into a charge. This was not only unhelpful to his plans, it was the exact opposite of them. He wanted steady defensive lines that the enemy would have to slowly push back uphill. Instead, he could see the formations falling to pieces already.

"Lima!" he yelled over his shoulder.

"Here, Third."

"Get our horses ready. We're going down."

"Already ready, Third."

By the time he, Lima, and Pim reached Handersonn's headquarters, the first waves of panicked soldiers were already running past.

Nico's instincts were to attempt to rally them, but logic told him to get a grasp of the big picture first. He located the general's open canopy and galloped toward it, practically launching himself from horseback to ground in his haste, bellowing to get the man's attention. "General Handersonn, what are you about? Your orders were to…"

He stopped himself. There was no point in continuing, for the general was clearly drunk. The nose redder than ever, dark veins blazing forth from waxen skin. "Third, welcome! We drive the enemy back... Isn't it glor…glorious?"

The general's aide was a quiet young woman named Anika. She had seemed capable during their brief exchanges in the past. Now, Nico addressed her stiffly. "Captain, please take command of the center. Pim, the general is under arrest. Please see him back to the city, find someone you trust and turn him over, then come back. I might need you."

He was aware that words were spoken in protest, but Nico focused on the young captain who suddenly found herself in command of an entire third of an army. She stared at him anxiously, but showed less surprise than he might have expected. He wondered if she had known this outcome was inevitable.

He stepped toward her, away from the curses and insults now being leveled in his direction. "Captain, let's see if we can get this rout under control."

"Yes, Third."

The other officers were willing enough, but it quickly became obvious that no one was going to be able to slow the mass exodus of fleeing troops. As a last resort, Nico leapt back onto his horse and called to the troops as loudly as possible, just to get their attention. Some stopped, but most ran on. He did not blame them, for he saw the enemy cavalry not far off, pushing ahead, hacking down scattered pockets of resistance. Behind them came rows of infantry, moving at a brisk pace. Handersonn's center had all but dissolved.

The first missiles began landing on the rapidly shrinking field between Nico and the enemy, and he became aware of the precariousness of his own position. Then a Lorester cavalryman was struck by a ballista bolt and knocked from the saddle, and Nico realized the incoming projectiles were friendly fire. This was the furthest reach of those on the walls and towers.

Of course. He now recalled how the enemy crossbows were concentrated in the wings—which was a good thing, for Nico had overloaded his own with the cavalry that were so dangerous to missile units. Nevertheless, he found himself wishing he had kept a few more horsemen in the center, for emergencies like this.

"Third!" Anika called out. "We must pull back now."

Nico watched her mount her own destrier, pointing out the direction for the rest of the headquarters staff to head. Then he looked back at the Loresters, looming closer and closer. The cavalry had pulled back to tighten their ranks, forming a giant wedge. Soon they would be upon this very position, with the infantry just behind.

He wanted them to come, closer to the city walls—and his own sword. He reared his horse on its hind legs, hoping to make an irresistible target for their attention.

"Fool!" Lima spat as she grabbed his reins and pulled him after the others. With her single arm, she could not control both his mount and her own, so Nico accepted her lead and galloped back toward safety. He was heartened to see some semblance of order being restored. Many of the most frightened continued to run toward the walls, but Anika and her officers had managed to reform patchwork groups of infantry. Not enough to counterattack, but perhaps enough to slow the enemy's advance.

He and Lima cleared the front rows and saw the spears fall into position behind. The Loresters continued to come on quickly, undaunted by the thin defensive line. But each step brought them farther into the kill zone, closer to the crossbows and ballistae, and the effect of the missile fire was beginning to show. The Lorester line slowed at last, and sporadic cheers erupted from the Akenberg troops.

Once the opposing lines clashed, however, the advantage of the city walls would be lost. The missiles would stop firing for fear of hitting friends. Nico looked about for Pim, hoping that the two of them might be able to charge into the melee, if for no other reason than to stiffen the resolve of the outnumbered defenders.

He heard horns sounding all around, and looked expectantly at the oncoming Lorester forces. Signals to charge, no doubt.

But they were not charging at all. Instead, their lines were breaking into disorder as some soldiers kept coming while others turned around. Disorder quickly became panic, and Nico could now see fighting in their rear and on their flanks. Beyond flew the banners of General Freilenn's Second Army.

Nico's wings, pressing in, enveloping the enemy at last.

In terms of pure numbers, the Loresters probably still held the advantage. But nothing affects a soldier's morale quite so much as being unexpectedly hit from the undefended flank. And the Loresters were now being hit not only from both flanks, but from behind. Their soldiers did not know which way to turn, for danger lay all around, and some of them lashed out so indiscriminately, they must have hit each other.

Nico turned toward Captain Anika, but she was already issuing orders to attack. He watched the emboldened defenders run ahead, the formation compensating in enthusiasm what it lacked in precision. Drawing his sword, Nico prepared to join them.

A hand grabbed his reins, tugging back, and he looked into Lima's censorious glare as she shook her head. "Nay. You stay here."

His help was not needed, in any case. The outcome was clear even before the Lorester standards came down. Some tried to run back down toward the lake, but most dropped their weapons and surrendered. A few continued to fight, and the bulk of the enemy cavalry managed to punch a hole through the chaos and escape to the west. But these were mere trivialities to Nico's racing thoughts.

One battle won, the capital safe for the moment. But what were the ramifications? He would demand complete surrender, of course, but could the Loresters be induced to leave the war entirely? Even if so, that was only one enemy down. There were two more to go. *And after that, barbarians and demons.* There would be more battles in the future, and under less favorable circumstances than today's. It was difficult to feel encouraged.

He remained mounted, stationed between Lima and Pim, watching the clusters of prisoners march up the slope and into the city. They were mixed intermittently with jubilant groups of the victors, a few still in formation, others in cheerful disorder.

Some more cheerful than others. One decimated company in

particular marched in weary step through the slick grass and crushed snow just ahead. Exhausted, but maintaining a straight line as their deep-voiced captain barked orders at them. Their heads were bowed, and Nico nearly did not recognize one blood-spattered face.

He rode forward, reaching down to touch the shoulder once more. Kip's face looked up in surprise, his thoughts pulled away from whatever dark place they had occupied.

"It's good to see you alive, Private." Nico had nearly said what he really meant. *It is surprising to see you alive.*

"Aye, Third." The nose sniffled, but the smile that followed had not nearly the exaltation of the previous eve's. "I...killed one, I think."

His corporal stepped forward. "He killed three, by my count. A true hero of Akenberg, this one."

"You all are," Nico said. *Best that they feel appreciated now.* He would be asking far more from them in the coming months.

But first, there were other matters to attend. Things he could not put off any longer. A general to punish, another to commend, a servant to speak to. Let the others celebrate this victory. Nico had a city to run, a kingdom to defend, an empire to protect.

GOTHENBERG

The snowstorm had long since stopped, but not before ruining the harpa's clever canopy and damaging two wagons. Now the caravan was moving again, but at a creeping pace far too slow for Yohan's liking.

Redjack led them northeastward, toward a path through the Triumphs separate from the one they had traversed. Yohan was still unclear how the bearded soldier had found them, so far from his starting point and in the middle of a blizzard. Redjack himself seemed hazy on that point, as he was on many others, the fog of fear and desperation clouding smooth recollection.

Yohan would later recall these days as a sort of lost opportunity—the break in the weather, a clarity of purpose, and the greatest companionship of his life. And on the periphery of awareness, he knew these things were true. But of course it was impossible to appreciate them, for Jena had cared enough to come after him, and that was all that mattered.

There was never any possibility that he would not go after her, but the longer he considered the choice, the more he wished he had never spoken to anyone about the decision. He had known that permission would be denied, yet the instinct to follow a chain of command was too strong to resist. And then, just as the reality that he had wasted his chance at a rescue was sinking in, Summer miraculously turned the entire caravan around to salvage his hopes.

So now Yohan was responsible not only for Jena's current sufferings but also any ills that befell his current companions.

He could not pretend to understand why Summer had decided what she did, other than the simple truth that she was a good person at heart—all the harpa were—and clearly recognized that he needed their help.

The strange thing was that Yohan agreed with Mercer—this was a personal quest and an unnecessary risk for the group. Yet the corporal's commands were overridden by Summer's, with a result that the unlikeable leader of the Vilnians was completely emasculated in front of his soldiers. The resentment was palpable, but Yohan had no time to deal with it. There was only a single concern on his mind. A single person.

By the time they neared the mountains again, the snowfall had resumed. As they reached the road that cut through, winding a difficult path up into formidable peaks, the sky was already a premature black. Another storm, and another delay to frustrate Yohan.

Only when he noted the traders' distress did he recall that the protective canopy was no longer available, so now people, livestock, wagons, and contents were all subject to the capricious whims of a merciless nature, a situation all too common to his experience.

This time Redjack offered a solution, practically yelling to Corporal Mercer through howling wind and whipping precipitation. "Caves. At the base of the mountains. Not far from the road." Ice thickened his beard, turning the intense ginger color a paler shade of despair.

Mercer nodded and passed the suggestion on to Summer. Without words, they focused their efforts on leaving the road for the natural, protective cover. Sure to his word, within an hour Redjack brought them to a pair of overhangs, barely deep enough to be true caves but sufficient to cover human and beast. The wagons would necessarily need to remain exposed until the storm passed and the caravan could move again.

Brody assisted Meadow with her wagon, Krisa aided Silvo, Kelsey Patrik, and Yohan Summer. The strain and worry kept them silent at first, but he had come to know her well enough that a few words and gestures were all they required to communicate. First they carried the food crates to the makeshift camp, then her bundles of clothing. By the third armful, her natural cheerfulness reasserted itself, and he caught her smiling down on a small wooden box. He stopped to admire that smile, remembering that this was the sort of behavior that brought him to appreciate her people—a contagious joy for life that could never be repressed for long. He desperately needed a dose of that now. "What is that?" he asked.

Without looking at him, without acknowledging what he had asked, Summer began to speak. "You asked me before why we don't believe in the gods. I don't think I ever answered you properly. It's not that we don't believe they exist, but rather our legends maintain that they aren't worth worshiping. Instead, we find inspiration from simpler things. The stars and moon. From the pleasure of music, the song of the lark, the bark of a dog. From each other. From family. From those we meet who improve our lives. Those we think of, even when apart. From everyday objects that are all around, their beauty overlooked.

"As a girl, this was the first thing that inspired me. I've kept it, for it's given me much luck. I always believed I would find someone who needed its power more than I."

She opened the box, lifting a small object wrapped in plain cotton. At last she smiled at Yohan, handing it to him. "Here. For your search."

He accepted it, opened the square piece of cloth, and stared at a large rough stone. A bright blue embedded in dull gray. As he looked back at her, Yohan could see the pleasure she received from the giving. Nevertheless, the transaction felt unequal. "I wish I had something to give back."

Summer laughed. "That isn't necessary, Soldier Yohan. I feel better knowing you have it. Perhaps, when you've found what you seek, you can give it back to me."

An uncharacteristic hint of embarrassment marred her lovely features, as if she worried he would reject this modest offering.

He nodded and slipped the stone into his pocket. Yohan was not good at exchanges like this, and in any case had more work to do. He motioned toward another large crate, soaking in the snowfall. "This one, too?"

"Aye, that's the last." He was aware that her gaze followed him as he hauled it into the cave.

Shivering by a campfire kept weak for fear of the unpredictable wind, Redjack accepted their thanks with a melancholy acquiescence. "It was a cave very similar to this where doom befell my squad. In a storm much like this one."

Kelsey stared out at the wagons, where Silvo and Krisa worked to secure the last of the valuable goods. Yohan noted that the big man tucked the mahogany box containing his precious lute under an arm and brought it with him into the relative warmth and dryness of the cave. If this meant the lute was finally going to be played that night, that was merely one more thing for Yohan to regret. He did not intend to be there to hear.

"In a storm like this?" Kelsey asked Redjack. "How could you see anything? I can barely make out the oxen." The beasts were less than a dozen yards away, huddled together and clearly discomfited by the weather and tight surroundings.

Yohan did not hear the reply, for he was already making his way to the corporal. Once more, he made a request to his superior. Once more he was turned down. And once more the harpa came to his aid.

"Our responsibility is to the caravan," Mercer said. "We go where the wagons go, and if the wagons don't enter the mountains, neither do we."

"I understand, Corporal. I'm not asking the caravan to go, only that you grant permission for me to go alone." He did not see how the man could refuse this much. If nothing else, it meant he would have one less hated underling to irritate him. Probably permanently.

But Mercer still refused. "Denied. We need your sword. We're short-handed already, since Bostik failed."

Within the confines of the cave, there was no way for their conversation not to be overheard. The other soldiers made an attempt to appear disinterested, but the harpa did not. In particular, Summer watched the exchange with a pensive look. Patrik joined her and put an arm around her shoulders, as if preparing to shield her from the soldiers' argument.

"I'm going anyway," Yohan told his superior. "You know none of the others will stop me."

"They will if they don't want to be in my report. Try to leave, Private, and I will make sure you are court-martialed. Along with anyone else who refuses my orders."

Yohan believed him, yet was still torn. He did not particularly care about his own future in the army, but he did not want any of the others to suffer on his account. Enough of that was already happening to Jena.

Summer looked up into Patrik's face. Cheerlessly, he smiled down on her and nodded, then turned to address Mercer. "Corporal, my mistress has asked that I scout ahead for a larger cave. I request someone to accompany me." His head turned, as if just now detecting Yohan's presence. "Private Yohan will do." Then he turned away before the corporal could think of an appropriate response.

Yohan's gear was already prepared, he simply gathered a fresh hooded cloak and met Patrik at the entrance of the cave. He saw the other man accept two cloaks from Summer, one for his head and shoulders and the other to wrap around the longbow he tucked beneath one arm. The two men nodded to one another, then Patrik stepped out into the snowy night.

Before he could follow, Yohan heard a heavy whimpering from behind. He turned to see a familiar black face looking up at him expectantly, red tongue hanging over the vicious row of teeth. "Nay, Lullaby. You stay here." The dog growled at him, annoyed, then turned her back.

He sighed. At least he would not need to worry about her following into the hazardous storm. *Perhaps I'll find a treat to bring back.* Then he laughed at his own foolishness. Between the storm, the mountains, and the barbarians, there was very little chance that he would return.

By midnight, Patrik wished he had stayed at the camp long enough to sup. He had not been hungry at the time, of course—his stomach constricted to the size of a pea as soon as he volunteered to come out on this fool's errand—but he should have known to force something down.

With just the two of them, they made good time. Assuming no patrols would be out during the storm, they stayed on the road until well into the mountains. The snow and darkness hindered their vision, making every shadow loom ominously, but early on Yohan had pointed out that poor visibility worked in their favor. They had the advantage of surprise, so long as they remained undetected.

They spoke little, but that was more than a tactical decision. The soldier's had always been a cold, distant personality—difficult to know and harder to like. Patrik could understand Summer's sympathy for the poor man, but not the pleasure she derived from his company. Yet that was one of the many things he loved most about her—the amazing ability to find the good in anyone. That was a talent he had never possessed for himself. In fact, he was close to the opposite, despite harpa culture and expectations.

It was not worth delving into the reasons he was here. Why he had volunteered to help. She had wanted him to, and that was all that mattered. Now he would simply focus on making it back.

The snowfall lessened noticeably by first light of morn. And there, in the distance, much sooner than he had expected to see it, lay the fort. It was a squarish, two-level structure built into the mountainside. A narrow tower stretched above to a point where it had collapsed in on itself. The whole did not resemble any of the imperial architecture he had seen in his travels, though that may have been due to its advanced state of decay.

With the fort and mountain covered in a layer of white that reflected the burgeoning sun, the fresh fall of snow giving the air a crisp cleanliness, the scene before the two men should have been one of peaceful serenity. Instead, the pall of death hung over the eerily quiet landscape, the sight of the ambushed harpa caravan and the bearded soldier's story lingering in their thoughts.

A strange place for us both to die.

If the road had ever reached up to the ancient stronghold, that time had long since passed. Now a difficult climb over snow and stone hindered their approach.

"I wish the snow had not stopped falling," Yohan said. "Without cover, we're a pair of target dummies out here."

"I don't see anyone."

"Nay. They'll be huddled inside, somewhere warm." The soldier's voice carried the certainty of experience. "I just hope no one decides to come out for a piss."

"Shouldn't we wait for night?" Patrik asked, conceding the other's superior knowledge of tactics.

Surprisingly, his words were met with a shake of negation.

Yohan was already shrugging off cloak and hood and tightening his sword belt.

"If we go barging in recklessly—"

"I'm not going to make her suffer one minute longer." The tone brooked no argument.

Patrik nodded, understanding the sentiment that drove a man to this point. Yet as he took a step from the road onto the slope, a hand shot out to roughly stop him. He turned a questioning stare toward the soldier, who gave a dismissive shake of the head.

"I thank you for what you did in camp." Yohan never took his eyes away from the fort. He did not speak often, and seldom looked at his companion when he did—an irritating habit that made Patrik feel insignificant. "You should go back now."

Patrik could do as Yohan suggested, of course. He could return to the others, to Summer, where he belonged. No one would think him a coward.

Yet he had learned to follow an inner voice, one that told him to continue. Whether he admitted it or not, Yohan needed all the help he could receive. Little Patrik he relished the thought of perishing in these desolate hills beside this disagreeable near-stranger, he never really considered the alternative.

"I've come this far."

"I'm serious. This work is for soldiers, not traders." He did not intend the comment to be offensive, Patrik knew. Nevertheless, the harpa's ire was instantly roused.

"Yohan, look at me… Has Summer taught you nothing, after all? You can't do everything alone."

At last his dour companion gave him what he asked for, turning those emotionless eyes directly onto Patrik's as he spoke. "This may or may not be the same group we met, but there are enough of them to overwhelm an entire squad. Twenty? Thirty? Anyone who goes in there isn't coming back. I *have* to try. You don't. Go back to your caravan."

The other man's stare was rather more intense than expected, making Patrik wish he had not asked for it, after all. At last Yohan looked away, once again studying the fort, then crouched and began to move toward it, leaving the trader alone on the road.

Patrik listened to the sound of his own chaotic thoughts. Without making sense of them, he unwrapped his bow and nocked one of five arrows he carried in a belt quiver. He may not be good with a sword, but there were other ways to fight.

Yohan was already moving up the slope, leaving deep impressions in the drifts. Although the snow was more than a foot deep in places, his boots did not make the crunching sound that Patrik's now did. The soldier heard and turned back. His own ire was audible in the warning he hissed. "If you make any more noise, they will kill her. Then us."

Standing on a snowy bank in the brightening sunlight, Patrik suddenly felt very, very exposed. His gaze drifted between Yohan and the fort, which was within easy range of a bow or crossbow. Out in the open like this, the two men made easy targets.

He fought back the urge to duck behind the nearest snowbank, instead watching the structure for archers or lookouts. Yohan resumed his lonely trek up the slope. Patrik watched the big, surprisingly stealthy man reach the halfway point, then followed behind. By taking advantage of the pre-made bootprints, he managed to minimize the sound of his own clumsy footsteps. Meanwhile, his eyes never ceased scanning the small windows and decaying ramparts of their destination. With every stride nearer, he expected to hear a hue and cry, followed by a rain of arrows or a mad charge of bloodthirsty barbarians. Instead, his ears only picked up the unwanted sounds of his own heavy breathing and the thunderous pounding of his heartbeat.

Ahead, Yohan's body stiffened, hit by a silent arrow. Then the same gust of wind hit Patrik, and he stiffened as well. Yohan moved forward once more, unharmed. There had been no attack, only a panicked imagination.

They reached the structure and pressed close to the uneven

stone bricks that formed the misshapen wall. Now the easy part was behind them. Entering the enemy's lair came next. With that, fighting of a kind Patrik had never before experienced.

He released the breath he was holding and sucked in another. His companion began to slide toward the nearest ground-level window. Not yet ready to go on, Patrik paused, giving his heart an opportunity to return to something approaching normalcy, and his mind an opportunity to wonder why he had insisted on coming.

Yohan peeked into the window, then slipped past. Patrik followed suit, quietly as he could manage, caught between a desperate desire to make no noise and another to get out of the open as soon as he could. As he passed by the same window himself, a quick glance inside revealed only that the interior was too dark to make out in any detail. At least no one saw him and yelled.

With some relief, he watched Yohan reach an opening in the crumbling wall. Sword drawn, the soldier ducked through, leaving Patrik alone outside. He waited one moment, expecting to hear yells of surprise, of anger, of pain.

Nothing. Not even the sound of Yohan's footfalls, for his boots padded silently. Patrik listened for a few more seconds, then followed into blackness.

It took several seconds for his eyes to adjust from sunshine to dusk and shadow. During that time he remained completely motionless, focusing on his ears to warn him to danger, fingers tight on the string. He made out motion, then discerned Yohan cautiously creeping along the far wall toward an open doorway. Their eyes met, and the harpa was struck by the calmness on his companion's face. The man might have been searching for breakfast.

On a second glance, Patrik revised his impression. It was less calm than determined. The soldier expected to confront evil, and wanted to get it over with.

Looking around, Patrik noticed a fireplace. No fire was lit, but there was wood inside, and a thick pile of ashes beneath. Recently used, clearly. Just beyond, hidden in a deeper shroud of shadow, was the top of a narrow stairway down.

Patrik remained stationary. His own ears could register every sound he made, all the way to the slightest movement, which meant that staying motionless was the only way to be sure the enemy could not hear him. He watched Yohan pass through the doorway into greater darkness, leaving him alone again. A quick swallow and slow steps to the other side, then the harpa entered that darkness himself.

A thin beam of light from outside was all that illuminated this smaller chamber, forcing his eyes to adjust still more. Now his nose detected a subtle change, the stale air picking up a distinctive but unidentifiable addition. The outlines of shapes began to form. One long table, a cupboard against a wall, two chairs pushed into a corner. Then more details, things he wished to unsee. A ribcage on the table, and a thick sheet of coagulated liquid that looked deceptively black in the darkness.

Was the ribcage human? It was about the size of a small person, but Patrik was no expert. He wanted to believe it was not.

Then his eyes made out the rags of a garment where the floor met wall—the remains of a dress, recognizably harpa even without seeing the bright colors. That explained the fate of his harpa sister, and probably the Vilnian princess, as well.

He felt an onrush of sympathy and remorse, until realizing his own fate could be the same. Every moment inside this deathtrap made that outcome more likely. Patrik could not shake the prospect from his mind, nor pretend it was not terrifying.

He sighed audibly, and Yohan's face flashed an angry warning. Patrik swallowed his breath and castigated himself. He had made a mistake coming inside, that much was certain. The soldier was right, this was no place for traders. Best for them both that he go back.

Patrik calmed his mind, then his pulse. He was in this to the end.

Yohan paused a moment, listening. Then he stepped to the table and dipped a finger into the blood.

How fresh? Patrik wondered, but the other did not so much as look his way. Instead he moved toward a corridor, and beyond it to the base of a stairway.

Yohan was halfway up by the time Patrik reached the bottom. He aimed the bow at the upper landing, saw no targets, then followed.

They crept cautiously up the stairs, the growing whipping of wind disguising their footfalls. Bow raised and ready, Patrik reached the landing at Yohan's side. A violent gust dislodged the arrow and forced the trader to turn his face away until it subsided.

Their vision cleared, revealing more of nothing. There were two rooms upstairs, one containing steps into the tower. But the two men did not make any move to explore them, for the ruined state of everything made this level uninhabitable.

Yohan looked at Patrik blankly, then whispered so softly it was barely audible over the whistle of swirling drafts. "Another way?"

"A basement..." Another frigid blast stung his cheek. "Where they can stay out of the elements."

"Where?"

"Where we came in."

Those intense eyes stared back. "Show me."

As they retraced their steps, Patrik felt guilty for regretting that he had mentioned it.

Stopping at the fireplace, Yohan extracted a length of wood, then took a minute to pull flint and tinder from his backpack. Thankful to be able to help, Patrik crept back to the kitchen where the dress lay discarded. Cringing at the sound, he tore off a strip of cloth, then brought it to Yohan. The soldier looked at him, nodded, and wrapped the top of the makeshift torch before lighting it.

The flame made more sound by itself than their footfalls combined. The harpa could only assume Yohan knew what he was doing as he descended, torch in one hand, sword in the other, ignoring the shadowy shapes formed on every surface by the flickering light.

Patrik followed, bow drawn, ready to fire at anything that attacked. Hoping for a target, wanting to fire, desperate to fight back against the never-ending fear.

The stairs curved, the bottom as yet unseen, and the two men moved even more cautiously than before. Drawing strength from his companion's steady demeanor, Patrik felt his own nerves settle. The fort was cold, dark, and sinister, yet he became slightly more hopeful. They had discovered only one body so far, suggesting that the princess may be alive, after all. Patrik mourned for his sister, but one victim was not so bad.

The bottom landing came into view, then suddenly they went down the last few stairs in a rush. Weapons ready, into a wide chamber, dark movements bathed in sudden torchlight.

The two men stopped, staring at the shadows dancing on the walls, mocking their anxiety.

Or Patrik's alone—Yohan did not seem to have any. He raised the torch, his face expressionless.

There were more shadows than their own, though the others hardly moved, cast as they were from a half-dozen thin, papery objects hanging on hooks wedged into the ceiling.

One wall was blocked off by rows of vertical bars. Inside those bars, shackles were suspended from the stone by rusted chains similar to those that hung from the ceiling.

The two men were the only ones present. Alive, at least. Bones lay all about the floor, strewn inside and out of the cells. More discarded clothing, tattered and stained, lay piled in one dank corner.

This was not a basement, Patrik realized. It was a dungeon. And those who had died within numbered too many to count.

The stench was overwhelming. It reached his nose only after his eyes took in the sights, but lingered even more powerfully. He grimaced to stop from coughing, looked at his companion, and wondered how the other man managed to look so unperturbed.

Yohan stepped into the room, avoiding objects both hanging and underfoot, briefly glanced at the rags, and headed toward an open doorway in the center of the wall opposite the stairs.

He took the light with him, leaving Patrik no choice but to follow. Already the area around him was falling back to shadow, and his first step came down on one of the bones that littered the floor. He yanked his foot back as he heard the snap, then felt one of the papery objects hanging from the ceiling brush against his shoulder and cheek. It was cold and wet, and his contact set it in a gentle motion that nonetheless creaked loud in the unpleasant silence.

Patrik stopped its swing with his hand, then caught a better look at the clammy surface, covered in a thin lair of hair and marred by moles and blemishes. Near the top were two holes where the eyes would have been.

He recoiled in disgust, kicking another bone in the process. His bow shot up, ready to fire should the commotion bring these savages out of their hiding place. Yohan was nearly across the room, but Patrik lingered a moment longer, certain an attack was imminent. He felt a prickling sensation all over his skin. Skin that was soon to be flayed off and hung by hook in this chill, damp abyss.

Something tapped his knee, freezing him in place. But it was just the limb of his bow. He was unsure exactly when his hands had started shaking.

The light was nearly gone, for Yohan had not stopped to wait. Patrik hurried after, catching up to the soldier halfway down a long, downward sloping passageway. They reached a corner and

Yohan swung the torch from side to side, revealing only more tunnel. This one took them a few hundred steps farther from the fort and dungeon, and deeper underground. Closer to hell, with less chance of ever coming back.

They moved on, a little more urgency entering their pace.

The passageway turned again, descending ever further. Now Patrik had to stow the bow to keep up with Yohan's quickening strides. The soldier was racing toward damnation, so why did Patrik blindly follow along?

At last they saw a closed door blocking the hall. It was wooden and damaged, with signs of recent repair. There was a lock, but the whole frame barely looked stable enough to stay upright.

Patrik took a deep breath as he stared at it, certain they had reached the culmination of their search. How many enemies were on the other side, and how many more dead innocents?

He looked at his companion, ready to ask how they should prepare, and saw that the soldier already had his leg raised. The foot shot forward, hard against the wood, and whatever held it in place snapped with a crash. The hinges creaked and twisted, and the door flung open in a surge of sudden light. They turned away, momentarily blinded.

It was sunlight, reflected from snowy ground. They stepped outside, recognized the depression they found themselves in, and looked back up a slope toward the fort. The empty fort.

At last, the imperturbable expression on Yohan's face showed signs of strain. The soldier looked south, in the direction they had come.

Patrik lacked Summer's gifts of empathy and cheerfulness, but even he could see the despair growing inside his companion, and felt the compulsion to be reassuring. "They cannot have gone far. The storm just ended."

"They haven't been here for a while." Once again, Yohan did not bother looking back as he replied, but Patrik was less annoyed than disturbed by the soldier's thoughts. "Why would he lead us back this way? This feels very wrong to me."

"What do you mean?"

Yohan only shook his head.

A terrible thought occurred to Patrik, alongside a growing revival of the fear that had just subsided. "Should I be worried about the others?"

"I am."

Meadow, Silvo... Summer.

"Come on. Let's hurry back." Yohan set off at a brisk run, back to the road. Patrik hurried behind.

The footprints showed that the attack had come from the east. Clearly, the enemy had moved from the old fort to a new base.

There were twelve bodies in total, not including the dead oxen and dogs. Four were barbarian tribesmen, all succumbing to stabs and slashes. Judging by proximity, two of them had fallen to Brody—for his body lay nearby, between them and Meadow.

The other two tribesmen were interspersed among the rest of the Vilnian contingent: Ledo, Kelsey, Duffey, Krisa, and Mercer.

Silvo's body was near his wagon, lying on top of his shattered lute, not far from the stashed bow that he had been unable to reach. His corpse—like Brody's and Meadow's—still bore the crossbow bolts that killed him.

Yohan felt surprisingly little emotion. Instead, he felt dead inside.

Marek's company. Jena's squad. And now this. Far too much to be coincidence.

Those bolts particularly bothered him. Captain Marek had been killed and Jena wounded by crossbows, and Yohan had yet to see a single tribesman use one.

There had been other signs, if he had only paid attention. But he had been too deep in self-pity to notice.

"Summer isn't the only one missing," Patrik said, able to form coherent sentences again. The utter terror that had overwhelmed the trader was subsiding, Yohan noted.

"Nay."

"Your bearded friend..."

"Redjack," Yohan affirmed. "Not a friend at all, it appears."

"What are you saying?"

"He led us into a trap. It wasn't the first time." Yohan sat on a broken wagon wheel, allowing his tired legs to rest. A very brief rest.

They would pursue, of course. He and this harpa civilian, for whatever that was worth. Whether they ever caught up remained to be seen, but they would certainly follow. And the sooner, the better.

"What are you looking for?" he asked impatiently.

Patrik was searching Summer's wagon. She was gone, clearly. Taken, most definitely. There was still a chance to rescue her and Jena both. But that chance was already minuscule, and every delay made it shrink still more.

"She had a giant blue sapphire," Patrik said. "A gemstone, uncut. She loved it. She wouldn't want it left behind."

Yohan stood, reaching into his pocket. At least he could give his last remaining companion some consolation. She had said it bestowed hope. May it work for Patrik better than he.

The trader's voice was near tears. "She said it was her heart. That she would give it to me when we were finally married. I... can't leave it behind."

Yohan froze. *Oh, Summer.*

I can't show him this. It would only hurt the man, and he is in enough pain already.

His legs felt weak, so he sat back down.

"Don't you even care?" Patrik accused. "She risked everything to help you."

More than you know, Yohan thought. *And more than I realized.* But showing his feelings was not going to help. It might have before, but not now.

The useless search went on for a few more minutes. "Not here," Patrik cried in frustration. "The thieves found it." He stared eastward, after the footprints. "We're going to chase them, right? And kill them all."

"Aye. Get whatever you need. We're leaving in five minutes." Yohan stood again, taking his turn to contemplate the footprints leading away. Dozens of them. The odds kept getting worse.

What had she told him? *I believe that when love is before you, you have an obligation to take it.* But what if you do not see it until too late?

I will never understand why people behave in a manner so clearly against their own interest, she also said, yet had done everything in her power to help him go after Jena. Had, in fact, risked the entire caravan to do so. Why?

Because she wanted him to be happy. Happiness was important to these harpa, a lesson he had begun to learn before turning away.

He raised his eyes from the marks in the snow, his gaze continuing on into the distance. Toward the enemy's homeland, where prisoners—those who were not summarily eaten—were likely to be taken, and the mountains that stood in the way. The Stormeres—those old familiar friends. He had the feeling he was going back.

Circumstances would be different this time, however. Yohan could already feel the change in the air, born from a shift in purpose. For as long as he could remember, he had tried to protect others from the omnipresent dangers that hunted them. Now that need to protect was gone, for those dangers had finally materialized, closed in, and taken everything. He had been as powerless to stop them as a goat stalked by wolves.

The helplessness ended now. There was nothing he could do to change what had happened, but he would do everything in his power to end these misfortunes. The wolves would come to know the hunt from a new viewpoint, for he was the tiger, and he smelled blood.

EPILOGUE

NEUBLUSTEN

From his perch on the balcony, Hermann watched the small line of soldiers file through the front gate of the castle. All of them familiar, the one in the lead most of all. His son, Nicolas, heir and acting commander of Neublusten. The dour boy and crippled girl with whom he always surrounded himself. General Freilenn was a surprise, and Captain Reikmann even more so. They gave the group an extra air of authority, of legitimacy.

Their purpose was written clearly enough on their faces, visible to an old man's eyes even at this distance. And so he waited those last moments with a mix of emotions. He could not help but feel a sense of regret, even a little fear. Surprise, of course, at how quickly the wheel turned. And somewhere, deep inside, a sliver of pride.

He heard a commotion in the antechamber. His chamberlain, performing the useless duties of office. Demanding respect or requesting leniency, it mattered not which. It was merely one last pointless service at the end of a lifetime's worth. Hermann regretted the delay, for he was ready to get this over with.

At last the door opened, and his remaining son strode into the august chamber, leaving the others behind to have a moment alone with the king. Trusting in the forbearance of a known manipulator, or simply in his own capability to handle himself. Either way, it was another foolish error by a staggeringly naive child.

How much does the prince know, I wonder? Best just to assume the answer to that was everything. That way there would be no surprises.

Nicolas opened his mouth to speak, but said nothing. Hesitant, unsure how to begin. Not a good sign, for any of them. Despite all that had happened, the boy still showed irresolution. Weakness.

Well, there was one last lesson Hermann could provide.

"You should have known what you were going to say before ever you entered," he rebuked.

Nico's shoulders stiffened. "I did. I'm giving you an opportunity to speak your piece first."

Hermann shook his head. "Unnecessary. You spoke to General Cottzer. You know where the ground lays."

"You deny none of his story?"

"I do not. Even you will have seen the truth in things, regardless. It was a fair plan, save for the treachery of others."

"You know treachery when you see it, Father."

"A good king should."

Nico glared back, and the level of hatred contained within that stare made Hermann shiver. Or perhaps that was merely the chill breeze blowing in from the open balcony.

"Your betrayal of me means not half so much as your murder of Arturo," Nico said calmly. The rage had been contained. It was still there, but the boy spoke without its controlling him. That, at least, was a good sign.

"You spoke to the girl?"

"Pris? Yes. The Third was a great man. She did not wish to poison him, but you forced her to."

"No, you did, Nicolas."

There was the anger again, flashing in the prince's eyes. Hermann hammered home the point, leaning forward in his chair. "With your reckless decisions. Surely, you see that a ruler cannot allow his kingdom to rise and fall on such trivial whims." He leaned back, shivering again despite himself as another winter breeze blew in.

"Your whims are more trivial than mine," Nico said defensively. "And more reckless by far. As much as anyone, you plunged this empire into civil war. I am saddened that you don't see that." He looked away from Hermann momentarily, locating an object in the room. He stepped to the blanket and unfolded it while he continued speaking. "Your actions were for personal gain. Mine were for the good of the empire."

Nico came forward to spread the blanket on his father's legs. Hermann allowed him to do so, for it was a gesture reminiscent of another son, another time. And even his hardened heart resonated at the poignancy.

He smiled, banishing the anger from the discussion. "I always believed you were more ambitious than you let on. I am pleased to see that my actions are justified."

"Justified? Sacrificing your own son?"

"Had I done nothing, you and Markolas would certainly have clashed, and in so doing ripped this kingdom asunder. My actions saved Akenberg from being torn in two."

"You exaggerate to shield your ego from the truth. You failed yourself, this kingdom, and your family."

Hermann snorted. "Have I failed? I don't see it that way. My son will be emperor, after all. Even if it isn't the one I expected."

The brief silence that followed loomed profoundly. He found it telling that Nico did not attempt to deny this destiny. The natural progression was clear enough, even to that obstinate mind.

Nico paused to consider his words. Exactly what was

expected from a good ruler, and another promising sign. "The future will bring what it brings. I'm not trying to shape it."

"You don't really believe that. Ever since you returned, you've seized power at every opportunity."

"The difference between us is that you see power as treasure, to be collected and coveted. But power isn't treasure, it's more like a sword. To be used only when needed, and treated with respect. With honor."

"This foolish code of yours makes you take unnecessary risks, young prince. Those risks will catch up to you, sooner or later. And when they do, where will your precious honor leave you?"

"Honorable."

Hermann's eyes narrowed. At first, he thought his son was making game of him. Now he could see the boy was earnest.

"You're not Eberhart, Nicolas. Leave the heroics to the heroes."

He could tell those words had stung. Not that Hermann wished to be cruel to his only living son, but it appeared that was the only way to get the message through.

Once more, Nico needed a moment to rein in his embattled emotions. Then he called out in a loud voice, "Captain Reikmann."

Hermann's old friend entered the chamber, striding boldly to the prince's side. The king greeted him with a smile. "You have joined with the boy, Reikmann?"

"I side with winners, Hermann. The Third has proven himself to me, as you once did."

The Third. Bah. When did that become more important than blood and friendship?

Nico cleared his throat.

Here it comes. Will it be death, then? Or banishment? Public humiliation, perhaps?

"Captain Reikmann, my father is unwell. He sees the

importance of strong leadership in a time of war, and relinquishes his duties to those better able to perform them.

"Yet he is to be respected for all he has done to benefit Akenberg. Maybe there is still time for him to learn that respect —the giving and receiving—is more valuable than power.

"He is confined to quarters until the transition is complete. After that, ceremonial duties can resume.

"Does this suit you, Father? Do you 'know where the ground lays?'"

Not death, then. Not even a trial. Smart, for the boy would not benefit from certain secrets being revealed.

It was far more than Hermann expected, and probably better than he deserved. Perhaps he still had more service to provide his kingdom.

"Very well, then, I abdicate. Rule with my full support, for the time I have left. What's in a title, anyway? You seem to accumulate them faster than one can keep track. Prince, Thane, Commander, General, Third.

"I suppose you have one more to add to your list, *King.*"

The following is a sneak preview of *Shield and Crown: Empire Asunder Book 3*

NEUBLUSTEN

The eagle soared far overhead, gracing the blue sky with golden majesty, tracing a path from the walls of Neublusten to the sparkling lake for which the city was named. Once over the water, the bird circled back, flapping its wings but once, then gliding lower over the melting snows of the field where a thousand soldiers were forming, always in motion, in the spirit of all animals everywhere, hunger compelling its eternal search for prey.

As he watched, King Nicolas of Akenberg silently wished it luck. He felt little sympathy for the hare and marmot, for this was simply the way of things. The blessed prospered, the weak succumbed. It was unfair, but so was life.

Farther and farther away, the image lost clarity. Now little more than a speck, the great bird abruptly changed directions, back toward the heights, as a volley of bolts flew into the sky.

Nico frowned. Crossbowmen, making sport. He could barely make out the projectiles from this distance, but had no doubt what they were. He also knew they would have to be lucky, indeed, to take down an eagle in flight.

One was, and the swift speck of gold ceased its upward

trajectory and fell to earth. The noblest of creatures in a moment of transcendent glory, snuffed out in an instant.

"That's a lesson for you," Leti told him. "Appreciate all of life's precious moments, for you never know when they will end."

"As My Princess commands," he replied, leaning in for a kiss.

"There's no time for that, boy," Renard admonished. "You have a kingdom to lead. Nay, an empire."

Nico closed his eyes regretfully. When he opened them again, the other two were gone. He still had the beauty of the lake, however, and the welcome warmth of sunshine. The tranquility of the scene was not to be lightly disregarded.

But in times of war, springtime meant new offensives, and he had ordered this one himself. Now, it was his obligation to see the troops off.

From a respectable distance away, two others watched him stand. Seeing him mount, they followed suit. Then, as he cantered toward the Fourth Army, they galloped to catch up. Lima took position on his left, Pim his right. Neither spoke a word, but he felt their presence so keenly he almost stopped missing his ghosts.

He loved them more than he could let them know. Nico owed them much, for he never would have reached the position he was in without their aid, and their friendship.

Exactly what position was he in? A king, but more than that, according to the rumors. A reluctant hero to his homeland. The man who turned a war around, who summoned hope from despair.

And a ruler only a few steps away from being emperor. Win this civil war he unwillingly found himself fighting, and he would become the obvious candidate. Akenberg's former enemies would have little alternative but to support him. Such was the price of defeat.

If Akenberg won this conflict. One battle did not make a war.

The siege of the capital was over, but three enemies remained, and more fighting was yet to come.

Soon his escorts were joined by another. Captain Mickens of the Kingshields, Nico's personal guard, saluted his leader and fell in behind the others. Nico glanced back to see the man beaming at his former comrades. And why not? They had all gone through trying times together, and all had much of which to be proud.

Pride did not sit easily upon Nico's head, however, for there was always one more obstacle in his way, one more problem to push through, one more responsibility to fulfill. This had been his life ever since being tasked with a modest errand to a neighboring kingdom, two seasons and a lifetime ago.

Words were not necessary for the foursome to enjoy each others' company, and the brief gallop across the scenic plains was more rousing than the grandest orchestra.

Nico located the commander near the front of the formation, twenty companies of infantry and four of cavalry, plus the ancillary aides and adjuncts that made an army function. A formidable force with which to turn the tides of war, and much better than what Nico had returned to at the beginning of winter. An army with more tendays training at its back. And, even more importantly, a victory.

Overseeing this massing of eager young men and women was the man Nico came to see. He slowed his destrier, but did not dismount, and spoke in a loud, authoritative voice. He wanted as many of the staff and soldiers as possible to hear the respect he had for this officer, the true savior of Neublusten.

"General Freilenn, I wish you and your troops a fast and successful journey."

"Thank you, My King. You honor us with this duty, but not so much as you do with your person. We are all very pleased that you send us off personally." He smiled, enjoying the exchange. For a commoner, Freilenn was becoming quite adroit with the formalities of etiquette.

Moving closer now, Nico lowered his voice and spoke in the casual manner of friends. "Remember, drive them back as needed, but avoid bloodshed where possible. We want them deterred, not dead."

"Aye, Third. I understand the circumstances."

He did not, of course. Or at least not all of them. Freilenn was aware of the three conflicts inflicting the empire—not only this civil war, but the rumors of a demon infestation in the north and a Chekik invasion in the east. Every able soldier was needed for the latter two, which meant every death in the former was doubly tragic. Thus Akenberg's unfortunate war with her neighbors needed to be resolved as quickly and bloodlessly as possible, then resources shifted to the other fights.

These strategic necessities had been explained to Nico by Third Arturo, just before his death in a duel between the two. The result was that Nico took on the responsibilities and the title of the other, along with an overwhelming sense of guilt.

All this Freilenn knew. But there was more that he did not, that he could not. Nico had made a promise to Princess Letitia of the Asturians that they would never be enemies. Events had already made him an unwilling liar, and he had no desire to become a willing one.

The Fourth Army was marching south, against Asturia. The Loresters, to the north, had already lost one battle and were open to negotiations. That left only Daphina for Nico to confront with the remainder of his forces.

"I trust you above all others, Freilenn. You're the right man for this." Nico spoke from the heart, as the other well understood. "But I'll miss having your counsel."

The general nodded. "Let's be sure to speak again soon." He smiled. "In Cormona, preferably."

They saluted, then Nico backed away while the man issued orders. Soon two-thousand boots were marching in unison, filling the late morn with precision stomping like the drums of an endless symphony. Freilenn was taking the best of the recent recruits, leaving a mob of misfits for Nico and Lima to whip into shape.

He turned to his long-time, one-armed aide. "Well, we should get to work."

She nodded. "Aye, Third. General Reikmann is waiting."

Once the leader of King Hermann's royal guard, Reikmann had been promoted following General Handersonn's debacle at the Battle of Neublusten. Nico had hated to cashier that drunken officer, for he genuinely liked the man and believed in second chances. But not third.

Handersonn had tried, and mostly failed, to turn the influx of recruits into an effective fighting force. Now that responsibility was Reikmann's, for which the man had obvious mixed feelings. An old friend of Nico's father, he was torn between a genuine desire to please and a regrettable attachment to the old ways. He accepted Nico's reforms without complaint, but lacked originality of his own.

To help the new general transition, Nico assigned Captain Anika to his staff. She had proven herself capable in relief of Handersonn in the recent fighting, and she would be next in line should any of the current generals fail. Or fall.

That left Cottzer. Once a highly respected officer, he had risen to field command beside Nico's brother, Markolas. Now he was a broken man, for not only had Markolas' army been defeated and Cottzer captured, but he had been party to the betrayal of the younger prince. Nico forgave him for the slip, but the general had more difficulty forgiving himself.

"Are you ready for this?" Lima asked as they neared the city walls. Nico looked from her to Pim, who grinned like a proud fool at the king's discomfort. Mickens was only slightly more successful at concealing his mirth.

Nico lowered his head, then sat up straight in the saddle as the gate opened before them and they rode inside.

"Hail, Nicolas the Great!" the gathering crowd cheered. The familiar refrain followed the entourage through the streets, and would go on all the way to the Rechshtal, the headquarters of the army that had become more of a home than Castle Neublusten itself. "Nicolas the Great! Nicolas the Great! Nicolas the..."

He had mixed feelings about the cheers. On the one hand, love and respect was something he cherished, even though he could never be comfortable with such outward demonstrations. The cheers themselves never failed to lift his spirits, and had literally saved his life in the duel with Arturo. These people had been with him through that, the subsequent battle outside the walls, and his hurried coronation. Their support had stayed with him while he recovered from many difficult wounds.

His physical wounds, that was. There was another that would never heal, the one in his spirit, for he had not defeated Arturo fairly. Long after the duel ended, after the battle won, Nico learned that the Third had been poisoned.

The Swordthanes lived by a particular code of conduct, and Nico had been made an unwitting participant in that code's violation. Every man must die, and to die by the blade of another thane was the highest honor of all. There would have been less shame in dying to Arturo than there was in defeating him unfairly.

Not only did Nico not deserve to be Third, not only should he be dead, but the act denied a great warrior of the righteous honor that should have been his due. All Nico could do was hope the man had not known the truth before his last breath. It was a guilt that would poison the young king's heart as long as it continued to beat.

There was one other general that Nico had all but forgotten, until the man presented himself at the Rechshtal that eve.

Lima came into his office looking uncharacteristically

nervous. "Third, General Koblenzar wishes a word. Should I send him off?"

Nico leaned back, considering. Koblenzar was the former commander of all Akenberg forces, and the man Nico had summarily dismissed as soon as he took that role for himself. There was little love lost between the two of them, and even less respect, but Nico's curiosity was piqued. "No. Send him in." *I want to see what he is about.*

He was about pleading for a job. Nico never would have guessed the man had a scrap of humility, but here it was on full display. "Should you give me the opportunity to serve Akenberg once more, I shall do so faithfully, to the best of my abilities."

"Alas, we have no command positions available."

"There are other ways I might serve, other functions I can provide."

"Such as?"

"For one, I was the head of the intelligence service. It is a responsibility not many are qualified for, requiring a network of discreet informants built up over time."

Along with a moral pliancy beneath most, Nico thought. Yet the man had a point, for the gathering of information was a greatly underappreciated duty. Even Lima, who hated the man, would attest to that.

"Suppose I appointed you on the morrow. What would you do, General?"

"I understand that Crown Prince Matheus managed to escape our capture, but there are surely others worth interrogating. I would start there."

"I hope to make Lorester see the value of peace, not fight them to submission."

Koblenzar scowled. "It may be wise to press your advantage while they are weak."

I intend to—at the table, not on the battlefield. "What else?"

"Our other enemies, Daphina and Asturia. I have contacts in

both. A steady stream of information, troop deployments, the tendencies of commanders."

"Very well, General. I see your point. I will take this into consideration. You understand if I think the matter over?"

"Of course, My King." The man bowed and accepted his dismissal, even going so far as to nod at Lima. Perhaps the recent victory—the changing fortunes of the kingdom—had earned the old officer's respect.

Nico turned to his aide for advice. "I think I should speak to my father about this. What do you think?"

"I think you should trust your own mind," she replied. Then considered. "On second thought, that's a terrible idea. You should speak to your father."

He laughed. "Make an appointment. First, let's see the Loresters." He stood up.

She shook her head. "Not so fast. You have another visitor to deal with."

Nico sat back down and waited impatiently. He was finding a king's busy schedule to be even worse than a general's.

Yet this visit was due to neither. A handsome young face peeked into the room, grinning like a jester. The man it belonged to was no courtly fool, however, that much was clear from the moment he sauntered into the room and crossed long arms over a powerful chest. "So this is the man who defeated my esteemed Patron, and to whom I now owe fealty. Do wonders never cease?"

The meaning was clear enough. This was a Swordthane, the first one Nico had met who was beneath him on the hierarchy. The Order of Swordthanes had only one First, whom two Seconds served faithfully; each Second three Thirds, making Nico one of six; and each Third three untitled thanes of their own.

When he defeated Arturo—or rather, when Arturo died during their duel—Nico assumed the other swordsman's position. That included the three subordinate thanes, though he had never attempted to contact them. Something must have compelled this man to seek him, instead.

I wonder if he intends to challenge me? According to the code of the Order, Nico could rightfully decline until a year passed since his last bout. Nevertheless, he already decided that he would accept any challenge. Win or lose, it would ease the burden of guilt.

Whatever his purpose, the man's appearance was a welcome distraction from the morbid duties of war and the petty affairs of state. Nico stood, extended an arm, and offered the guest a place at the table. "Please, Thane, sit. You honor me with your presence."

The eyes crinkled in silent laughter. "Are all kings so courteous to former thralls?"

Nico recognized that he was being teased, but knew not whether it was intended to provoke, or as simple merriment. He shrugged. "If you find courtesy disagreeable, you've come to the wrong place."

The stranger lifted an eyebrow, and his smile lost its touch of ostentation. But he accepted the offered seat. "My Third—"

"What is your name, Thane?"

"I am Fawkes, at your service."

"I am Nicolas, at yours." The brow lifted again, but the man listened patiently. "No doubt you know more of me than I of you, Fawkes. But I hope you will rectify that. My responsibilities here, in the midst of conflict, have forced me to neglect my functions in the Order more than I might have wished—but that does not mean I take them lightly. In fact, I hope your arrival here will go far in helping me fulfill my obligations. Am I correct?"

"Aye, My Third. I come from Second Devero, who desires that I answer all your questions. And instruct you as to the Order's wishes." As he spoke, lithe fingers danced animatedly—or perhaps nervously—on the pommel of his sheathed sword, as though he possessed too much energy to remain stationary in the manner of courtiers.

"Just so. I've not had the pleasure of meeting the Second, so please tell me all about him. Why do you laugh?"

"*Her.* The Second is the proudest woman I know, and the finest warrior. Though I've not met the First of Swords, of course."

Nico grinned. He had a habit of making silly assumptions that came back to bite. If nothing else, these blunders kept him humble and attentive. "Where is the Second now?"

"In Falkenreach. Fighting demons."

"Yes, Arturo told me of the infestation. How fares the fight?"

"Too soon to tell. When Arturo failed to return, I was dispatched on this mission before the real fighting began. Naturally, I will return to the battle as soon I leave here."

"I hope you can stay a few days, at least. I have much to learn."

"A few days, aye. Longer, impossible."

Lima opened the door and caught Nico's attention. "Your pardon, Third. Chancellor Thamos desires a word."

He nodded, then looked at his peer. Solidly built, squared shoulders, but an easy manner. Confident, and no doubt capable. "As you can see, Thane, I find my time is not my own. But come to my office this hour each day, from now until you leave. We will speak as long as my aide allows. I want to know everything. In the meantime, I hope you'll enjoy the comforts of the castle."

"Your pardon, Third, but I prefer the comforts of the tavern."

Nico smiled. "We have those, too."

The city had been in no position to house a thousand prisoners so soon after a siege, therefore most of the Lorester solders were paroled and sent back home with orders not to take up arms against Akenberg again. A few, feeling no particular hatred for their neighbors, had willingly joined the Fourth Army's march to

Asturia. Only the officers remained in Neublusten, and only the general staff imprisoned in the Rechshtal's adjoining gaol.

Nico entered without fanfare, wanting a few minutes to observe the dynamics of the prisoners. One thing he had discovered in recent years was just how much could be learned from watching people when they did not know they were being watched.

He spotted one familiar face right away—Fineo, the envoy of the crown prince, who had once crushed Nico's soul with the information of his family's betrayal.

Besides Fineo, there were six others in the communal cell. All of them wore the uniform of Lorester, gray and brown, prominently emblazoned with the proud lion of Chissenhall.

All were men. Two of them, one young and one old, were sharing whispers with the foppish captain. Three others sat together, playing cards and occasionally swapping banter with the first three. The last, a white-bearded old man all but shunned by the others, sat alone in a corner.

Nico wished he had thought to bring Cottzer along, if for no other reason than to get a sense of the personalities and importance of the people here. The insignia on their uniforms indicated that three were captains, three commanders, and only the quiet old man a general.

An odd dynamic was at play here, for it was strange to see an officer—and a general, at that—neglected by peers. No doubt the others held him responsible for the recent, unexpected defeat.

Nico waited for someone to notice him and the talking to diminish. Only then did he motion the guard to open the door and let him in.

"Captain Fineo. How pleasant it is to see you. How pleasant, indeed."

The once-brash officer looked quickly at the young commander he had been speaking with. Then he smiled sheepishly at the Akenberg king, a man whom he had not treated well when last they spoke, yet who had assumed an air of polite cheer. Caught somewhere between a frown and a smile, Fineo stepped forward.

"Thank you, Prince Nicolas. That is to say, King."

At the sound of the name, all seven prisoners stopped what they were doing to watch the exchange.

"Are you treated well?" Nico inquired. An answering nod, as was to be expected. "In that case, I have a favor to ask. I require a dependable man to deliver a message to King Maximil." *This is the sort of man who will recommend himself. To abandon other prisoners in order to escape his own imprisonment.*

Another glance exchanged, then Fineo smiled broadly, reassuming the false air of good cheer that was so irritating. "Of course, Prince Nicolas. That is to say, King. May I recommend Commander Tomas, who is the finest rider amongst us, and as dependable as any Lorester alive."

That may not be saying much, Nico thought. He nodded. "You may recommend him, indeed." He turned to his companions. "Lima, please escort this Tomas to the Rechshtal. And summon Generals Reikmann and Cottzer. I suspect we have our crown prince, after all." *I cannot believe I didn't do this already. An oversight that might have cost us greatly. Perhaps I need help more than I thought.*

"Pim, take the captain to General Koblenzar for interrogation."

Fineo attempted to protest, grabbing Nico by the arm. "You err, Prince Nicolas...that is to say—"

He stopped and stared at the array of swords raised all around him, the guards only waiting for a nod from their king.

Nico looked at the hand clutching his arm, then into the other man's eyes. "I suggest you accept the change in circumstances a little faster, Captain. For your own good."

Then he faced the old man in the general's uniform, watching from the corner. "You there. What is your name, Commander?"

"Farrel, King."

"Just so. Commander Farrel, come with me. I need you to carry a message to Chissenhall."

To Nico's surprise, Fawkes brought a flagon of wine to their second meeting, and took intermittent sips during the discussion. Yet his face showed none of the markers of heavy drinking, nor his voice the signs of intoxication. The pleasant jocularity remained, reminding Nico in many ways of Mip, Pim's twin who had been the delight of the Threeshields until his sad death at Cormona.

Much like Nico's sessions with Arturo, the two men spent most of their time bent over a large map of the twelve kingdoms.

"Second Devero is here." Fawkes tapped the southeastern portion of Falkenreach, where forest thinned to plains. "Or was, when last I saw. She intended to move north with Thane Vasturo, to challenge the horde before it swept south."

"What do you mean, challenge? Surely she does not mean to fight all the demons herself?"

"Nay. I mean, aye." He took another swig of wine. "They speak of a man who commands the demons, and this man is her target. She seeks to kill the leadership and see the rabble descend into confusion."

Nico had his doubts that things would be so simple, but he was here to listen and learn, not to offer objections.

"How soon?"

"As soon as she learns his location. Reports are frustratingly wild and contradictory."

Considering the range of outlandish rumors he had heard—all manner of foul creatures witnessed in the dark woods, rogue beasts turning suddenly hostile, perpetual storm clouds filling the skies—Nico could well imagine how difficult it was for the Second to distinguish fact from fiction. "Your best guess?"

"Very soon. Perhaps as we speak." Fawkes took another swig. "I...am anxious to get back. I wish to be at her side, not a kingdom away." He hesitated. "Your pardon, Thane."

Nico dismissed the apology with a wave. "What of the other Second? What can you tell me?"

"Second Garrett is east, aiding the Vilnians." He pointed to Northgate on the map.

"Against the Chekiks?"

"Aye. They received warning of the invasion before the enemy could get the bulk of their forces through the mountains. The fight is thickest here, at Halfsummit. Thus far, the Vilnians hold them at bay."

Nico stared at the markings in the mountains. "There are two other passes, however."

Another swig, heavier than usual. "There have been no reports from Soul's Pass, in the north."

"And Sea's Pass, in the south?"

"A massive lake obstructs the way, right in the middle. A beautiful sight, if rumors be true. The surface freezes for much of the year, naturally, but not enough to allow an army to cross."

"Not an army, but the Chekiks would be foolish to send no one at all."

"Aye, and they have. Raiding parties only. Gothenberg reports they have already taken care of them. It's clear that the invasion's heaviest thrust is in the center, and so it's there we have focused our forces."

A logical plan, but one that worried Nico immensely. It assumed much based on little evidence, with the existence of the empire at stake. "One final question for today, Thane."

"Aye?"

"May I have a swig of that wine?"

. . .

"And so I believe Koblenzar deserves a second chance," King Nicolas informed his predecessor.

"Did you learn nothing from what happened with Handersonn?" Hermann raged.

"I did, but that was incompetence."

"Disloyalty is a far graver concern than incompetence."

"General Koblenzar has not yet been disloyal."

Hermann glared back at his son. "Even you aren't this naive, Nicolas."

"Even you understand the need to hear voices that don't only say what you want to hear. It's a mistake many leaders make, and I don't intend to. I need information, father. It will take too long to replace Koblenzar's network. We need every ally we can get."

"Not every ally is a friend. Some smiles mask deceit."

Nico's exasperation grew. "Then I'll be careful with what he tells me."

"And what of what he doesn't?"

"I cannot run a kingdom with nothing but suspicion and distrust."

Hermann sighed. "How did I ever raise such a fool? At least Markolas knew when to listen."

"Yes, that worked out well for us all."

This conversation was even more painful than expected. His father's frequent contempt was currently even more irksome than usual, for this time it was deserved. This whole notion to reappoint Koblenzar was foolish, but Nico was going through with it, anyway. He had no choice. He had to believe in second chances, because he needed Leti to give *him* one.

Regardless, he was ready to end this conversation. Whatever advice the good king Hermann might provide was not worth the price.

. . .

"Captain Mickens, I am sending one of the Loresters to their king with a message. Please choose two troopers as escorts."

"Aye, Third." The young trooper saluted and turned away, but not before Nico noticed the man sported new facial hair to hide his homely face.

Nico looked over his shoulder at Fawkes, whom he had invited to today's dispositions. The thane would be leaving soon, and Nico wanted him to report to the Second that Akenberg was doing all it could to end one conflict and help with the others. "The terms are generous. We don't seek Lorester's humiliation, nor any of their land, but only their aid in the coming wars."

Fawkes nodded, looking more sheepish than usual. "Aye, My Third."

Cottzer was next. For this, Nico stood to deliver the orders. "General, I haven't an army to offer you, but this duty is just as important as any field command. We need updates from the war in the east. You will take two companies of light cavalry to Northgate, with a double complement of horses. From there, use discretion in your dispositions—but I expect your main force to continue to Halfsummit. Avoid the fighting unless you really can help, and send regular reports to me."

Most of these points were being repeated for emphasis, the general having already received a full briefing the eve before. Nevertheless, the repetition made Nico feel better. Whereas the man had been quite distracted at the prior meeting, he seemed much sharper today. Small wonder, coming on the heels of a good night's sleep with the secure knowledge that the king was salvaging his career.

"I also want scouts sent north to Soul's Pass and south to Sea's Pass. We need a continuous watch on each." In war, as in other things, surprise could be deadly.

"Understood, My King. I'll begin at once." The general saluted and briskly moved away, showing none of the tears of joy and gratitude that overwhelmed him last night.

Nico studied the other Swordthane once more, attempting to read the man's mind. The appealing face carried an air of gravity that mixed with its natural cheerfulness, creating a curious amalgam.

"Thane Fawkes."

"Aye, My Third?"

"I cannot talk you into staying longer?"

"Nay, My Third. I appreciate the offer, but my duty is elsewhere. I ride north and west later this morn."

Nico nodded. "I know. I will be headed west soon enough myself, Thane. You are welcome to accompany my army—"

"Your pardon, Third, but I prefer not to delay."

"Just so. In that case, I hope you will accept an escort. I can spare only one squadron of troopers, but the Second may find them useful in a fight. And can consider them only the start, for I will send more as soon as I'm able."

"You send troops away while you still can use them here? I… cannot refuse aid, Third." He looked as though he wanted to say more.

"Lima, Pim…will you excuse us a moment?" Nico waited for the door to close. "Continue, Thane."

"My Third, I must say, my time here did not go as expected."

"No?"

"Nay. I assumed you would order me to join this war against your neighbors. A Swordthane is a valuable resource, yet you never seemed to consider it."

Nico remained quiet, letting the man speak his mind.

"Third Arturo was the finest man I knew. He lifted me from servitude to become what I am today."

I'm not sure I like where this going.

"I thought to hate you, King Nicolas," Fawkes said abruptly. "By the gods, I wanted to hate you. But I find I cannot.

"When I arrived, I meant to challenge you. To avenge my Patron, or die trying." He looked like he wished for another flagon of wine. "I no longer feel such compulsion, however. The empire is better off with you fighting for it."

Nico was touched by the candor. Here was a man who had not wanted to like him, yet did despite himself. Of such beginnings could friendships grow, and Nico was in constant need of reliable friends.

"Thank you for those words, Thane." *Though I'm not sure I deserve them.* "Please, go with my best wishes. Tell the Second I desire nothing more than to end my kingdom's selfish war, and join her in the north."

KINGS CLUB

Want to know when the next book is out? Or the audiobook? How about free bonus materials, and a heads-up when special offers are running? Join the Kings Club, and become a part of the growing Empire Asunder community.

Members receive free bonuses to supplement the novels, currently including a full-size, full-color version of the map and a copy of *Empire Unveiled: The Complete Sourcebook for the World of Empire Asunder*.

The sourcebook grows with each novel and contains background information about the characters, places, and culture that fill the Empire of Twelve Kingdoms.

The map is available as PDF and the sourcebook in both PDF and ebook formats.

Kings Club members also receive monthly announcements from me about special offers, the progress of the series, and are invited to join my Launch Team, who receive copies of each novel before publication and are an important part of each book's launch.

You can join online at:

www.MichaelJasonBrandt.com/Offer

ABOUT THE AUTHOR

Michael Jason Brandt is a specialist in history and geopolitics. Born in Washington, DC, he has lived, worked, and studied in the US, England, and Spain. He received his first degree in business from Shippensburg University of Pennsylvania. After a decade in the corporate IT world, Michael returned to academia and received degrees in International Relations from George Washington University and The London School of Economics and Political Science.

Now dedicated to research and writing, Michael is a co-founder of Casus Belli Books. He currently lives in Maryland.

His first novel, *Plagued, with Guilt*, is the story of five friends confronted by war, disease, and the end of humanity. The *Empire Asunder* series, inspired by his time in Europe, is his second writing adventure and first sojourn into fantasy.

ALSO BY MICHAEL JASON BRANDT

The EMPIRE ASUNDER saga continues with BOOK 3: SHIELD AND CROWN, coming in November.

Some champions rise, while others fall...

From prince to king, commander to general, Nico's rise from obscurity to power has launched him closer and closer to the seat of the emperor itself. But he is still a young man, untrained and unprepared for the countless pressures of ruling a land at war. Will the struggle to protect his people, help his friends, and preserve his love for his enemy's princess become too much for him?

Fed up with the endless sacrifices of friends and loved ones, housethrall Jak begins a personal quest to bring down the mysterious devils that hold the empire in their malicious grip. As he seeks to find safe refuge for his companions, however, he discovers that they are not so willing to let him go on alone. Soon he learns that he needs their aid, and that from unexpected new friends, to have any chance of success. And so he must risk more sacrifices from the very people he wishes to save...

The ravages of war have left soldier Yohan bereaved and bereft. Left only with one unwanted companion and a heart full of anger, he begins the hopeless quest to rescue two women from the enemy tribesmen terrorizing the empire with surprising impunity. Outnumbered and exhausted, rejecting friendship in favor of revenge, he faces a personal battle as much as an external one. Does his transformation into a single-minded killer make him as evil as those he hunts? Will he rescue the women he loves, or will he lose them along with his humanity?

Or, if you're looking for a change of pace, why not check out his first novel?

PLAGUED, WITH GUILT

Five personal journeys through war, disease, and the fragile line between human and animal.

Dr. Ben Appelstein and his archaeological team unwittingly unleash an ancient plague on the modern world, derailing their promising lives and threatening to destroy life as we know it. Against a backdrop of war and disease, four friends fight through transformative journeys both personal and monumental: Rich, a brilliant gay athlete struggling for esteem; Wendy, a querulous coed caught between two men and an uncertain future; Halfus, a quiet hero with a tragic past; and Ernie, a fun-loving charmer with aspirations of grandeur. Bound together and pulled apart, they struggle to save all they hold dear from impending doom.

Plagued, With Guilt is the critically-acclaimed, character-driven epic novel about the best and worst tendencies of humankind. Tackling the difficult themes of terrorism, abuse, and mental illness, and providing insight into history, science, politics, and psychology, the novel is a must-read for anyone interested in a deeper understanding of the complexities of today's world.

"At once a fierce academic thriller and a powerful meditation on humanity... A striking, powerful debut that heralds the start of a promising career." —Kirkus Reviews